Bernadette's Dashing Doctor

THE BOOKSHOP BELLES
BOOK FOUR

CATHERINE BILSON

EBONY OATEN

Content Advisory

- Emotional abuse from relatives
- Medical scenes with blood and a broken bone
- Short medical scene with lancing of a boil
- Herbs being used to terminate pregnancies
- Rampant unfairness and sexism because women were considered second-class citizens
- Cats breeding uncontrollably as desexing pets had not been invented

Catherine and Ebony strongly advise readers against making or consuming any of the herbal treatments mentioned in this book. While Bernadette's salves, teas and lozenges are loosely based on mixtures people might have taken 'back in the day', they could make a person awfully sick too. Some are semi-useful but disgusting (like clove tea) while others range from useless to downright dangerous. Especially treatments taken to bring on a woman's 'courses' for whatever reason. Just because something is made from natural ingredients does not mean it is safe or effective.

Also, we'd like to apologise what, to modern eyes, may appear to be the poor treatment of cats in these books. Our understanding of their care and enrichment of pets has changed a lot in 200 years. Responsible owners keep them indoors or have 'runs' in the gardens so their cats can't kill wildlife. The authors both have pet cats that are desexed and live entirely indoors. They are fed cat-specific diets and Ebony even has a water fountain for her kitty because it mimics a natural stream. Both Cath's cats were adopted from the RSPCA, where she worked as a volunteer for several years. Desexing of pets wasn't an option until at least the 1930s. And of course, USB-powered water fountains came much later.

CHAPTER 1

Stirring up Trouble

Early March, 1815
Hatfield, Hertfordshire

Bernadette Baxter, the youngest and definitely the most helpful of the four Baxter daughters of Baxter's Fine Books in Hatfield, Hertfordshire, kept a close eye on the pot of bubbling honey and lemon mixture on the stove. She added a dozen whole cloves into the mix, careful to avoid getting her hand too close to the simmering liquid. Experience had taught her that the ensuing burn would hurt agonisingly if she made a mistake. The syrup smelled deliciously sweet as she stirred it three times one way, then three the reverse, breathing in the fragrant steam. The cloves would impart their pungent healing oils, but remain intact for her to tweezer out of the lozenges before they set.

The doorbell to the bookshop tinkled, and she heard her sister Louise give whoever had arrived directions to go to the kitchen.

Light footsteps pattered up the stairs, followed by a slim boy with a shock of scruffy brown hair.

"Oh good, Brutus, you're here!" Bernadette was delighted to see her young cousin - her favourite, but then there really was no competition in that regard - had arrived to assist.

"It smells much better than the binding glue Louise cooks up!" he said, face full of cheer.

"It's almost ready to pour. Would you like to do the honours?" She lifted the pot off the stove carefully and placed it on the iron trivet on the kitchen table.

"Yes please!" he said, coming forward eagerly.

He was a fast learner and eager to please, always ready to lend a hand no matter how dirty or smelly a task they might assign him. More than that, Bernadette had become grateful to have Brutus accompanying her around town. He was young enough not to be threatening to the women she helped. He stayed out of the way, but most importantly, he helped her carry the produce home that her customers provided as payment. Sometimes her basket was so full of fruit, honey, meat or other items given to her by grateful patients she could barely lift it by herself.

Brutus was a meticulous sort of boy, and soon became adept at pouring the cooling mixture onto the wax paper under her directions. One by one he dolloped a teaspoon-sized amount onto each paper, then moved on as Bernadette followed along behind him with her tweezers, carefully picking out the whole cloves. Moments later, they had a bench full of individual sweets.

Bernadette gently waved one of her hand fans to keep them cooling. Once they set, it required only a quick twist to close the wax paper and the lozenges would be ready to take to Mr Lennox the apothecary.

"May I have one?" Brutus asked, opening his mouth and pointing to the back of it. "I think there's a tooth coming through at the back."

Bernadette brought him over to the window for better light and peered into his mouth. "The gum does look red. I'll make some clove tea."

He winced.

"Yes, I know it tastes awful," she agreed. "But it's the best thing to remove the pain."

"Can't I just have a lozzy?"

She tried not to roll her eyes. Young people took such liberties with language! She ignored the fact that she had barely seven years on Brutus, but then she had been raised in a well-educated household, whereas Brutus could not honestly be said to have been raised at all, considering he was ignored by his parents and bullied by his ghastly older brother. It was truly a surprise that Brutus was turning out as well as he was; she could overlook some casual informalities in his speech.

"Yes, for now." She glanced over the bench and picked up the most oddly-shaped one, handing it over to him. "I'll get the clove tea brewing and by the time we get back it will be nice and strong."

His shoulders slumped even as he popped the lozenge into his mouth. "Thanks," he mumbled around the sweet, and Bernadette smiled. Brutus had sweet manners, even if she suspected he wouldn't thank her after she made him gargle the pungent clove tea. He willingly helped her load up her basket and hefted in manfully, shaking his head when she checked if it was too heavy. She packed up a second, slightly lighter, basket for herself and they made their way downstairs.

They waved goodbye to Louise as they passed her at the counter and then the two of them made their way through Hatfield to Mr Lennox's business.

"Ahh, the Baxters! How wonderful to see you!" The apothecary always greeted them with a smile. He did not get to his feet, however, and remained sitting behind his counter. Try as she might, Bernadette had not been able to make any kind of medication that might help the dear man. He'd lost a leg below the knee during valiant service with the Navy years before, and now walked with a peg leg. He suffered constant pain in his lower back if he stood for more than a few moments, but flatly refused to take laudanum, saying with a dark look on his face, "that road leads nowhere I care to go," on more than one occasion when Bernadette suggested it might help.

They greeted his assistant, who everybody called "Young Devon," with a smile and a wave, but didn't interrupt as he dealt with several customers.

Mr Lennox's eyes gleamed at the sight of the basket, and he quickly reconciled the herbal sachets, lozenges and salves Bernadette laid out on the counter, and paid her.

Bernadette thanked him and said, "While I'm sad we lost Dr Rasley, I must confess, I've never been so busy."

"I concur," Mr Lennox said, reflecting a suitably sad expression. "Terrible loss for the town. But now I'm so busy, I need Young Devon here every day."

Bernadette leaned in and mentioned, quietly, "I set a broken wrist last week." She was quite proud of herself. The young boy who'd been tree climbing had fainted, but she was quite sure she had done a good job and he would heal with no troubles.

Mr Lennox chuckled. "Good for you. We never stop learning, do we?"

"That we do not!" She readily agreed. "It's a shame the nearest doctor is in St Albans - there are some people in town with ailments that truly do require a proper doctor's skills and they aren't able to travel to him."

"Dr Edmonds isn't fond of coming this far," Mr Lennox agreed. "We'll get a new one soon, I'm sure."

Dr Rasley had tragically perished in a suspicious fire just a few weeks earlier. A new doctor had been hired in London, supposedly, but hadn't arrived yet… perhaps he was waiting until the doctor's cottage had been rebuilt, Bernadette thought. And in the meantime, she, Mr Lennox and Hatfield's three midwives were very nearly run off their feet.

They parted on excellent terms and waved to Young Devon on the way out.

The rest of the morning Bernadette and Brutus were kept busy, walking from house to house to visit the women who needed help.

She kept track of each one in her notebook, but used her own special code for their names, just in case the book ever fell into the wrong hands. Like her Cousin Joshua's, or Reverend Millings'. They'd get a sermon to curl their ears if *he* ever found out the full scope of her activities.

The women paid Bernadette with produce or herbs they grew in their gardens. Sometimes eggs from their chickens, or best of all, honey from a nearby hive. The coming spring would bring out the meadow flowers and bees, once the weather warmed a little more.

Returning to the bookshop after several hours,

CATHERINE BILSON & EBONY OATEN

Bernadette and Brutus deposited their baskets on the counter with a sigh of relief. The baskets were even heavier now than when they'd gone out!

Brutus said, "What a morning!"

"The clove tea will be well-steeped by now," Bernadette said with a grin.

"It doesn't hurt any more," he said quickly.

Louise chuckled and said, "Welcome home, both of you. Mrs Poole has made soup for lunch."

There was a fresh cob loaf of bread in one of their baskets. It was delicious spread with freshly churned butter and eaten with Mrs Poole's thick parsnip-and-carrot soup. Bernadette ate hungrily, knowing she'd be busy again all afternoon. She had several more patients to visit.

The new doctor couldn't arrive soon enough, though she certainly hoped he'd be a little younger and have more up-to-date training than old Doctor Rasley, Lord rest his soul.

Wednesday was Bernadette's regular day to visit Lord Ferndale and Miss Yates at Ferndale Hall, which was almost ten miles from Hatfield. Although the visit took most of her day, she wouldn't miss it for anything, being extremely fond of the elderly brother and sister, who had been friends of her family for many years and were now relatives-by-marriage. The carriage arrived soon after breakfast to collect her. She waved to Mrs Bell as she climbed into it, just coming out of her house directly across the street from the bookshop. Mrs Bell was one of three midwives in Hatfield, who were all exceptionally busy at this time of year, what with it being about nine months after the various midsummer festivities.

She could call back in to see Mrs Bell on the way home and check if any of the women needed assistance, perhaps with herbs to help to bring in the mother's milk, treat mastitis or childbed infections.

It was lovely to see Lord Ferndale, who insisted that she must now call him 'grandfather' since her sister Estelle had married his grandson Felix, and Lord Ferndale's sister Miss Yates looking so well. Bernadette couldn't stop fretting about them during the cold winter months, but they'd come through the worst of it well. Ferndale Hall's butler Mr Thorne and the housekeeper Mrs Sykes were grateful for the jar of clove tea, which Brutus hadn't used in the end.

In the glass house, the gardeners were happy to see her and helped with harvesting a few tubers of ginger that Bernadette had planted there a few months earlier. It was a temperamental plant and needed lots of warmth, which made it expensive and difficult to buy. But it was so good for expectant mothers in the early months for keeping their retching at bay.

"Grandfather, I can't thank you and the gardeners enough for growing the ginger. You're making people's lives so much better." She looked happily at the small basket of ginger root the gardener handed her. "It would cost a fortune to buy this much, and I would have to charge far more than most people could afford. Growing our own means I can help so many more people."

"I was thinking," Lord Ferndale said, "I know you usually make a tea or cordial with it, but what if you added the ginger to a lozenge? Would that make it easier for people who can't keep fluids down?"

Bernadette's eyes sprang wide. "That's brilliant! I should

have thought of that! Oooh, I think I might call it 'Ferndale's Ginger Relief'."

"An excellent notion, my dear. Now do come inside, Florence will be waiting for us!" He patted her hand kindly and they went indoors for nuncheon.

<hr />

Back in town later in the afternoon, Bernadette crossed the street to Mrs Bell's house before going back into the book-shop. The midwife looked weary, resting her feet on a foot-stool as she sipped on a cup of herbal tea. No doubt she'd been getting little sleep of late, with all the births in town. Babies always did seem to come at the most inconvenient times.

"Is there anything I can help with, Mrs Bell?" Bernadette asked.

"Aye, I saw Mrs Pennyrigg today." Mrs Bell sipped her tea and shook her head. "Mr Pennyrigg won't leave her alone, I'm afraid."

"But she has nine children already, and the eldest is barely ten!" Bernadette said, horrified.

"Aye." Mrs Bell eyed her over the rim of her teacup. "She's only just missed her courses, though."

"I'll call in and see her tomorrow," Bernadette said imme-diately. While it was not an infallible remedy, she had learned of a very particular combination of herbs from her mother, which when steeped into a strong tea and drunk at the correct early stage of one's first missed course, could prevent the pregnancy from progressing any further. Poor Mrs Pennyrigg needed a rest from being pregnant… and

Bernadette would take a moment to tell Mr Pennyrigg to leave his wife be for a while too!

Every woman of marriageable age in Hatfield knew what Bernadette's herbs were capable of, and not one of them, not even her ghastly cousin Phoebe, would ever breathe a word about it in the hearing of a man. It was women's business and none of men's, and a woman who betrayed that code would likely find there was suddenly no midwife available if she should happen to need one.

"I've a tonic for you," Bernadette said then, digging in her satchel and handing Mrs Bell a bottle.

"For me?" The midwife looked surprised. "What ever for?"

"For when you get called out in the wee hours and are struggling to find the energy to get out of your warm bed." Bernadette smiled at her. "Might put a hop in your step."

Mrs Bell laughed, but she tucked the bottle away and thanked Bernadette. "You're a good lass, and no mistake."

Making her way back across the street, Bernadette turned her face up to the sky, enjoying the warm spring sunshine. It had been a miserable winter and a wet early spring; today's sunny sky was a pleasant change.

She re-entered the bookshop at the same time as the maid Rosie, who held the door open for her with a friendly smile. Rosie was shy around some people, but could be positively garrulous if she liked someone. She talked a good deal to Bernadette, who had found that Rosie was very well-informed in what people around town were getting up to. Between their housekeeper Mrs Poole, the midwives and Rosie, there wasn't much that happened in Hatfield that Bernadette didn't hear about sooner rather than later.

"Got some news for you, Miss Bernadette." Rosie beamed at her. "New doctor's here."

"In town?" Bernadette stooped to prevent Crafty, the bookshop cat, from dashing out through the open door.

"Arrived this morning, like. Took a room at the Red Lion, on Lord Ferndale's account, since his cottage ain't ready yet." Rosie nodded importantly, obviously pleased to have imparted interesting news.

"Well done, Rosie," Bernadette beamed with the fresh information. A doctor in town at last was so very welcome. There was Farmer Allom, whose shoulder was still not sitting properly after falling from a barn roof. Bernadette had studied diagrams in a medical text and knew the theory of what she attempted, but when she tried it in reality, she lacked the brute strength required to reset the shoulder properly in its socket.

She hoped the new doctor would not be too old and frail for the heavy work that would be required in a town as large as Hatfield.

She marched upstairs and bundled her fresh herbs to hang, then put away the ginger grown at Ferndale Hall, as well as several little treats Miss Yates had insisted she bring home. The lemon biscuits had been particularly excellent; Bernadette considered another one, but she'd had three earlier. She'd leave these for Louise, Brutus and Mrs Poole to enjoy, it was only fair.

Now, where was that list she'd nearly completed? A little more rummaging and she found it.

No time to waste, she skipped down the stairs, waving to Louise and Mr Jackson writing in the ledger behind the counter and headed to the Red Lion.

The landlord, Mr Haye, was delighted to see her and asked what she might need.

"I heard the new doctor has arrived. Which is his room?"

Mr Haye smiled broadly and said, "Aye, you're right! Top of the stairs, last on the right."

Just as she was about to take herself up the stairs she paused to quickly ask, "What's his name?

"He goes by Williams," Mr Haye said.

With that knowledge, Bernadette took to the stairs and arrived only slightly out of breath. What with rushing from house to house to help people, she was used to putting on the pace.

She knocked on the door and called out, "Doctor Williams? Are you there?"

There were footsteps, then the door opened a little. She had been hoping for a doctor younger than Rasley, but the face she saw appeared far too young to be a doctor at all. Perhaps this was the doctor's son. He might have brought him along?

"Hello?" The man was a little over middle height with dark hair and eyes, and skin that appeared to have a tan far too early in the year. As if he'd lately returned from sunnier climes, like Portugal or Spain.

"I'm looking for Dr Williams," she said. "I'm Bernadette Baxter from Baxter's Fine Books, which is just next door."

"I am Doctor Williams," the man said.

"But you can't be. You're only four and twenty if you're a day!"

"I can be, and I am. You're right about my age, though. Good guess." He opened the door a little wider and she could see past him into a comfortable room and a badly damaged open travelling cabinet with different sized drawers.

"Gosh, what a beautiful cabinet, but why is it so scuffed?"

He turned and looked back at it. Some sections were polished to a high gleam, but there were large chips of timber missing from the sides and two buckled belts held the whole cabinet together. "It got me through the war."

"Can't imagine you were in service very long?"

"Three years," he replied with a slow blink of those dark eyes that seemed to see through her. Then he added, "Three *very* long years."

Bernadette nodded and still couldn't quite fathom how he could look so young. People who returned from war looked haggard and older than their years, in her experience! He must have signed up fresh out of the school room.

Still looking at that intriguing cabinet, she said, "We have a good number of skilled tradesmen in Hatfield, but they are busy with repairs after the ah…" she stopped herself. Dr Williams would know why. "Anyway, I brought a list of patients who I think you should see first."

She handed it over with a flourish, walking just over the threshold of his room, but standing near the open doorway.

Dr Williams looked at her in a slightly puzzled way and shook. "That's all very well, but I'm here under the auspices of Baron Ferndale, so I only take orders from him."

Bernadette puffed herself up to her full height, which really wasn't much, and said, "I'm Lord Ferndale's granddaughter, he asked me to provide you with this list."

Dr Williams tilted his head with suspicion. His voice was accusatory. "I understood he had only one grandson, who is currently in Ireland with his new bride."

Bernadette beamed at that. "Correct. The bride is my sister, Estelle Baxter, and now Lord Ferndale insists we all call him 'Grandfather'."

His confidence dimmed, shoulders slumping slightly.

She inwardly cheered her success. "The list. See to it."

"Now see here," he said.

"No, *you* see to the list." She put her hands on her hips and stared at him.

Really, this was a dreadful beginning! If the new doctor wasn't going to listen to her, how would he ever learn what the people of Hatfield needed?

CHAPTER 2

Meddlesome Chit

Glynn Williams had met any number of officious people who thought they knew better than a doctor, more often than not the patients he was trying to help, but he'd never had a young girl knock on his bedroom door and attempt to order him about before. She placed her hands on her hips and tried to stare him down, some feat as she was significantly shorter than he was.

"How old are you anyway, little girl?" he said a little mockingly. She might be Lord Ferndale's granddaughter by marriage or some such connection, but he doubted she was more than sixteen. Playing at nursing to keep her busy, he suspected, like several of the idle, wealthy young women he'd met in London.

"I'm almost nineteen, and my name is Miss Bernadette Baxter, not *little girl*," she said indignantly.

Glynn failed to smother a laugh, which made her hazel eyes snap with annoyance.

"Do not laugh at me, sir! You know nothing of the people of Hatfield, whereas I have lived here all my life!"

"All *eighteen* years of it," he said mockingly.

He could swear he nearly saw steam coming out of her ears. Her teeth ground together quite audibly, but her voice when she spoke was commendably level.

"Eighteen years longer than you. Do you even know the ailments of your employer, Lord Ferndale, and his sister Miss Yates? That Lord Ferndale has a cough brought on by changes in the weather, but eased by a tonic of…"

He held up his hand to stop her. "What can you know of such things? You're not an apothecary, or a midwife; you're far too young to be either."

"My mother was an extremely well respected herb woman," Bernadette said with great dignity. "I'm proud to carry on her caring tradition."

"Oh, your *mother*," he said, not missing that she spoke in the past tense. "And I suppose she gave you her book of recipes?"

"Yes she did. And trained me in all her knowledge," Bernadette declared proudly. "May her soul rest in peace."

"Let us get one thing straight. You're playing with people's lives if you attempt to diagnose and treat them without training or qualifications and I will not have it!" Even as he spoke, Glynn realised he could be making an error. She was Lord Ferndale's granddaughter, after all, even if it was only an honorary relationship, and Lord Ferndale was his employer.

Nevertheless, Glynn meant every word. He'd seen too many people sickened or even killed by those who meant well but didn't understand what they were doing.

"I'll take your list," he said, as a small peace offering, "and consider your suggestions." She was right that he did not know the people of Hatfield, and local knowledge was something he needed. But he would prefer to get it from people who were actually qualified. "Can you tell me who the local midwives are, and where to find the apothecary? And who is the doctor who has been providing services since Dr Rasley's passing?"

"Mr Lennox is the apothecary; his shop is around the corner from here. Go past the bookshop and take the next turning right. The midwives are Mrs Bell, who lives almost directly across the street from our bookshop, in the house with the green door, Mrs Tristan and Mrs Leywood…"

"And the doctor?" Glynn prompted.

"There is no doctor here, not since Dr Rasley's passing. Dr Edmonds in St Albans will not travel this far. A few people who were well enough and wealthy enough to travel will have visited him, but most of your patients could not afford to do so."

"Can they afford medical treatment at all?"

She stared at him. "Why should they pay you for medical treatment? You are paid by Lord Ferndale!"

Glynn paused, readjusting his thinking. "You're quite correct." He'd just spent two months working beside another doctor in a practice in London, being paid to attend to wealthy fainting ladies in their salons. Mr Jackson offering a steadily-paid job where he could attend to real people with real ailments had been exceptionally appealing. "I am being paid by Lord Ferndale, but I had assumed that he would…"

"You make a lot of assumptions, Doctor. A habit I'd advise you to get out of."

Why, the little madam! Annoyed all over again, Glynn almost tore the list into pieces right there and then.

"Thank you, Miss Baxter. Good day to you now." It was

getting late, and he was tired and hungry. He hoped the Red Lion served a good dinner.

"I shall see you soon, Doctor." Bernadette gave him a knowing little smile before turning on her heel and walking out of his room.

"Not if I see you first!" Glynn muttered under his breath, closing the door firmly.

The memory of that knowing smirk stayed with him all evening.

The next morning, after a hearty breakfast courtesy of the Red Lion, Glynn packed a valise and made ready to set out to visit some patients. He grimaced at the list that *smirksome* young girl had given him. He had to concede that it was a fair list; it seemed to have been arranged in an order of priority that he didn't think completely inappropriate. Top of the list was a farmer whose shoulder had not set properly after a dislocation. There was a chance they could reset it, but if the injury had happened weeks earlier, the arm joint might not go back. The sooner he attended to that matter, the better. He packed a bottle of laudanum and asked Mr Haye for directions. Then he collected his horse, Canterbury, from the livery stable behind the Red Lion. Lord Ferndale was paying to have Canterbury boarded there.

He arrived at the Allom property just a little out of town. A pretty place redolent with the unmissable smell of fattening pigs.

"Right good of you to come out, sir," Mrs Allom said, showing him into the thatched-roof farm cottage and then into the bedroom. It had a low ceiling and he had to hunch down to avoid whacking his head on the beams.

"He's been in dreadful pain," the farmwife said, wringing her hands. "Miss Bernadette did what she could, like, but she said she didn't have the strength to put it back in. She warned us not to touch it, because if one of the labourers did it, he might do it wrong, like?"

"Hm." Glynn examined the man's shoulder, noting the sheen of sweat on Allom's upper lip as he gently manipulated it. Glynn hated to admit it, but Miss Bernadette had been correct in her diagnosis - *'shoulder out of socket'* was written neatly on the list - and equally sensible in her assessment of the injury as both beyond her abilities and too hazardous for someone untrained to attempt to remedy. And Mr Allom would have been in no condition to travel to St Albans for proper treatment, even if Lord Ferndale had paid the bill for them.

"Well, I am here now," he said briskly, putting his annoyance with Miss Bernadette aside to focus on the task at hand, "so let us have this back where it belongs. I shall strap it tightly after that and you must not use the arm for at least two weeks, do you understand me?"

"It's been five days already," Allom grunted, but he nodded at Glynn's raised brows. "Aye, I'll mind you."

"Very good. Bite down on this." Glynn handed Allom a padded stick. "It's going to hurt, but it'll be quick." Carefully, he placed two fingertips of his left hand on the misshapen joint, took hold of Allom's thick biceps in his right hand, and with a deft twist and shove put the shoulder back into place.

Allom fainted.

"My word," Mrs Allom said in admiration.

"Keep him out of action, Mrs Allom. I mean it," Glynn advised as he took a bandage from his bag and began tightly wrapping Allom's shoulder joint. "And not straight back into the heavy work after two weeks, either. You make him mind."

Mr Allom groaned as he came around. The sight of Glynn standing over him startled him, and then his wife quickly explained.

"The new doctor has come, and he's fixed your shoulder," she said.

His eyes flew open. "It doesn't hurt!"

"But you're not to use it, at all all, for at least two weeks," Glynn warned him again. "Then light duties only for a good while longer."

"Yes, Doctor," Mrs Allom said, answering for her husband.

Glynn saw the resolute glint in her eye. She'd take care of him.

He'd learned from experience that men generally did recover much faster when there was a woman about to make them mind the doctor's orders. He gave instructions for small amounts of laudanum - Allom would be in considerable pain for a few days - but advised that it should be taken for no more than five days, and both husband and wife listened carefully to his instructions, nodding in agreement.

"Can I offer you a cup of tea, Doctor?" Mrs Allom asked, but Glynn shook his head.

"I've a lot more patients to see, ma'am, thank you kindly. Have your husband call into town next week and see me... I'll be arranging a consulting room as soon as possible, check at the Red Lion and they'll be able to tell you where."

Mrs Allom accepted this, but pressed a pork pie on him

as he left, which Glynn happily accepted. He folded it into his clean handkerchief and tucked it in his coat pocket. It would make a good lunch.

After visiting some more injured and sick townsfolk, in which Bernadette Baxter's name was spoken often and with praise each time, he headed to visit the apothecary to introduce himself. The two of them would do well to get along, if at all possible. His patients would need proper medicines and compounds. It would also give him a chance to see what out-dated tinctures and brews were still for sale. They did more harm than good, and perhaps he could persuade the apothecary to take them off the shelves.

Mr Lennox was a cheery older fellow and walked on a prosthesis with a crooked gait. Happy to show Glynn around his shop and discuss his product range, he hissed slightly as he made the last step towards a cabinet where he showed off some of the goods for sale.

"Mr Lennox, I've noticed your leg is giving you discomfort." Glynn tilted his head to look at the peg leg.

"Aye," Lennox said. "Hasn't been right for a while now, but I manage."

"Would you like me to take a look? I fitted a good many men with new limbs after amputation. They can be tricky to get right."

"Were you a sawbones?"

"That I was, with the army in the peninsula. Then I came back to England and went to medical school," he confirmed, as he looked at the apothecary from the front and then the side. "I think one of your hips is higher than the other. Has it always been like that?"

"I don't think so," Mr Lennox shook his head. "Was all

right to start with, but in the past few years it's been getting worse."

"Can't have that," Glynn agreed. "I think perhaps you've worn down the sole of your shoe on your good foot, and now your prosthetic leg is too long."

His eyes widened. "I stopped wearing boots! Well, *a* boot. It must have had a thicker sole."

"I think the answer is to either trim a little off the bottom of your prosthetic or slip a riser in your shoe to get level," Glynn suggested.

"I'll try the shoe riser first, and see how that goes," Lennox said. "Well, I am jolly glad you made time to see me today. Fortune smiles upon Hatfield indeed. Now, is there anything I can get you for your assistance?"

"Your happiness is my thanks, Mr Lennox. I am being amply compensated by Lord Ferndale - I even have a horse at my disposal. He's called Canterbury, but he generally likes to walk."

Mr Lennox laughed at the pun. "He's a good one, Lord Ferndale, but I still want to give you compensation. You noticed something Dr Rasley completely missed."

He directed him to a shelf of jars filled with wrapped lozenges, a basket with sachets of herbal mixes for headaches and another piled high with little tins of honey balm for cracked lips. Glynn was impressed with how sensible they were, and the ingredients were safe. He didn't recognise any of the packaging, though. Not supplied by any of the big London firms.

"They're some of my most popular items, all made locally by Lord Ferndale's granddaughter, Bernadette Baxter."

Glynn stifled a groan at hearing *that* name yet again. The meddlesome wench apparently knew everyone and had a hand in everything.

And most vexing of all, she was using the right kind of ingredients that would genuinely help people. Where had she learned these skills? It was deeply annoying to find himself incorrect in at least one of the assumptions he'd made about her.

"Has Miss Baxter been supplying you long?" Glynn asked.

"Took over after her mother passed four years ago, God rest her soul. Michelle Baxter had forgotten more about herb healing than I'll ever know, I reckon." Lennox nodded sagely. "Bernadette has the knack for it too. She's been taking good care of the folks of this town for a long time. Don't like to speak ill of the dead, but Dr Rasley... well, he didn't bestir himself much. It's why Lord Ferndale decided to pay the new doctor a regular wage; folks as couldn't pay in cash weren't getting help. Miss Bernadette don't mind if they pay in eggs or honey or potatoes."

"So, she's been treating people who should by rights have seen the doctor?"

Mr Lennox stared at him. "Weren't you listening, son? If the doctor wouldn't see them because they hadn't the blunt, what were they supposed to do? Just up and die?"

"No, of course not!" Glynn flushed red. "Well, since Lord Ferndale is paying me to see anyone who needs it, you can just let everyone know to come to me now instead of Miss Baxter."

Mr Lennox looked quite amused, but he tipped his head in a nod. "I'll do that. Good to meet you, and thank you for your recommendation about my leg. I'll try the riser in my shoe and let you know if it works."

Glynn bade the apothecary a polite good day and exited the shop, silently stewing. It had been obvious from Lennox's expression that quite a few people would continue going to Bernadette Baxter for her herbal remedies rather than see an actual doctor, which was quite ridiculous. He needed to put a stop to that, and soon.

Marching along the street and around the corner, he stopped outside Baxter's Fine Books. He'd been told by any number of people that it was where Bernadette lived, in the apartments above the shop.

"Give her a piece of my mind," he muttered. "Tell her she needs to send patients to me first, and stop meddling where she's no business!"

Opening the bookshop door, a bell tinkled gently above his head. Glynn closed the door and stood still for a moment, letting his eyes adjust. While it wasn't dark in the bookshop exactly, it was much dimmer than the bright sunshine outside.

"Hello, there," a deep voice rumbled, and Glynn smiled as he spied Shaun Jackson, Lord Ferndale's man. He'd been the one to interview and hire him in London. Jackson was standing at the counter, in conversation with a tall young woman, who despite being at least a head taller was so much like Bernadette she could only be a sister.

"This is the new doctor, Louise, Doctor Williams. Glynn, this is Miss Louise Baxter." Jackson's voice softened as he said her name, and it only took a single glance for Glynn to realise that the two were sweet on each other.

"Welcome to Hatfield," she said.

"A pleasure to meet you," he said, bowing.

"I hear you've already met Bernadette." Hazel eyes sparkled teasingly.

Glynn smiled tightly. The old adage *'never come between sisters'* reverberated in his head. "Indeed. Would she be about, by any chance? I'd like a word."

Jackson laughed quietly. "A kind one, I hope."

Apparently, Bernadette hadn't wasted any time sharing her opinion of him. Glynn took a slow, deep breath, well aware that Jackson worked for Lord Ferndale too. He needed to watch what he said, or he'd put the entire town against him.

"She's been doing a fair job of taking care of folks," Glynn said, honestly if rather unwillingly, "with obviously limited resources at her disposal, but I'm here now. I'd prefer she left treating patients to me."

"Would you, indeed?" a light voice said behind him, and Glynn turned, startled. Bernadette had appeared apparently out of nowhere and stood with her arms folded across her bosom, looking up at him with that annoying little smirk on her face. "I'll be sure to tell all the ladies with feminine complaints that the new doctor will be most sympathetic."

"If necessary," Glynn said through gritted teeth, "though surely that is a job for the midwives?"

"Perhaps you'd like to discuss that with them." Bernadette's smirk grew wider. "Mrs Bell lives just across the street, the house with the green door."

"Yes, you mentioned that last night." Glynn realised he'd better leave before he lost his temper and said something he'd regret. Jackson was watching him warily. Yanking the door open, he nodded a little curtly. "Good day to you all."

"Crafty, no!" Bernadette yelled, and Glynn blinked at her, bemused.

"I beg your pardon?"

She flung herself forward, lunging low - at his knees? - and Glynn looked down just in time to see a furry black streak dash between Bernadette's reaching hands, jump over his feet, and race out into the street.

He'd let a damn cat out.

CHAPTER 3
Escapades

B ernadette had actually been rather enjoying provoking the new doctor, who was far too stiff-necked for such a young man. Dr Williams was clearly trying to restrain his temper, and equally failing and deciding to leave before he said something regrettable.

Unfortunately, he stood in the doorway holding the door open while making a tight-lipped nod to politeness, and Crafty took her opportunity to escape. It was springtime, and Crafty had been in heat for the last two days, yowling and generally making a nuisance of herself.

And while Bernadette's herbs might work on humans, she'd found nothing yet that could help with a cat.

Bernadette was just too slow to catch the cat as Crafty made her dash for freedom, and Dr Williams stood gaping like a fool as Bernadette almost fell flat on her face right at his feet.

And then, oh horrors! There was a squeal from a startled horse, a great clatter of hooves, then crashing and shouting just outside.

There was a veritable stampede to get out of the door as Louise, Bernadette, Mr Jackson and the doctor all rushed out at once, to be greeted by a dreadful scene. Crafty had apparently run right in front of a carriage coming along the street drawn by two horses; at least one of the horses had spooked and pulled the carriage across the street straight into the path of a rider coming in the other direction, who had then fallen off his horse.

Mr Jackson, former soldier that he was, jumped into action straight away, catching the now-loose horse. The driver of the carriage had his horses back under control, and Mr Thomas the ostler came hurrying out of the Red Lion to take their heads.

Dr Williams wasted no time running straight to the fallen rider, and Bernadette was right on his heels. The man was evidently injured, bright blood spilling onto the cobblestones from his head and one leg bent at a dreadful angle mid-shin.

"Easy there, don't try to move," Dr Williams said crisply, kneeling down right in the middle of the street. He dragged his coat off and rolled it up, shoving it under the injured man's head. "I'm a doctor."

Mrs Bell came out of her house just a couple of steps away, obviously summoned by the commotion, took one look and disappeared back inside. Bernadette knew the sensible midwife would return in moments with bandages, but moments could be too late, considering the amount of blood she could see flowing. She snatched off her apron, wadded it up and pressed firmly on the man's head wound.

Dr Williams spared her a glance, then nodded. "Keep pressure on that," he ordered. "Can you tell me your name, man?"

"Ned," the man mumbled, blinking vaguely. "Ned Fellowes."

"You've broken your leg, Ned, and your head is bleeding. Don't try to move and we'll take care of you." Dr Williams looked down at Ned's leg, pursing his lips. "I don't like the look of this. Mr Jackson, we need a large board. An old door? We'll have to move him."

"He's in no condition, surely…" Bernadette began, horrified.

"If I don't perform surgery on this leg, and quickly, he'll lose it. And this is no place for surgery." Dr Williams flicked a quick glance around, at the crowd of bystanders who had gathered.

Ned cried out in horror, trying to move away from them.

"Hold him still," Dr Williams said firmly, and willing hands came down to help.

Mrs Bell arrived, going to her knees by Bernadette. "Get him inside my house," she suggested. "There's a big flat table in the front room."

"This is Mrs Bell, the midwife, Dr Williams," Bernadette introduced hastily.

"Can you stitch?" Dr Williams didn't look up.

"Yes," Bernadette said.

"I wasn't talking to you, Miss Baxter."

Well, that was just rude! She gaped at him, quite shocked.

"Miss Bernadette sews a much finer stitch than I do," Mrs Bell said reprovingly.

Bernadette saw the doctor's jaw clench, but he nodded without speaking. Mr Jackson re-appeared carrying an old door by himself, and Dr Williams directed how Ned should be moved onto the door and then carried inside Mrs Bell's house.

Ned fainted while they moved him, which meant he wouldn't try to fight them at least.

The poor man lay pale and still as the door was put atop Mrs Bell's table.

"Now, everyone move away," Dr Williams ordered, "except Mrs Bell, Miss Baxter, and you, if you'd stay, Jackson? Might need someone to hold Ned down if he comes around."

Annoyed with him though she was, Bernadette couldn't help but admire his calm, commanding air. He seemed utterly competent as well as confident in his abilities. She just hoped he really did know what he was doing. Ned's leg looked ghastly.

"Can you get hot water, Mrs Bell?" Dr Williams was rolling up his shirt sleeves and opening the valise he'd been carrying, pulling out a rolled-up piece of leather. He opened it to reveal a number of surgical instruments.

"What are you going to do?" Bernadette asked, horrified at the sight of the blades and saws.

"The broken end of the bone is poking out of his leg, and may be splintered. I'll shave off any shattered pieces and then realign and splint the whole thing, but likely I'll have to make an incision in the leg muscle to get things back into place." He paused, looked at her, and then came to Ned's head. "Let's have a quick look at this head wound."

A warm hand came down on Bernadette's, to where she'd been holding the wadded-up apron against poor Ned's head the whole time, and she jumped slightly and let go. Dr Williams removed the apron and nodded.

"As I thought; that's not too bad at all. A simple cut, but head wounds do bleed a lot. A suture or two would be best, after cleaning it with some alcohol. Can you handle that while I tend to the leg?"

His eyes were very dark, Bernadette noticed as he looked directly into hers, so dark a brown it was hard to see where the pupil ended and the iris began. He seemed incredibly calm, much more so than she felt after seeing the awful angle of Ned's leg. She nodded.

"Have you done surgery like this before?" she asked as he took an already-threaded needle out of a case and handed it to her.

"More times than I care to count." A rueful little smile crossed his face. "My father was a surgeon with the army. I went with him as his apprentice when I was twelve, was performing surgery myself by sixteen."

"Oh! But… you *are* a *doctor*?" Most doctors considered surgeons to be little more than butchers, Bernadette knew.

"Indeed. Quite by chance, one of my patients in Spain turned out to be… well, I shan't name him, but someone extremely wealthy and influential. He was quite determined that I had saved his life, and equally determined to give me his patronage. Sponsored me to return to London and study medicine."

Bernadette was right to assume he'd enlisted straight out of the school room, as he'd more or less confirmed that, but there was no more time to think about his qualifications or his experience as she set to cleaning the worst of Ned's head wound and stitching the thin pieces of skin together. She made three stitches, not to show off, but to make sure they were evenly spaced and under the same amount of pressure.

Keeping her eyes on this small wound meant she would not be distracted by what was happening at the other end of poor Ned.

As predicted, he did come around, and Mr Jackson spoke to him in reassuring tones while holding him down. Mrs Bell came over with some whiskey for the pain, and Bernadette poured some onto a clean rag and wiped it over the stitched head wound.

When it was mercifully over, and Ned's leg was patched and splinted tightly, Doctor Williams' white shirt was covered in blood.

"We'll need to get you some crutches," he told Ned, "and don't put any weight on the leg at all. Mrs Bell, is it all right if Ned remains here for the night so he doesn't move? I'm just across at the Red Lion. I'll make a quick change and will come back to clean the room."

"I can watch him," Mr Jackson volunteered, "my room is only upstairs."

Light poured in through the windows and Bernadette thought this room would be perfect for the Doctor to see his patients. She'd ask Mrs Bell when they had a quiet moment.

"We have a pump in the courtyard behind the bookshop," she said, taking in the hideous sight of the doctor's clothes. "I can give you one of my father's old shirts if you need one."

He looked down at himself and made a face, obviously recognising what a sight he looked. "Much appreciated. I think perhaps I'd best not go back into the inn looking like this."

"Cold water is excellent for getting rid of blood," she added, trying very hard not to smile at just how cold the water might be from the pump.

Bernadette spotted the crowd gathering outside and quickly grabbed Mr Jackson's coat to put on the doctor to cover the blood.

"What's this for?"

"To cover you up so that they don't faint," Bernadette said, pointing to the window.

"Oh! Good thinking." He shrugged himself into the dark coat, which mercifully covered all the blood on his shirt.

"Thank you, for your quick actions," he addressed the crowd as they walked away from Mrs Bell's.

As Bernadette thought, the bystanders walked away from the house and appeared to follow them. Good, that would leave Ned in some peace and quiet.

"Ned's leg is badly broken, but his head injury isn't serious, and he should be fine," Dr Williams said, his voice calm and steady. He did have a very good manner with patients, Bernadette thought; a shame he had apparently decided to be obnoxious to her!

There were audible gasps of relief at that. People began to thank him even as he tried to walk away, but he held up his hands to stop them. "You will understand, I need to write this up in my medical record, and I should do that while the event is fresh in my head."

With that, they both slipped into Baxter's Fine Books and heaved a sigh of relief.

"Let's clean you up. I'll get soap to get the stains out," Bernadette said as she walked him through to the courtyard. Louise sat up behind the counter and gave a nod, the understanding between them that Bernadette would fill her in on the details later. Or perhaps Shaun would, if he came back earlier.

Bernadette's hands were none too clean either, and she must have left her apron behind at Mrs Bell's. There were blood stains on the front of her dress.

She left Dr Williams to care for himself and hurried up to

the kitchen, where she washed her hands. Then in her room she found a fresh dress and changed into that, with a little help from Rosie.

"I'll clean this as good as new, Miss Bernadette," Rosie declared as she bundled up the stained one.

"Thank you," she said, then headed to her father's room where she grabbed one of his shirts. A few moments later, she stepped into the courtyard, completely forgetting that a doctor washing bloodstains from a shirt he'd been wearing, would most likely remove that shirt to do so.

He stood there scrubbing at the fabric, naked from the waist up, quite taking her breath away.

She had seen shirtless men before. Countless numbers of them, far more than any unmarried woman would expect to, because she'd spent so much time treating them for various ailments and injuries, but somehow none of them had ever caused her eyes to almost pop out of her head in the way they were doing right now.

Dr Williams wasn't a particularly tall man, only a little over average height, nor was he especially broad, but he did appear to be exceptionally fit and strong, his torso all lean, wiry muscle. His biceps bunched and flexed as he scrubbed at the bloodstained shirt, and Bernadette could not look away.

"Oh, thank you." He saw her standing there and came to accept the shirt from her, apparently quite unconcerned about his state of undress.

"Uh, if you would like to leave your shirt, our maid Rosie is very good at getting out bloodstains. She can launder it and return it to you," Bernadette gabbled, hastily averting her eyes as the doctor shrugged into the clean shirt, causing his chest muscles to move in ways that were exceptionally dangerous to her peace of mind.

This is just stupid. I don't even like this man. Why can't I stop staring at him?

Turning on her heel, she marched hastily away before he realised she was discomposed.

The next morning, Crafty cried at the front door to be let back in. Bernadette rolled her eyes at the thought the family mouser would be pregnant with another litter. Opening the door to the High Street, she cursed to herself as Crafty rubbed against her leg. "It's just as well you're a good mouser," she grumbled under her breath.

There were no mouse entrails to clean this morning, as whatever Crafty had caught in the night - aside from a tomcat's lustful gaze - remained somewhere out there.

Rosie arrived only moments later, her smiling face appearing as the door tinkled open.

Bernadette knew the maid's cheeky expression could only mean one thing - exciting gossip awaited! They headed to the kitchen, where Bernadette could sort and pack herbs, while Rosie tackled the week's washing.

Mrs Poole pretended to ignore their chatter, but when the subject veered onto Phoebe Baxter wanting to get on the hospital committee, she quickly joined in.

"Not happening," Mrs Poole said very firmly. "She pushed her way on to the gardens committee and is giving us all megrims already, after only one meeting!"

"That's what I thought, too," Rosie said. "But she's

sending cakes and pork pies to everyone on the committee to sweeten them up."

"I'll wager she didn't make them," Mrs Poole said, "nor did her housekeeper. That must be why Mrs Langford was asking for the best place to get pork pies last week."

"Alloms," Rosie and Bernadette said at the same time.

Mrs Poole chuckled and said, "She can try all she likes, but there's no way Miss Yates or I will let Phoebe Baxter on the hospital committee. I can't imagine why she wants to be, that woman hasn't the slightest hint of compassion."

Bernadette was satisfied with the finality in that sentiment.

Rosie pulled out a man's shirt from the dirty basket, some weakened bloodstains still showing on the white fabric. "I'm sure this has a story behind it!"

"Yesterday's accident," Bernadette said, feeling horribly guilty that their cat was the cause of it. Crafty had a particular enmity with horses.

"I heard Ned was recovering well at Mrs Bell's," Rosie said as she pushed the fabric into the cold water.

Rosie knew more than she! "I'm very glad to hear it. I should head over and check on Ned myself, and see if Mrs Bell needs anything."

"This is Doctor Williams's shirt, I take it?"

"Yes, he ah, cleaned himself up in the courtyard and I gave him one of Father's shirts." All the while her head was full of complaints about the town's newest resident. *The man has no manners at all. He is completely dismissive of the work I do. He may be a doctor, but he is certainly no gentleman. At least not to me...* but still, she couldn't keep from thinking about how calm and competent he'd been, or how cleverly he'd performed the surgery on Ned's leg.

Louise called up from the bookshop below.

She headed down and saw Mr Allom himself waiting at the counter, with his arm secured tightly to his body. "Mr Allom, how are you faring today? It looks as if Dr Williams has been to see you?"

"Aye, he has. Set it to rights. Erm," he looked a little embarrassed so Bernadette walked him over to a quiet spot in the bookshop. "Was celebrating my good fortune last night and now have a shocking head. Saw the doc having breakfast at the Red Lion and he told me to sleep it off. But there's too much work to catch up on."

"You're not using your bad arm, are you?" She frowned sternly at him.

"The missus would skin me alive if I dared. But have you got anything for my head?"

"Wait here," she said, suppressing a laugh as she turned to go back upstairs. She returned with a stoppered bottle and said, "Drink this when you get home. It's disgusting and you may wish to be outdoors in case you can't keep it down."

"Much obliged," he said as he put his hat back on. Then he reached into his pocket and withdrew two pork pies wrapped in a square of linen as payment.

"Very much appreciated," she said with a warm smile. They really were the best pies in Hatfield.

Mr Allom made his way out, and Bernadette went over to the counter to see what Louise was doing. "Do you need me to check the figures?" she asked, seeing the accounts ledger lying open in front of her sister.

"No, Shaun was just here." Louise looked a little dreamy, and Bernadette smiled. It was quite lovely to see Louise in love! And Shaun Jackson was a good man who seemed to feel the same way about her; Bernadette just hoped he wouldn't wait too long to propose and make Louise a happy woman.

The bell tinkled, and both sisters winced as their cousin Joshua marched into the shop, his wife Phoebe behind him, their youngest son Barnaby in her arms. Barnaby was really getting too old to be carried, but Phoebe spoiled him absolutely rotten. Bernadette's eyes narrowed as she saw the telltale signs of jam around Barnaby's mouth. She was quite sure Phoebe deliberately gave him sticky foods before bringing him into the bookshop and letting him loose to put sticky hands all over the books.

"Hello, dear boy!" She intercepted Barnaby as Phoebe put him down. "Dear me, what have you been eating, you're all over sticky!" She sacrificed another clean apron to clean him up, already mentally making an apology to poor Rosie who would have to wash it, but better a dirty apron than sticky books.

Phoebe scowled, thwarted. Bernadette smiled at her, thinking happily of Mrs Poole's insistence that Phoebe was not going to get her way about the hospital committee.

"And what are you looking so happy about?" Joshua snapped at her. "You girls should be in mourning!"

"If you are yet again going to claim that our father is dead without the slightest shred of evidence to prove it, you can turn yourself around and get out of our shop," Louise said, not even making the slightest pretence at politeness.

Louise had always been the bold one, but being courted by Mr Jackson made her absolutely fearless. She no longer seemed to care a whit what Joshua said or did. Bernadette admired her for it.

"Well!" Joshua puffed up with outrage, his eyes glittering. "Mark my words, girl, you'll regret it when word of your father's death does arrive. Remind me again; when did you last receive a crate from him?"

Louise made no answer, just marched over to the door and opened it with a pointed glare. Joshua and Phoebe perforce had no real option but to collect Barnaby and leave again.

Once they were gone, Bernadette said in a small voice, "It was January. The beginning of January."

Crates had arrived from their father on a fairly regular basis before that; every two weeks or so, though he had rarely included so much as a note inside, to their intense frustration. But now they were well into March, almost Easter, and Louise and Bernadette were beginning to fear that Joshua's doom-laden predictions that their father would never come home might come true after all.

"Don't!" Louise said quickly, but Bernadette could see the fear in her eyes too. "He's coming home," Louise added. "Soon. That's why we haven't heard; why there's no more books. He's travelling, and he'll be home soon."

"I wish I had your confidence," Bernadette said under her breath as Louise marched away and began unnecessarily rearranging the lending library shelf.

Well. Wherever their father was, there was work to be done here, and it wasn't getting done while she stood about in the shop. She wanted to go over and visit Ned and check that he was showing no signs of fever or infection. She had some salve to go on his stitches.

Taking off her sticky apron, Bernadette made her way back upstairs again to fetch another clean apron and collect her basket.

CHAPTER 4

New Lodgings

The rooms at the Red Lion were so comfortable, Glynn felt refreshed every morning. He didn't mind so much that his residence wasn't available yet, as the food here was good and the people of Hatfield were unfailingly friendly. Except for that one meddlesome girl.

Mr Jackson found him finishing his breakfast, and Glynn invited him to join.

"I'm afraid I can't stay," Mr Jackson said, crushing his hat in his hands. The huge man's brow was sternly creased with worry. "I've rejoined the army, and I must be off."

"Goodness, are we at war again?" Glynn asked, startled. "Who's it with this time?"

"Napoleon escaped and is raising merry hell," Jackson said. "It's all the returned soldiers can talk about. They're all joining back up as well. Walk with me? I need to talk to you."

Glynn quickly paid for his meal and followed Mr Jackson back to Mrs Bell's so he could finish packing. The road was wet from fresh rain and sparkled in the sun.

"I must ask you a favour," Mr Jackson said, "Would you please look after Louise and Bernadette while I'm gone?"

Glynn pulled up short as they reached Mrs Bell's door. "That virago?"

Shaun's eyes rounded in shock. "Who, Louise?"

"No, not her," they walked in and greeted Mrs Bell, then headed to Shaun's room where he'd already half-filled a carpet bag. "I mean Miss Bernadette."

Shaun stopped packing, obviously confused. "She's a sweet, quiet little mouse."

"She's a harridan," Glynn objected. "Meddling with people and playing with medicines she doesn't understand."

Shaun sighed and shoved the last few items into his bag. "I've spoken with Mrs Bell, and she's more than happy for you to have my room. She offered her front room as your consulting room."

"Until my house is ready?"

Shaun shook his head. "The men repairing the doctor's house are joining as well. There won't be any more work done on repairs for a while, unless you're good at carpentry yourself?"

It hit him then. He wouldn't have a house or consulting room until this latest skirmish with Napoleon was over. Even then, not all the men would make it back.

Should he be signing back up as well, for that matter? He felt guilty for not wanting to, but he was needed here, especially with Jackson gone.

Added to that fact, he was being paid to remain.

Mrs Bell dabbed a handkerchief to her face as she bid Mr Jackson farewell. He waved them off and closed the front door behind him.

"Lor' bless and keep him," Mrs Bell said. "He's a good man, for all he's the appetite to go with that big frame."

Glynn grinned, amused. "He's praised your cooking any number of times, Mrs Bell. I'm looking forward to sampling it. I'll bring my things over from the inn in a little while, if that's all right?" While the rooms at the Red Lion were comfortable, he wouldn't be sorry to get away from all the hustle and bustle of the busy coaching inn.

"It's all a little last minute, but I never use this room, and I know Lord Ferndale will pay me a nice rent so you can use it," Mrs Bell said, opening the door into her front parlour. "I've moved a chair in here and a table you can use for a desk."

"Goodness, it's perfect, thank you Mrs Bell." He was impressed with how quickly she'd arranged the room. The table was long enough that somebody could lie on it for examinations or even surgery, just as they'd used for Ned the other day. Glynn could put his medicine cabinet in the corner; the table was a luxury, a proper desk! He'd used his medicine cabinet as a desk during his time in the army.

"Tea?" the midwife asked.

"Thank you, that would be lovely."

Mrs Bell bustled out and left him alone in the room. There was a charming fireplace that he hoped he might not need to use until autumn. Along one wall was a picture rail where he could hang his certificate. There was also a comfortable couch where his patients could sit while relaying their ailments.

He sat down in the sturdy wooden chair and gazed upon his new consulting room. Satisfaction spread through him. Life was suiting him very well.

Then he looked through the windows and realised he was directly overlooking Baxter's Fine Books.

He muffled a groan of anguish.

Mr Thomas set the medicine cabinet down where Glynn suggested, then said a polite farewell to him. Glynn thought the brawny man might walk straight back to the Red Lion, but instead he visited the bookshop.

If Mr Thomas had a sore back or shoulder, Glynn could have helped. Instead, he feared the man would ask Bernadette for some kind of healing tea.

The view kept changing as a post carriage arrived with travellers and boxes of goods. Then people would often visit the bookshop for a while, before leaving with packages. He also watched as the occasional townsperson visited the bookshop. To his surprise, one man who'd just walked into the bookshop then walked out only a couple of minutes later, making a bee-line for his consulting room.

Glynn opened the door himself instead of putting Mrs Bell to any trouble, and greeted the man with a friendly smile.

"Miss Bernadette said I should see you," the man said, "so I came right over. Are you busy?"

"I always have time for the people of Hatfield, Mr, ah?"

"Black, Horace Black, I run the printers, with my brothers."

"Mr Black, come in," and he showed him to the room. He opened his ledger and began taking notes. "What's troubling you today?"

42

"Well, y'see, it's me finger. Not sure what I've done," the man said, holding his palm out.

Glynn's eyebrows shot up so high it stretched his face. "It looks completely flat," he said, taking in the spade-like end of his index finger.

"Oh, that! No, did that years ago, never came good, but can't feel it neither so it don't bother me none. No, it's the little one on the end here."

Looking now at the correct finger, Glynn noticed it bent at a strange angle at the knuckle. He gently examined the joint and felt the tell-tale warmth underneath the skin.

"It has all the hallmarks of arthritis," he delivered the news as calmly as he could. It was hard to guess Mr Black's age from his weathered face. He could be anywhere from 40 to 60, depending on how much manual labour he'd done over his lifetime. "Any other joints bothering you?" Glynn asked gently.

"Well, now that you mention it, my knees aren't as good as they used to be."

Glynn was pleased that Mr Black trusted him for further examination. As the town printer, he would know a great many people, and would spread the word about how the doctor had helped. Alas, there weren't too many good reme-dies for arthritis aside from staying warm and resting. Not possible for a man who was on his feet all day.

"Did Miss Bernadette offer you willow bark?" he asked.

"She said Mr Lennox would have some, but to come here and see you first."

Glynn nodded, and said the words he really didn't want to say. "Miss Bernadette is right. I'm very glad to see you and let me know if things get any worse." He grabbed a small piece of paper and wrote down, *willow or Jesuit bark for arthritis, drink with tea in the mornings*. "Take this to Mr Lennox and let him know I sent you. It's willow bark, sometimes called Jesuit bark, and you take it steeped in tea. It's a good remedy for painful joints. If you have it in tea with your breakfast, it should help. I hope it gives you a few hours' relief. In the mean time, wear a glove on your bad hand and perhaps wrap your knees with scarves to keep them warmer?"

The man nodded and said, "How much do I need to pay?"

"Nothing at all, Mr Black, Lord Ferndale has employed me to serve the people of Hatfield. It may be a few pennies at the apothecary." He considered telling Mr Black to ask Mr Lennox to put it on Glynn's account, but looking at the man's clothes, and considering he owned the printer, decided the man could afford to pay for his own medication.

The man beamed with delight. "Much obliged, and a pleasure to meet you, Doctor!"

As he waved Mr Black off, he saw Miss Bernadette leaving the bookshop with a basket on her arm. Glynn nodded a greeting her way, but she darted off and mustn't have seen him.

Well, he would do as Shaun Jackson had asked and keep an eye on her. It wouldn't be too difficult since he could see the bookshop door from both his consulting room window and his bedroom window, as he discovered that evening when he made his way upstairs after a good dinner with Mrs Bell.

Over the next week or so, as trade resumed after the Easter Holy Week, several more patients came in to see him. Frustratingly, every single one of them had visited the bookshop first. Glynn supposed he should be grateful that at least Bernadette was sending people over to him, though it did irk him that they were going to her first - everyone must know there was a new doctor in town by now, Mr Black had even put an article about him in the local newspaper! Plenty of people had begun greeting him when he walked down the street, at least; Hatfield seemed to be full of friendly folks. Walking to church the next Sunday morning, Glynn received any number of friendly nods and smiles.

He was a little early for the service, and spied the vicar in his cassock talking to some parishioners outside. Perhaps he should go and make himself known to the clergyman? Their paths would cross regularly after all, at either end of life's journey for the people of Hatfield.

Glynn hesitated in his step as he saw a familiar, small figure pause in front of the vicar. He didn't particularly want to get into yet another argument with Miss Bernadette in front of Reverend Millings; he'd heard the clergyman was quite the martinet and had no need to be hauled up for being impolite to a lady, and he'd managed to avoid arguing with Bernadette all week only by dint of keeping a scrupulous distance.

"Reverend Millings," he heard Bernadette say earnestly, her voice carrying on the light breeze, "may I inquire after your health?"

The vicar looked down his long nose at Bernadette. "I am perfectly well, Miss Baxter. The Lord cares for his own."

"Well, that is good to hear, sir, only..." Bernadette hesitated. "I cannot help but note that you look a little sallow. A touch of jaundice, perhaps? I have an excellent liver tonic…"

"I want none of your witchcraft, woman!" The vicar's voice was low, but vehement enough Glynn could make them out clearly.

Glynn frowned. That was no way to speak to a lady. And a liver tonic was not witchcraft; the best ones were simple like radish water and fresh mint, or gooseberries crushed and steeped with basil leaves.

"Good morning, Doctor!" A cheerful voice interrupted his thoughts, and Glynn turned to find Lord Ferndale approaching, his sister Miss Yates on his arm.

"Good morning, my lord." Glynn bowed. He'd gone to Ferndale Hall to present himself to his new employer before even coming to Hatfield, and had been charmed by the elderly brother and sister. Lord Ferndale was a perceptive, kindly man determined to do good works for his community, and Miss Yates was, Glynn thought, far more clever than her slightly vague, gentle demeanour might suggest. "Miss Yates." Glynn bowed to her too, and was favoured with a sunny smile and Miss Yates reaching out to take his arm.

"It is so nice to see you again, Dr Williams! Now you must come and sit with Arthur and I in church, mustn't he, brother?"

"Of course," Lord Ferndale acquiesced comfortably. "Plenty of room in our pew, and we have a few minutes before service will begin, do tell me how you are getting along. I hear you have opened a consulting room at Mrs Bell's, and are staying there now that Mr Jackson has gone off to deal with the Corsican again?"

Glynn was not the least bit surprised with how much

Lord Ferndale knew already. The man was his employer, and he owed him a great deal. "Mrs Bell has indeed delivered me a great boon," he said. "Her front room is in a convenient location for the townspeople to find me. I'm keen to hang out a shingle as soon as I can find someone to create one for me."

"Yes," Lord Ferndale nodded, opening up his hymn book. "We are short of good craftsmen again. A couple of my gardeners have signed up, too. I could not hold them back from this most valiant cause."

Guilt pricked at Glynn. "Should I rejoin too? I have served before."

"Don't you dare even think about it!" Miss Yates interjected. "Hatfield needs your skills. If anyone dares lure you to another town, send them to me and I'll give them what for."

He had to smile at the elderly lady's vehemence, imagining Miss Yates setting about the miscreant with her reticule.

Just as the service was about to begin, Bernadette and Louise Baxter joined the Ferndale pew. Bernadette hesitated when she saw him, then made a last-second detour to make sure Louise sat directly next to him instead of herself.

Lord Ferndale leaned in and quietly said, "Do try and get along with Miss Bernadette. It will be so much better for all concerned."

The man missed nothing. Heated embarrassment warmed Glynn's neck as he realised Lord Ferndale must have seen Bernadette's diversion. He also figured somebody from the town had probably said something to the baron about their animosity. That his behaviour had reached his employer's ears felt like a personal failing.

"Of course, my lord," he said, and added honestly, "I owe her my thanks for sending a steady stream of patients to my door."

Any residual guilt Glynn felt evaporated at great speed as Reverend Millings launched into his sermon about the evils of disobedient women who thought to step outside their places as servants of men.

It was one of the nastiest sermons he'd ever heard. That it was so soon after Easter had him thinking the goodness of Holy Week had worn off very quickly.

He caught a glimpse of Lord Ferndale's bowed head. The elderly baron looked in pain and he was grimacing. It would not do to turn his head and stare at others in the congregation, so Glynn couldn't tell whether others were enjoying or enduring it.

But one thing that was incredibly obvious was the way the reverend deliberately looked towards Louise and Bernadette sitting next to him before launching into an even more pointed tirade about pornographic literature!

It really was getting too much, and it was obvious to anyone with ears that the lesson was deliberately making an example out of the Baxter sisters.

Horribly unfair.

Neither of them deserved such scorn. Why, young Bernadette had only a few minutes earlier kindly offered the vicar a tonic! Looking at the vicar now, the man's face should have been red from excitement and anger, as he invoked the story of Eve and the apple and temptation. Instead it did have a yellow tinge to it. Was it the man's liver making him so angry?

By trying to help him, Bernadette had instead made herself a target.

As much as Glynn might personally disagree with her activities, she didn't deserve to be singled out like this in front of the town.

On the man raved for a painfully long time. When it was eventually time for a hymn, Glynn quietly checked with Louise to see if they were all right.

"He's been getting worse," Louise said under the noise of people singing.

It was unfair, not to mention unconscionably rude, and he felt sure others in the town would feel the injustice of the situation. "Please let Miss Bernadette know she was completely correct to offer him a tonic for his liver. He does not look well."

Bernadette peeked out at him from behind Louise and said, "Thank you," in a soft little voice.

She looked so small next to her robust sister. Glynn felt a rather peculiar sensation in his chest… was that protectiveness he was feeling?

When the service was mercifully over and they were once again outside and out of view of the vicar, Miss Yates turned to Lord Ferndale and said, "He really exceeded the bounds this week. Arthur, you must speak to him."

Lord Ferndale sighed and nodded his head reluctantly. "I have put it off for far too long. I kept hoping he'd tamper down the brimstone. Today was too much. He'll scare people away."

Glynn didn't want to eavesdrop, but he was standing very close by. "I'll second Miss Yates' suggestion. I'm yet to explore all of Hatfield. Is there a Methodist community here?"

"A small one," Miss Yates confirmed. "They come to our services and then have a kitchen gathering afterwards, but after this week I can't imagine they'd want to come back. Are you Methodist, Dr Williams?"

"I was raised in the community," Glynn admitted. "It's not just my name that's Welsh. I grew up in a small fishing village near Pembroke."

"You don't have an accent at all!" Miss Yates looked surprised.

"I worked hard to lose it while I was studying." He left unsaid the fact that it had marked him out; he was common-born and knew it, and among the sons of gentlemen at university he had stuck out like a sore thumb. Learning to mimic their upper-class English accents had enabled him to blend in far better.

Miss Yates nodded before turning back to her brother. "Arthur, please speak with him, he's not bringing the community together; he's singling people out for damnation."

Lord Ferndale's chin puckered for a moment as he realised he had to do something. "Back in a moment," he said with a little sigh.

Glynn saw Louise and Bernadette meeting with friends in a small gathering nearby. Each woman embraced Bernadette with comfort and consolation. Mrs Bell was with them, hands on her hips, looking quite furious.

At least they had defenders, Glynn thought. And plenty of customers in the shop, if the number of people in and out of their door every day, most of them carrying purchases as they left, was any guide. He probably should go in himself and see if they carried any medical texts of interest.

"Would you like to come to dinner at Ferndale Hall today, Dr Williams?" Miss Yates asked. "Our carriage will bring you back to town afterwards, of course, with the Miss Baxters."

He had been opening his mouth to say yes, thinking that a nice dinner at Ferndale Hall with these lovely people would be a pleasure, but closed it again on realising that of course Bernadette would be there. She was considered family. And though he was feeling rather more charitable towards her at this precise moment, he still didn't quite trust himself to manage to be polite, especially not if she deliberately provoked him again. He didn't want to be made to look a fool in front of Lord Ferndale.

"You're very kind," he said instead. "Perhaps another time."

Miss Yates gave him a penetrating look, but graciously accepted his declining the invitation and left him to go and join the cluster of women around Louise and Bernadette.

CHAPTER 5

Making The Best Of It

Louise was so glum and mopey Bernadette wanted to scream. She was sure customers were avoiding coming into the bookshop because of Louise's miserable face behind the counter. Their sister Marie had been exactly the same before the Earl of Renwick had come to his senses, realised he was in love with her and swept her off to be his countess and live in his Cumbria castle.

If this was what love did to a person, Bernadette was quite sure she didn't want any part of it.

At least Marie had known that Renwick was all right. Louise had no such assurances about Shaun Jackson. The news coming out of France was quite terrifying, Napoleon having amassed a vast army in an alarmingly short span of time.

"Why did he have to go?" Louise sobbed into her hands one morning at breakfast. "One man isn't going to make any difference and I - *we* - need him here!"

Bernadette patted Louise's shoulder, sharing a despairing look with Mrs Poole. Both of them felt quite helpless. Not to mention the fact that Bernadette was growing more afraid for their father's welfare with every passing day; Matthew Baxter was somewhere in France too, almost certainly behind enemy lines. Though he could speak the language perfectly and hopefully pass for a local, his life must be in constant danger. Bernadette refused to even think of the alternative.

"Why don't you stay upstairs today?" Mrs Poole suggested kindly.

"Someone has to mind the counter," Louise sniffled.

"I can do it," Bernadette said stoutly. She was less busy since Dr Williams had come to town; people were beginning to send for him for major injuries and illnesses at least, and folks with minor complaints would know where to find Bernadette. "You stay upstairs and just rest. I know you're not sleeping well."

Louise lowered her hands and looked at Bernadette from reddened eyes, before nodding.

"And tonight, I'm going to give you a tea before bed and you're to jolly well drink it," Bernadette added firmly.

"All right," Louise conceded quietly.

"And you're going to eat this breakfast, too!" Mrs Poole added, pushing the plate of buttered crumpets under Louise's nose.

Louise picked up a crumpet and nibbled at the edge, and Mrs Poole and Bernadette exchanged another worried look. It was awful to see Louise, normally so strong and determined, being meek and miserable like this.

Bernadette just hoped that Cousin Joshua didn't come into the shop today. She wasn't nearly as good at shutting him up as Louise. Well, if he did, she'd just have to put on her big girl boots, stomp her feet and tell him she wasn't

CATHERINE BILSON & EBONY OATEN

putting up with his nonsense. She should see where the crowbar was, on the off chance she might need it.

Letting Rosie in, she turned the Closed sign on the door around to Open, checked Crafty's scratching pad and looked at the usual pile of mouse entrails behind the counter with a grimace of disgust.

The doorbell tinkled as her young cousin Brutus came in, and Bernadette looked around at him hopefully. He saw what she was looking at.

"Let me get that," he said obligingly, fetching the dustpan and rags.

He was a good boy, Brutus, despite his awful parents. Bernadette could not understand how Joshua and Phoebe had managed to produce him... or perhaps it was simply because they ignored him, Joshua favouring his eldest son Benjamin, a ghastly bully, while Phoebe doted on little Barnaby.

The bell chimed again to announce the arrival of Ruth Millings. Ruth seemed to view the shop as her escape from a very strict home life. Her father didn't even allow Ruth to receive pay for her work; they had to put the money in the collection plate at church on Sundays, which had felt particularly galling last Sunday when the vicar had been so utterly nasty in his sermon.

"Good morning, Bernadette," Ruth said quietly.

"Good morning, Ruth. Louise isn't feeling very well today so I'll be here at the counter. If I have to run out for anything, do you think you and Brutus could manage the shop for a little while? Louise is just upstairs if you need help, and so is Mrs Poole, of course."

Ruth gulped, but nodded bravely. She did seem to be getting past the worst of her shyness; for the first few weeks in the shop she'd barely even been able to look Bernadette in the eye, never mind any customers!

A lad came into the shop but didn't want to acknowledge Bernadette when she gave him a cheery, "Welcome to Baxter's Fine Books, let me know if I can assist."

That had her on alert immediately. It did not surprise her that he made a bee-line to Ruth at the counter. The child was incredibly beautiful, and in several years when she became interested in courting, she would have young men falling at her feet.

But at the moment she was only a child, and she sat there mutely, looking rather scared.

"I like books," the new customer said, "Could I get one please?"

This was not the sort of thing people asked when they came in. If they were new to the town, they often walked in with a smile and mentioned the type of books they liked. Nobody simply "liked books." Not all of them. Even Louise had grown tired of Shakespeare.

Ruth's pleading eyes found Bernadette's.

Bernadette recognised him and intercepted. "It's Young Devon, isn't it? From the apothecary?"

He finally acknowledged someone else in the shop at this point, which was a relief. "Yes, Miss, but you can just call me Devon."

Bernadette had no idea if that was his Christian name or his family name, but it made no difference. Giving him the benefit of the doubt – perhaps he was merely awkward – she figured he could start with the lending shelves and try a couple of books for the short term. "Well, Devon, you may join our lending library, then you can borrow books and return them. Let me show you where they are."

As she led the boy away, she cast a glance back to a very relieved Ruth Millings.

She explained how the lending library worked, and the fees per month.

Barely five minutes later, another young lad came into the shop and appeared to wander about. Bernadette was still with Devon who didn't seem to know what sort of books he liked. "Take your time," Bernadette said, "I'll be back in a moment." Then she called out to Brutus to come and help Devon while she headed back to rescue a terrified Ruth.

She hadn't seen this lad in her shop in a long time. He might have come in with his mother at some point when she ordered a fashion periodical, but she hadn't seen him in here by himself. "Good morning, Master Burton," Bernadette said, recognising him as the solicitor's son.

The boy nodded, but his eyes never strayed far from Ruth.

As much as she was delighted that they had two new customers this day, Bernadette found her "benefit of the doubt" reserves drying out. The lad was virtually drooling at Ruth; far more interested in her than any books.

"You'll want to be joining our lending library as well, won't you?"

"What?" the boy asked.

A quick clear of her throat and Bernadette informed him of the monthly fees for the lending library. Then she guided him toward those shelves as well, which would block his view of Ruth.

He and Devon eyed each other suspiciously but didn't say anything. An uneasy feeling spread through Bernadette and she knew she could not leave Ruth in charge of the shop while she headed out. These lads were older and bigger, and it simply wasn't right.

It wasn't Ruth's fault she had the face of an angel; the girl was a child, and while she was in the shop, she was under Bernadette's protection.

Another young lad then came into the shop and sudden.y, Bernadette wanted to chase him out immediately. She let him in, but her blood was up. The boys had no intention of purchasing anything or joining the lending library. They were here to ogle Ruth.

Not on her watch!

"This is a shop that sells and loans books," she said quite sharply. "If you're not here for either of those two things, you can jolly well get out."

They looked at her, wariness flickering over their faces, but they did not move.

"I shall sign you all up to the lending service? Let me put your names in the membership list."

When she reached for the ledger to add their names and take their fees, she found all three of them standing around, forming something of a semicircle, not one of them putting their hands in their pockets to pull out coin. No wonder Ruth was terrified, they were all taller than Bernadette, and positively towered over Ruth.

It was on the tip of her tongue to call down for Lousie, and then she remembered. Lousie had a crowbar under the counter.

Bernadette reached for the crowbar and held it up, threatening them with it as she walked toward the three of them. "I said if you're not here to purchase or join the lending library, then you can *get out*!"

As one, they turned and fled from the shop as fast as their feet would take them.

Bernadette dropped the heavy crowbar on the counter, making a dent. Her arm ached like the devil, but she'd done it. She'd scared them off. She turned to check on the poor girl, who was white as a sheet. Somehow this made her even more beautiful than before.

"Are you all right, Ruth?"

The girl nodded.

Brutus chose this moment to step out where he'd been hiding among the bookshelves. "I don't like those boys, they're Benjamin's friends and they're all mean."

"Even Devon?" He seemed a little meek, if anything. Not the kind to hang around with bullies.

Brutus shrugged. "I don't know why Devon wants to be friends with them, they're mean to him as well."

Bernadette was grateful she'd been here to scare them off. But she started to wonder if she needed to always be in the bookshop to protect Ruth and possibly Brutus from the town bullies.

Maybe Louise would feel better soon, and be able to sit at the counter. That would help a great deal, and Bernadette would be able to get about town and see her customers. She had too much to do to babysit, and Ruth shouldn't need it. Bernadette chewed on her lower lip, thinking. A word or two to Mr Lennox would probably remove Devon from the field in short order, but the other two were probably worse… Devon's presence might actually make them mind their manners. What to do? She sighed in irritation. Why was this even her problem?

The bell above the front door tinkled again. Bernadette

steeled herself for cousin Joshua to appear. To her surprise and a fair amount of relief, it was the new doctor.

He was … smiling?

"Good morning, Doctor Williams," she greeted him. They had not begun on the best of terms, but after church he had been pleasant. One might almost call it conciliatory. They had withstood Reverend Millings' ire and were receiving plenty of support in the aftermath, including some gentle words from the doctor outside church. He had, however, declined an invitation to lunch with the Ferndales, which had her wondering if he simply wasn't accustomed to socialising.

What had he told her? That he'd followed his father from the school room to the battlefields as an apprentice surgeon, then endured several years of hideous conditions before being sponsored to train as a doctor. There would have been no time to learn the niceties of society.

"I came to browse, if that's all right," he said, tilting his head at the shelves of books.

It was a relief that at least he was not here to harass Ruth in any way. He'd not even noticed her at the counter. He only looked at the shelves of books, an expression of wonder on his face.

"Of course," she said, "Let me know if you need any assistance."

A pang of guilt surprised her, and she wondered if she had any books about society that might help in his new situation.

"This is marvellous," he said from behind a tall shelf. "This whole section is for lending?"

Bernadette headed toward the sound of his voice. "Yes.

Louise re-covers them to ensure they're robust enough for repeat borrowing. Would you like a lending membership?"

"Yes please." His face was alight as he looked at the shelves like a child looked at sweets. "Oh, and I was wondering where your medical section is."

"This way," she showed him to the single shelf with their range of health-related titles. "It's not as comprehensive as I'd like. I'm hoping Papa sends some home from France soon."

His face paled, eyes widening with horror. "Your father is in France at this moment?"

She found his concern comforting. There was no artifice in his expression at all. "He is, and we are, obviously, dreadfully worried about him. He departed last year when he heard that the crazed Corsican was safely imprisoned on Elba. If only he'd remained so."

Doctor Williams reached out momentarily before withdrawing his hand, as if he wanted to comfort her with a gentle touch on the arm. Bernadette appreciated the gesture and steadied her breath. "In the meantime, we have books to keep us gainfully educated and by turns distracted from the madness in the world."

"That we most certainly do."

By the end of their interaction, he'd joined the lending library and bought a book on arthritis, then suggested some more medical volumes they should order in. "It's so much easier showing patients the images in these books. I'm afraid I'm not much of a draughtsman and my illustrations tend to confuse them all the more."

Bernadette sighed with relief as he left their shop. It had only taken the best part of a month, but they'd had a suitable interaction where they had not come to verbal blows. How utterly marvellous!

What was not marvellous at all was that Bernadette had to put all the entries into the ledger herself and add them up. Louise was useless with mathematics and continued to be so, but Bernadette had to admit she wasn't much better.

Over the next few days, Bernadette tried to teach Brutus how to do the numbers, but his education was seriously lacking and she had to start with much more simple additions. Not his fault; his parents were only paying for Benjamin's education, not their second son's.

It would be impossible to leave the ledger until Mr Jackson came back. It could be months. Or... She didn't want to think about it.

One morning, Mrs Bell came over and asked Bernadette to come with her and visit her married daughter, Mrs Nettle, who had a sore arm. The small bookshop windows were open to draw air upwards, because Louise was making stinky glue. She was still crying and moping but at least she was being somewhat productive. Until the glue was ready, Brutus had little to do.

Mrs Poole was too busy, so Bernadette begged Ruth and Brutus to mind the counter. "The glue smell will probably keep customers away, so I doubt you'll have to do anything. And I'll be back soon to help. Just take people's names down if they have inquiries and I'll sort it all out later. If they buy anything, please make a note of the money and put it in the tin under the counter. Ruth, you're good at counting, I'm sure you'll have no trouble."

The young girl beamed at being given such responsibility, and Bernadette felt better immediately. "Call for Louise if any of those silly boys come in. Or run next door and get Mr Thomas, Brutus," she added in a flash of inspiration. "He'll toss them out if any of them start any nonsense."

Grabbing her basket, she followed Mrs Bell to Mrs Nettle's house, where they were both surprised to find Dr Williams already in attendance.

"Oh, good morning, Mrs Bell," he said, cheerfully enough. "I passed Mr Nettle in the street and he asked me to stop in."

"Ah," Mrs Bell said. "Well. I didn't think it something to bother you with, not yet anyway, I was going to ask Miss Bernadette to have a look."

Her tone had the doctor, who had been bending over where Mrs Nettle sat in a chair, straighten up and look around. Spotting Bernadette standing in the doorway, his expression changed from amiable to annoyed.

"Your daughter has an abscess in her armpit, Mrs Bell, most likely from an infected ingrown hair. It requires lancing, draining and thoroughly cleaning, and not by an untrained herb woman."

Bernadette bristled with fury. "Who do you think was handling this sort of thing before you came?" she snapped. "Dr Rasley would never have bestirred himself for such a thing!"

"Why ever not?" His expression was frankly incredulous. "This is a nasty infection!"

Mrs Nettle made a slight sound of distress, and Bernadette stepped forward to look past the doctor. What she saw gave her pause - the lump in Mrs Nettle's armpit was as big as a baby's clenched fist, an ugly shade of purple, with dark red streaks around it.

"Oh," Mrs Bell said, obviously seeing it too. "Hilda, you didn't tell me it was this bad! Why didn't you say something to me before?"

"Didn't want to be a bother," Mrs Nettle said sheepishly.

"You're not a bother," Bernadette said quickly, reaching to take Mrs Nettle's free hand and squeeze it gently.

"I'll take care of it," Dr Williams said firmly.

"The pair of you." Mrs Bell put her hands on her ample hips and frowned at them. "Stop bickering like children and take care of it *together*."

Bernadette flushed to the roots of her hair, and though she couldn't look at him directly, from the corner of her eye spotted that the doctor had turned a little red too.

"Once the abscess is drained, I have a poultice here that is very good for drawing out residual infection," she offered in a small voice.

"I appreciate that, Miss Baxter." The doctor paused, and then said quietly, "This is likely to be quite uncomfortable for Mrs Nettle. If Mrs Bell can hold her shoulders and you hold her arm…"

"Of course."

Bernadette was actually quite fascinated to watch as Dr Williams carefully cleaned a scalpel blade with what smelled like pure alcohol, before tucking some clean rags beneath Mrs Nettle's arm and making a single thin slice deep into the skin.

What came out of the abscess was quite unmentionable, and Dr Williams gently probed and prodded and massaged until Mrs Nettle was hissing with pain, but the fluids looked a much more natural colour.

"A good job," he said briskly, whisking away the soiled rags and wiping the cut with a fresh one soaked in whisky.

"Will it need a stitch in?" Bernadette asked curiously.

"No, I would prefer it continue to drain naturally. If you notice any excess bleeding, send for me," he told Mrs Nettle, "but otherwise treat it with the poultice Miss Baxter will give you for… three days?" He looked at Bernadette.

"At least three days," she agreed. "I'll call in each day to look at it for you. And I'll let you know, Doctor, if I think the infection is worsening."

"Thank you." He gave her a small nod, cleaning his scalpel and putting it away.

"There," Mrs Bell said in satisfied tones. "See, the two of you *can* work together."

Neither Bernadette or the doctor had anything to say to that, but she met his eyes as he gave her a quick sideways glance, and a little to her surprise, he smiled at her. A wry, sheepish sort of grin, but one which seemed to express the same things she was feeling - that perhaps they'd both been a little silly, building up a rivalry that served no good purpose.

She smiled back.

Returning to the bookshop a little while later, Bernadette found the smile staying on her lips. Dr Williams could be nice when he wasn't trying to lord it over her with his superior medical knowledge. There was no question that he was actually a very good doctor, far superior to old Dr Rasley. Not only his medical skills, but his bedside manner; he had been very kind to every patient she had seen him with thus far, quick and deft when a painful procedure was required and taking what steps he could to minimise discomfort.

Yes, although she'd had misgivings initially, she thought Dr Williams was going to be very good for the people of Hatfield!

Humming a jaunty little tune to herself, she smiled at Ruth as she placed her basket on the desk.

"I sold four books!" Ruth said, looking rather proud of herself.

"Oh, what a good job! To different customers?" Bernadette asked.

"Well, no, just Lord Ferndale. But he was very pleased with the selection I offered him!"

Bernadette resisted the urge to pat Ruth on the head. Lord Ferndale rarely left the bookshop with less than three books tucked under his arm, and was so kind he would probably have bought whatever books Ruth offered even if he owned them already. Ruth had still done well to interact with a customer at all, and she had written the transaction down perfectly, Bernadette saw as she looked over Ruth's shoulder at the ledger.

"Excellent work," she praised.

Ruth beamed happily. "Shall I go dust shelves now?"

Since Ruth had begun work at the bookshop, there was rarely a speck of dust to be found anywhere.

"I think we're very clean at the moment. Why don't I show you the catalogue? Now that those books are sold, we need to decide if we are going to re-order them for stock."

"How do you decide that?" Ruth asked.

"It depends on if we've sold them before, and how frequently..."

Bernadette continued to explain as she opened their

heavy book catalogue. She showed Ruth what she was talking about, and the younger girl nodded, listening intently.

"Bernadette, may I ask you a question?" Ruth said a little while later, as the two of them worked quietly, Ruth writing out a list of books for the next order from the London printer.

"Of course," Bernadette said.

"It's not about books…"

Bernadette smiled. "We're friends, Ruth. You can ask me anything, about any topic you have questions about."

"What are courses?"

Bernadette hesitated. "In what context are you asking?" she said cautiously.

"Well." Ruth glanced about furtively, even though the pair of them were quite alone, since Brutus was upstairs helping Louise at the moment. "I've heard some of the women come into the shop asking you for herbs to help with their courses. To bring them on, or to regulate them… and I'm not sure what they are."

"You're fourteen, aren't you, Ruth?" Bernadette checked. Why ever hadn't the girl's mother talked to her about this? Bernadette sighed inwardly. An awkward conversation, to be sure, but someone would have to have it. Maybe Mrs Millings didn't dare speak of such things to her daughter, for fear of her husband calling such speech sinful.

Ruth was looking at her expectantly, so Bernadette nodded. Better for the girl to have the knowledge, the *complete* knowledge, especially since her beauty meant she already had most of the young men in town tripping over their feet when she walked by.

"All right. I'll tell you. Let me get us a cup of tea, and I will stop talking the moment the bell rings, but I promise I'll explain everything you need to know about the functions of a woman's body."

Ruth's eyes got bigger and rounder the longer Bernadette talked, and by the end of the long conversation, her face was quite white. Bernadette's was rather pink. Factual though she had tried to be, it was still not a topic that she was quite comfortable discussing aloud with anyone!

Ruth shook her head when Bernadette asked if she had any questions, and Bernadette suspected she'd shocked the poor girl. Better too much information than not enough, though, or worse yet, inaccurate nonsense gleaned from other girls who didn't have the facts.

"It's quiet this afternoon. Why don't you take a book and go read by the stove?" she suggested kindly, guessing Ruth probably would like a little time to digest what she'd been told.

Ruth very nearly fled, making Bernadette smile. Perhaps she should give this talk to other young girls, she mused. It might lead to a few less unwanted pregnancies among the farm girls who flipped their skirts for boys without a thought and then came begging Bernadette for help when they didn't want to marry!

On the other hand, maybe not. If Reverend Millings found out she was delivering these kinds of lessons, the thunderous sermons would get even worse. Bernadette just hoped Ruth had the sense not to ever mention today's knowledge at home.

The bell chimed and Mr Thomas from the Red Lion next door popped his head in. "Letter came for you, Miss Bernadette," he said cheerfully. "From Ireland!"

"From Estelle!" Bernadette paid the postage and took the

letter eagerly. Their eldest sister Estelle had gone off to Ireland with her new husband Mr Yates the previous autumn to visit with Mr Yates' mother who lived there. Estelle had written regularly, every two weeks at least, and in her last letter had mentioned that Mr Yates was making enquiries about a ship to bring them home now that spring had arrived.

"Oh. Oh!" Bernadette read the letter in increasing shock, her hand going to her mouth. "Louise. Louise!" She shrieked it loudly enough that her sister came rushing down the stairs only a moment later, asking whatever was the matter. Bernadette held out the letter with a shaking hand.

"Estelle's pregnant!"

Louise's expression transformed from sad and slightly concerned, to shocked delight. She took the letter and read it, her expression undergoing another transformation as she got to the end.

"Oh… but she's not coming home!"

"Not yet," Bernadette qualified. "The morning sickness is making her quite miserable at the moment and she is in no condition to travel, but usually that eases after the first months and she should be able to come home then."

"Hm." Louise read the letter over again, leaning on the counter. "She sounds so happy," she said wistfully.

"As does Marie!" They'd had a letter just the previous day from their other sister, now the Countess of Renwick, blissful in her northern castle with her new husband after running off to Gretna Green with him when Cousin Joshua refused permission for them to marry.

"I am happy for them," Louise said with a loud sniff. She wiped away a tear. "At least we know they're safe so we don't have to worry about them."

Bernadette put a sympathetic hand on Louise's arm. No, they didn't have to worry about Estelle and Marie... but their father was another matter, and so was Mr Jackson.

"Hopefully *everyone* will come home soon," she said, and Louise nodded in fervent agreement.

CHAPTER 6
A Thaw In Relations

There was a tease of summer in the warm air as Bernadette headed back to the bookshop with a basket full of mint and lavender stems. She nodded to Louise as she took the stairs to the kitchen and found Crafty waddling around.

The moment the mint was on the table, Crafty leapt up - but only reached part way before the weight of her distended belly brought her straight back onto her paws. She'd grown so fat with her latest litter her belly nearly dragged on the ground. Bernadette took pity on her and stripped the leaves off a couple of stalks, then tossed the stalks on the floor. Crafty rolled her face in the herbs and wailed. She flopped onto the ground to really give herself a good scratch, but her belly rose like an uneven pie crust in the middle. Her abdomen was moving; the kittens would be here any day now.

With a sigh, Bernadette put the mint leaves in a cotton bag out of Crafty's reach and headed downstairs, where Louise was moping behind the counter.

"I dare not do the sums, I'll think too much about Shaun," Louise said.

"And Father," Bernadette goaded.

"Yes, yes, him too," she agreed.

"At least Joshua hasn't been stomping about," Bernadette said, as she reached under the counter for the cash tin.

"Do not even utter his name," Louise said with a noisy sigh.

They shared a dark laugh at that. In a few minutes, Bernadette had the last loan payment ready to go. The sisters had a world of troubles on their shoulders, but this at least was one less thing to worry about from today. "Should we have a toast to celebrate the end of Father's loan?"

"Gosh, is that really the last payment?" Louise looked genuinely puzzled.

Her sister at least wasn't crying the entire day, and was even capable of having short discussions with people before Ruth would step in and help.

"I'm proud of us," Bernadette said. "I know Felix helped before he and Estelle left, and we could have called on Renwick's man in London, but we did this, you and I. We kept it all going."

"We did," Louise managed a wistful smile that almost reached her eyes. "We certainly have a lot of news to impart to Papa when he gets home."

"Yes, 'when'," Bernadette emphasised the possibility. "I'm sure he's holed up somewhere and keeping out of trouble. I doubt anybody is getting any post at all from France at the moment."

These were the supportive fictions they told each other to keep their spirits up. They had not heard from Papa since his last crate of books had arrived in January, nearly four months ago.

It was lovely hearing from Estelle in Ireland and Marie in Cumbria, but it was unlikely Shaun would have time to write, and even less likely that any letter from him or their father might reach them. They simply had to keep hoping things would turn out for the best.

The alternative did not bear thinking about.

And although the loan would soon be in the past, Bernadette couldn't help but be suspicious of Cousin Joshua's absence. They used to be able to set their watches on him storming into the bookshop at least once a week, with a fresh accusation or threat. It had been a while now. It might have been three weeks since he'd last come in with a list of ridiculous demands.

He had to be up to something. She would talk to Rosie about it, see if the maid had heard any gossip.

Glynn had a spring in his step and a smile on his face as he and Mrs Bell put a note on the door to say they were at the Hospital Committee Meeting at The Red Lion if anyone needed medical attention.

The assembly room at The Red Lion echoed with their footsteps as Mr and Mrs Haye moved tables and chairs together so they could all face each other. Mr Haye set out teapots brimming with fresh brew and Mrs Haye had a tray of cups, saucers and biscuits.

"Is this usual for a committee meeting?" Glynn asked, taking a seat. "To feed and water us so well?"

"Of course," Mrs Haye said. "This isn't The Swan."

Glynn chuckled, having been warned from that establish-ment. It was natural that there would be rivalry between inns. He made a mental note that if The Swan did have a bedbug infestation problem as rumour said, he should examine the premises and the people. They could be unwit-tingly transmitting diseases, and that would not do under his watch.

He was pleased to see all three midwives of Hatfield in attendance, and Miss Yates, who would no doubt be Lord Ferndale's eyes and ears. Mrs Poole was also here, and took a seat next to Miss Yates. As the rest of the members arrived and filled each seat, he was surprised young Bernadette was not joining them. Was this a snub, or was Mrs Poole her proxy?

He would ask later, when he had the time.

Mrs Millings, the Vicar's wife, sat quietly on the other side of Miss Yates. He smiled and introduced himself, as he hadn't had a chance to do so yet. She made a shy acknowl-edgement. Well, he'd much rather she be here than her husband.

Mrs Poole poured the tea while Miss Yates called the meeting to attention. Then she listed the items they would be discussing on the agenda, in a serious tone. Mrs Millings took notes and the midwives each took turns delivering their concise reports. He was impressed with the quality of their work and how seriously they were taking the issue of where a hospital might be built. The optimum position would be somewhere close to the High Street, but that could hamper the hospital's growth in future because of existing buildings.

Miss Yates then asked if he had an opinion about where a hospital might go.

Goodness, he really lacked experience in this. "Well, I've

only worked in field hospitals, and they were all temporary and hardly robust. But a temporary hospital could work to tide us over … There is a grain store on the High Street that appears large enough."

The women nodded in thought, and then Mrs Bell said, "That's the trick of Hatfield, some buildings are empty for a good part of the year, but after harvest they are packed to the rafters."

Glynn nodded. "I wondered as much, you're right. I have not been here long enough to see how the seasons play out. Thank you."

Mrs Bell beamed.

In fact, they all smiled and appeared to relax at that. Had they thought he might refuse to listen to their counsel because they were all female? He was wiser than that.

Glynn rested his hands on the table and leaned forward, looking seriously at each woman in turn. "Ladies, I am here to learn. You know this town far better than I. Miss Yates, where do you think a hospital should be positioned? Does Lord Ferndale have any suitable vacant buildings, or an empty field in a location close enough to town?"

The discussion became lively as they shared their ideas around the table. Even Mrs Millings was encouraged to contribute. In a quiet voice she said, "I wondered whether the land beside the church residence could be used?"

"That's brilliant," Miss Yates said. "It's an excellent location, and not in a spot where the graveyard could be expanded to it."

"I think it was supposed to be a kitchen garden for the church. There were a few apple trees and such. Could they write to the bishop and request assistance? The Church owns the land, of course…"

Mrs Poole made a note and said, "I shall do just that, Mrs Millings. I can't believe I never thought of it."

"But please don't use my name, I have not spoken of this to the Reverend."

"Say no more," Mrs Poole said. "I will write to the bishop on behalf of Miss Yates and the Hospital Committee, that is all."

There was a supportive atmosphere to this meeting Glynn found fascinating. The women were working out the best way forward, together. Through their hard work, the town would benefit. While it was clear Miss Yates and Mrs Poole were the ones in charge, each attendee was treated with respect.

When they reached the part of the agenda where each midwife gave their reports for the last three months, he felt utterly humbled. A great many babes delivered, but so many losses.

"Is this the usual rate? To lose so many infants?" he asked. He knew babies delivered to camp followers of the army had an appallingly high death rate due to the conditions in which they lived, and often the poor health of their mothers. Somehow he had believed that was not the normal situation.

Miss Yates turned some pages back in her journal and checked her notes from a meeting at the same time last year, with a remark that more babies generally were lost in the winter months because of the cold conditions. "It's a little less than this time last year, but it's still not pleasant hearing," she confirmed.

He kept quiet for the rest of the meeting, feeling as if he suddenly had so much more to learn about women's work.

When the meeting came to an end, he thanked the

women for including him and then walked home with Mrs Bell. He sat in her kitchen for a little while, not hungry or thirsty, just turning things over in his head.

"The losses surprise me, and vex me a little, if I'm honest."

"They are a sad fact of life," Mrs Bell said. "That's why we started keeping notes in the first place, because we needed to know if things were getting better or worse. Some of the mothers are never right in themselves afterwards. It's a terrible sorrow for them."

In all his training, the topic of childbed, and the health of the mothers in the aftermath, truly hadn't been covered. Delivering babes was seen as women's work, not something for male doctors to get involved with.

He'd seen senseless deaths in field hospitals, but this had to be the cruelest loss of life for all concerned.

He wondered if the bookshop stocked any medical texts on childbed and the various ailments of women. And of infants, come to that; he'd treated few thus far. Perhaps he'd go over and take a look.

"Good afternoon, Dr Williams!" Bernadette said cheerfully as he entered the shop.

"Good afternoon." He paused. "I had rather expected to see you at the hospital committee meeting this morning, Miss Baxter."

"Oh, no." She shook her head. "I do not have nearly enough seniority in this town to be involved in any of the committees." Leaning in towards him with a conspiratorial air, she admitted, "Nor do I wish to, if I am honest. I leave all that sort of thing to Mrs Poole, she enjoys it."

"I see. Well, it was very informative... and made me

realise there are gaps in my education I should like to remedy. I'd like to browse your medical texts."

"Of course." She gestured him to the shelves in question, and returned to the counter to serve a lady who had followed him into the shop and was requesting some pamphlet or other.

The bookshop cat came by and rolled on Glynn's feet as he was browsing the texts.

"Hullo, my lady." He bent down to pet her, and frowned as he felt her grossly distended belly. "What is this, madam? Kittens on the way? I hope this is not a result of some disgraceful liaison after I accidentally let you out."

"I wish I could tell you it wasn't, but…" Bernadette said behind him, and he gave a half-laugh.

"Oh dear. My apologies."

"Crafty is a naughty girl. Her kittens are excellent mousers, though… perhaps you would like one once you are able to move into the doctor's residence?"

"I shall certainly take one of them off your hands," Glynn promised, thinking that was the least he could do. He should rather like having a cat for company, anyway.

"And have you found what you were looking for?" Bernadette looked at the books he'd already tucked under his arm. "Is that… *Burns' Principles of Midwifery*?"

"And his *Treatment of the Diseases of Women and Children*." He handed her the volumes. "Are there any other books you'd recommend on these specific topics?" Somehow, he was quite sure the shop wouldn't be selling the books unless Bernadette agreed with the general principles contained within

Her jaw was hanging open with shock. She shut her

mouth with an audible click, looked from the books to his face and back again.

"I, ah. Perhaps *Hamilton's Management of Female Complaints*?"

"Excellent." Spying the book among the other texts remaining on the shelf, he plucked it out and added it to the pile in Bernadette's arms.

"You didn't want to check the price?"

He grinned at her. "Put it on Lord Ferndale's account. Among his many other generous allowances to me, he told me that I could purchase any medical texts I pleased here and he would pay for them."

She laughed at that. "Of course he did. Dear Grandfather."

"You are very fond of him, I think," Glynn noted as they walked back to the counter together.

"Oh, indeed; even before Estelle married dear Mr Yates and he became family, Lord Ferndale has always been a dear friend to us." Bernadette checked the pricing in each book and noted it down in a ledger. "Would you like them wrapped in paper?" she asked.

"No, I'm only going across the street. Thank you."

As he left the bookshop with his new purchases tucked under his arm, Glynn reflected that it had been the first conversation he'd had with Miss Bernadette Baxter where one or the other of them hadn't become annoyed or defensive. It had been... nice. And she was really very pretty when she smiled, her eyes sparkling...

Careful, Glynn. He caught himself. *She's a bit young for you, and socially way above your class besides.*

Still, it was nice to appreciate a pretty young woman, and a clever one too, who had interesting things to say. Whistling quietly to himself, Glynn let himself back into Mrs Bell's house and made his way upstairs, hoping for once not to be interrupted by any patients that afternoon.

He had some excellent reading to do!

The next morning, he watched a stream of customers going into the bookshop and knew Bernadette would be too busy helping them to discuss his theories. He had a busy morning himself, seeing a host of younger women who had vague symptoms and strange ailments that didn't really match anything he'd heard of. The first woman, Miss Kilmartin, batted her eyes his way several times. The second, Miss Burton, the solicitor's daughter, affected a swoon. He'd seen so much of this lately.

"I believe Miss Baxter has exactly what you need," he said.

"Why would I need a herb woman?" She said the last two words in the same way a person might say *pestilence*.

"She is incredibly knowledgeable about these things, and has a far deeper understanding of the female condition," he said. He wrote a note that he knew Bernadette would understand. They'd developed something of a code of late. She would doubtless have a laugh to herself later.

Miss Burton was unhappy but nevertheless walked over to the bookshop.

His next patient was Miss Barnstable, and as he wrote the name down to begin a new record, a delightfully dark thought popped in. She was the undertaker's daughter, and if she thought they'd make a good alliance, she was sorely mistaken. Nobody in Hatfield could ever trust a doctor if he was married to an undertaker's daughter. Too much temptation to grow the family business.

That's what the women were here for, they were sizing him up as a potential husband: vague symptoms, smiling coquettishly at him and possibly catching up later to gossip about him.

He sent Miss Barnstable with a note to Bernadette as well.

After the general efficiency and pleasantry of the hospital committee meeting, Glynn was quite shocked by the town council meeting a few days later. Held in the same assembly room at the Red Lion, the only thing this meeting had in common with the other was the quality of the refreshments. The faces around the table were men, all prominent citizens, landowners and one or two professional gentlemen, including Reverend Millings, Glynn himself and Mr Burton, who was apparently a solicitor.

Lord Ferndale chaired the meeting, and it didn't take Glynn long to realise that the town council was split into two distinct, opposing factions, headed by Lord Ferndale on one side and the Reverend Millings and Joshua Baxter on the other. One might have thought that the younger men would be more progressive, but in fact the opposite was the case. The elderly Lord Ferndale was all for change and innovation, while the much younger Baxter and Millings behaved like reactionary idiots frightened of any change at all, probably including the wind and the tide, Glynn thought!

Lord Ferndale was as gracious and charming as always, but Glynn could see his frustration as the council split on just about every matter, several men stubbornly voting with Baxter and Millings even when their own interests would clearly be better served by a different choice.

"And next, the hospital." Lord Ferndale looked over his glasses at Glynn. "I have here a proposed budget for the fitting-out of the hospital; it is very comprehensive." He held up a sheet of paper with a long list of items on it. "I will pass it around for everyone to look at, but I find it to be very reasonable and funds have already been raised sufficient to cover these items."

"No point buying anything until there's a building to put it in," Reverend Millings said, folding his arms and refusing to accept the sheet of paper when Lord Ferndale tried to hand it to him.

"As to that," Glynn said, "the hospital committee…"

Joshua Baxter snorted loudly. "Bunch of yammering women."

"I will thank you to recall that my sister chairs the hospital committee, Mr Baxter," Lord Ferndale said in chilly tones. "And Reverend Millings' wife is a respected member of it, as is Mrs Burton, Mrs Platt, and Mrs Tinsley." He nodded at several of the other men present. "Let us not refer to our wives and sisters as 'yammering women'. And I will also thank you not to interrupt when Dr Williams is speaking."

Baxter subsided, but Glynn could see the simmering fury on his face.

With a polite cough, Glynn resumed. "The hospital committee proposed a temporary solution of using a currently vacant cottage, until a new hospital can be built." With a sideways glance at Reverend Millings, he decided not to mention that Miss Yates was writing to the bishop regarding the vacant land beside the vicarage. "The committee is in agreement that a purpose-built hospital is the ideal solution in the longer term, but we do need a facility now."

"They are all women," Reverend Millings said in tones of profound contempt. "What understanding could they possibly have of the matter?"

"I assure you that they have a very good understanding of how many of their number die in childbed, Reverend," Glynn said, trying to keep the snap out of his voice, "and they are well informed, in my *medically educated* opinion, as to how best to address the problem!"

And one of them is your wife, he didn't add, Lord Ferndale having already made the point. He quite saw why Mrs Millings was such a meek, terrified little mouse.

Glancing along the table, he met Lord Ferndale's steady gaze. *This is the kind of nonsense I have to deal with all the time,* the old baron's expression conveyed quite clearly.

"All in favour of the hospital being set up in the vacant cottage and the equipment purchased?" Lord Ferndale asked.

A few hands went up. Glynn counted quickly. Exactly half.

"Not you, Dr Williams?" Lord Ferndale asked, sounding surprised, and Glynn suddenly realised he'd not put his own hand up.

"I do beg your pardon. As I proposed the item, I thought I might not be eligible to vote on it."

"Quite the contrary," Lord Ferndale said firmly. "Else Mr Baxter would not have been able to be the deciding vote on the matter he brought to our attention today, now would he?"

"In that case." Glynn put his hand up, and Lord Ferndale smiled

"The motion is carried."

The reverend and Joshua Baxter both looked absolutely enraged. Baxter was red in the face, but Millings looked rather yellow... Glynn paused beside him at the end of the meeting.

"Begging your pardon, Reverend, but you look a little jaundiced. May I recommend some medication?"

Too late, he recalled Bernadette mentioning the same thing after church a few weeks previously.

"I want no help from you, charlatan! The Lord takes care of his own!" Millings snarled before storming out.

"Kind of you, but all you've probably done is set yourself up as a target for his next fire-and-brimstone sermon," Lord Ferndale observed dryly.

Glynn winced, before shrugging. "I'm not afraid of him. Besides, he targets the Baxter sisters often enough, and I do not see their business suffering. If he turns his ire upon me... people will still need a doctor when they are unwell."

"A wise attitude," Lord Ferndale said approvingly. "I'm glad you're a sensible man, Dr Williams. Shaun Jackson chose well when he recruited you." He sobered. "Talking of whom, I pray for his safety. Has Miss Louise chanced to receive a letter from him, would you happen to know?"

Glynn shook his head, expression grim. "So far as I know, she has not heard from him since he left for France."

Lord Ferndale looked grave. "The reverend would be better served praying for the King's brave soldiers rather than targeting our own. I'll speak to him, not that I think it would do any good."

"Perhaps the bishop...?" Glynn suggested tentatively.

"They will rarely remove a clergyman from his post for anything less than criminal conduct. A shame. He was a good man, a few years ago, but seems to have fallen into this strange mindset." Lord Ferndale shook his head and sighed, before making a polite farewell and departing, leaving Glynn alone with his thoughts.

CHAPTER 7
An Unlikely Thief

A most peculiar thing happened a few days later. Bernadette was on her way out with her usual basket of herbs when Ruth asked her to help a customer from London with a specific request. It was just the two of them in the shop, as Brutus was helping Louise bind another volume of Shakespeare folios.

Strange that Ruth could not do this for herself. There was a young woman waiting for Bernadette on the other side of town, and she was already running late. Ruth appeared to only want to sit behind the counter, which was unlike her. Then she suddenly remembered their excruciating but necessary conversation and wondered if Ruth was experiencing her courses? She left the young girl alone, thinking she might need a little privacy.

She helped the traveller with some reading choices and then made her way back to the counter. Just in time to see Ruth pull her hand back from the basket. She'd taken something, Bernadette was sure of it. It was very un-Ruth-like behaviour.

After she bid farewell to the customer, she reached for the basket and examined the contents. It was just as well she had, Ruth had taken the one thing her customer required.

She sighed, put the basket down and moved to the front door, where she switched the Open sign to Closed and snibbed the latch. Turning back to the counter, she looked at Ruth, who could not meet her eyes.

"Ruth, please tell me what's going on?" Bernadette said it as gently as she could, not wanting to scare the skittish girl.

Ruth dropped her head and snivelled miserably. Then she took the wrapped sachet of herbs from her pocket and put them back on the counter. "It's not f-for me. It's f-or a friend."

"Does your friend know how to use it?" Bernadette kept her voice steady, to get to the truth of the matter. Perhaps they were for Ruth's mother; Mrs Millings would be far too terrified of her husband to dare come to Bernadette herself. It would make sense.

"I… don't know… if she does."

Bernadette sighed and leaned onto the counter, then pushed the herbs towards Ruth to let her know she could have them. "There are no guarantees. There's enough in here for two doses. Divide it up and put half in a cup of tea. Not the pot, it will be too diluted, so put it in the cup. Let it steep for five minutes. Then strain it and drink it all at once. Twelve hours later, take the second half the same way."

Ruth nodded but said nothing.

"Look, why don't I come with you to see your friend, then I can see how far along she is and whether this will even work?"

"No!" Ruth sprang back as if Bernadette had struck her. "You can't come. I was sworn to secrecy. Nobody can know."

Cold fear moved through Bernadette. She had to speak carefully. "Ruth, you're not in trouble, but it sounds like your friend might be. Let her know I'd like to help. At the very least I could be a trusted person to talk to?"

Ruth shook her head, pocketed the herbs and said a timid, "Thank you."

Bernadette jogged upstairs to create another sachet of tea for her customer, and was soon heading out the front door, switching the sign back to Open now that she and Ruth had talked privately. The conversation and Ruth's furtive behaviour weighed on her mind, though.

She waved to Dr Williams as she walked past Mrs Bell's front window, but had no time to chat. She was even later now, and had to be back by closing to help Louise with the ledger.

By the time she reached her customer, Mary Ormiston, she was quite out of breath. They sat in her parents' kitchen and Bernadette was grateful this treatment required a cup of tea. She was parched. Mrs Ormiston fussed about, but she'd already got the water boiled for tea.

The rest of the male siblings were working in the fields, or had joined the war with Mr Ormiston.

"How long has it been?" Bernadette asked Mary.

"About eight or nine weeks, I suppose," she answered. The girl was despondent and had been crying. "I thought it was just nerves, and I've been crying so much since Alfred joined up. I thought he'd marry me for sure this time, but he up and enlisted anyway!"

One of Mary's younger sisters came in carrying a child of about one in her arms. The child was fussing and unsettled. Mrs Ormiston took the babe in her arms and patted her back until the little one burped. Satisfied and no longer in pain,

87

the babe closed her eyes and Mrs Ormiston handed the baby back.

"I'll make you some fresh scones as soon as we're able," Mary said.

"Don't worry about that," Bernadette assured her, pouring half the herbs into Mary's teacup.

Mary stirred them then moved to start drinking.

"Not yet, give it five minutes. It needs to steep," Bernadette said, folding the second dose of herbs away and giving them to Mary's mother.

"Mrs Ormiston, do you happen to have rhubarb growing? I'm running low and it makes excellent gripe water for babes." Bernadette knew the Ormistons had some, but it wouldn't be growing vigorously until later in summer.

"I have a good patch down the back that is reliable every summer. I'll dig you out a crown if you like."

"Oh no, thank you, I have nowhere to plant it, but two stalks, if you have any at all, will be excellent."

Once Bernadette deemed the brew had steeped enough, she nodded to Mary. "If you're only two months, it should work, but if you're further along, it might not."

Mary strained the drink through her teeth, then flicked the wet herbs into the cup. "Tastes vile."

"Take the second dose tonight," Bernadette said, patting Mary's arm. "You'll likely feel quite dreadful for a few days, I'm sorry, but hopefully you'll start to bleed sooner rather than later."

"Ow, I do 'ope so," Mary sniffled. "I wouldn't mind me a babe, but I need to be married first!"

"Mm." Bernadette tried to think if there were any young men who would marry Mary even if she was carrying another man's child. So many had gone off to war... but perhaps there was someone who might be persuaded? Better that than a home for unwed mothers. Or perhaps Mary and Mrs Ormiston could disappear for a while and Mrs Ormiston could pass the babe off as her own... Damn Napoleon and this stupid war anyway!

Mrs Ormiston appeared with five stalks of rhubarb instead of two. This was far more than Bernadette needed, but she appreciated the gesture and thanked the woman.

On her way home, she expected to wave to Dr Williams through the window as she passed, but he instead waved a news sheet at her and then came out the front door.

"What is it?" Her heart beat a tattoo in her head from fear.

"I wondered if you'd had a chance to see the latest dispatch from France?"

He looked pale. This could not be good.

Bernadette shook her head and he handed over the paper so she could read the awful news for herself. Terrifying battles taking place in towns she knew her father might be trying to traverse through to come home. There simply was no way of knowing if he was still alive and safe or in a ditch somewhere. And that was before she and Louise had time to worry about where Shaun might be.

"Dreadful business," Dr Williams said as she handed the newssheet back. "Before he left, Mr Jackson asked me to look out for you and Miss Louise. Is there anything I can do? Perhaps a meal at the Red Lion so you don't have to cook?"

"You are so kind," Bernadette said, thinking that he was being very decent these days and not throwing his educational achievements at her. "Mrs Poole, our housekeeper, will fret if she can't feed us a nourishing meal."

"Ah, I see," he looked at his feet.

"Wait. Why don't you come over and have dinner with us? And bring Mrs Bell, too. She can have a night off for a change."

His face brightened and he said, "Capital!"

The term made Bernadette laugh a little.

"Did I use the wrong phrase? I thought it meant 'Jolly good'."

"Oh, it does, but it sounds a little strange coming from you. I'll ask Mrs Poole what night would suit her."

"I should come and thank her for how well she and Miss Yates run the Hospital Committee."

Before Bernadette really knew what they were doing, they were walking across the street to the bookshop, chatting amiably.

The door tinkled and Ruth was not behind the counter.

A beaming Brutus Baxter was, so she was relieved to see somebody there.

Louise's voice carried down the stairs in a loud shriek of woe. "Oh no!"

Dr Williams sprang into action. "Is she hurt?" he asked as he rushed up the stairs.

Bernadette followed, and they were all soon in the kitchen, where she could put her basket down.

"Louise?" Bernadette called out.

"Oh dear." That was Mrs Poole, as she came into the kitchen from another room. "Oh dear, oh dear. That's ruined that, then." Then she saw they had company and came over all formal: "Good afternoon, Doctor Williams, everything all right?"

"Someone sounded hurt so I ran up?" he answered.

Louise came into the kitchen carrying a small wooden trunk.

Tiny mewling sounds sprang from inside.

She placed the trunk on the kitchen table with a huff. "Wollstonecraft, this is the last straw!"

Several heads from different directions all converged to look at what was in that box.

Crafty had delivered her five kittens in their box of beautiful fabrics Miss Yates had given them to make dresses for Estelle's wedding. They'd made a new dress each, but there were several lengths left over; Bernadette knew Louise had hoped to use one for a new dress for her own wedding to Shaun. Tears stood in Louise's eyes now at the death of that hope.

Bernadette shook her head. Those stains would never come out of the delicate silk.

Dr Williams gulped and looked guilty. "I can't help but feel this is my fault," he said. "I was the one who let the cat out…"

"She would likely have escaped anyway," Bernadette said kindly. "Don't distress yourself."

Louise was the one who was upset, Bernadette could see. She guided the doctor to the stairs and said Brutus would be able to assist if he needed any books.

"Perhaps I won't accept that dinner invitation quite so soon," he said as he reached the door, "I wouldn't want to upset Miss Louise any further."

After Dr Williams left, looking extremely guilty and contrite, Bernadette trudged back upstairs to assess the emotional damage. Louise was in a kitchen chair, her head in her hands, crying in earnest.

"Ah, pet," Mrs Poole said, with a look at Bernadette. "Here." She scooped up the trunk of kittens and took it out, perhaps thinking that if Louise didn't have to look at it she wouldn't feel so bad.

Bernadette knew better. She sat down beside Louise and put her arm around her sister's shoulders. "You've seen the newssheets?" she asked quietly.

Louise just sobbed harder.

"I know things are scary but you have to have faith, Lou. We've never stopped believing that Pa would come home, and you've got to keep believing that Mr Jackson will too." Bernadette tried to sound as confident and positive as she possibly could.

"What if neither of them do?" Louise cried.

"Then we're not alone," Bernadette said stoutly. "Estelle and Mr Yates will be home soon, and I know Marie is far away, but she and Renwick will send help if we ever need it."

Louise didn't even seem to be able to speak. She put her hand in her pocket and pulled out a crumpled letter, putting it on the table between her and Bernadette.

"What is that?" Bernadette peered at the letter, her brow furrowing. It looked… official, somehow. Like the loan letters from the bank. But they couldn't be getting more of those, they'd repaid the loan.

Louise gulped, and then she said in a small voice, "I think we need that help, 'Dette. I really do."

Bernadette couldn't make any sense of the letter, and Louise had to explain it to her; that one of their worst nightmares was about to come true. Cousin Joshua had gone to Chancery Court in London and requested to be made trustee of their father's estate; with their father gone to France, Joshua had claimed that two young girls, neither of them even of legal age, could not competently run a business.

Both of them knew too well what Joshua would do if he could legally gain control; there would be a pile of books outside in the street, probably on fire, and they'd be tossed out on their ears. Lord Ferndale would take them in, of course, but Baxter's Fine Books would be no more.

Over my dead body! Fury surged through Bernadette, replacing her initial panic. Joshua was not getting away with this, no matter what she had to do!

Leaving Louise to mourn the ruination of her not-even-created wedding dress, Bernadette set off downstairs with her writing things in hand and set about informing her other sisters. Marie and Estelle had both married men of influence; Renwick was an earl and Mr Yates the grandson of a baron. Either of them could bring their titled status to bear on the court to thwart Joshua, surely… they just had to agree to come. She'd go and see Lord Ferndale tomorrow, too. Grandfather would help. He might not have any legal standing to get himself appointed their trustee, not being actually related to them except by marriage, but he certainly had influence.

Determined, Bernadette bent over the paper, the scratch of her pen filling the quiet of the bookshop as she began to write.

CHAPTER 8
Brimstone

I f they thought the last sermon was bad, the Baxter sisters' ears were figuratively blistering at the next Sunday's service. Reverend Millings was in full flight. Considering his fury, his face should be as red as a scraped knee, but instead it had the colour of a decaying lemon.

There was a war on, so many men from Hatfield were in mortal peril at this very moment. Some of their wives had followed the drum to help provide meals and care.

Did he lead the congregation in prayer for a swift victory and the safe return of their neighbours? Not at all. Their vicar could only see sin in the people who remained. Bernadette looked directly ahead, trying not to flinch as he extolled the wicked nature of so many people who "gave in to sin at the slightest provocation."

"Interfering with God's divine will!" he screamed from the pulpit. "God looks after his flock, he needs no outside interference! If you are ailing, it is God's will! Let no man interfere!"

Bernadette had to suddenly concentrate. She'd felt sure

he was going to mention unsuitable reading material but he instead diverted sharply to talk about "prayer and faith being all people needed when they were sick".

As he continued, to her horror, she realised he wasn't pouring scorn on the Baxters this time. Instead, he was railing about the sin of modern medicine!

Proper medicines that a doctor like Glynn used for treating and healing people.

Bernadette could take it when Brimstone was harassing them; she and Louise supported each other, and they had Rosie and Mrs Poole at home. They also had the support of the Ferndales. But poor Glynn, he hadn't been here long. He might be in Lord Ferndale's employ, but he had no family in town. This was demonstrably unfair on the poor man. He didn't deserve to be singled out like this. She peered along the pew at him and saw him sitting rigidly straight, his face like stone. Beyond him, Lord Ferndale looked quite furious. The vicar had clearly not listened to Lord Ferndale's requests to tone down the brimstone and stop targeting his parishioners!

The end of the service couldn't come soon enough. When they were finally outside, the sun shone brightly and people were bidding farewell. Bernadette made her way to Glynn to offer him solace. "I am so sorry he targeted you this week," she said.

He made a rueful smile and shrugged his shoulders. "I'm glad he wasn't turning his ire on you, like he frequently does."

She shrugged and said, "I'm almost used to it. But it's not fair, what he said. You're doing good work here."

"Thank you. I feel a little politics might have played some part."

"Oh?"

He kept his voice low so they wouldn't be overheard. A lilting burr crept into his accent. "Yes, I voted against the reverend, and your cousin, at the last council meeting. They were displeased, to say the least."

"Oh dear!" She should be shocked, but instead felt a little camaraderie that the two of them were suffering the wrath of the same people. "Well, I hope it doesn't put anyone off coming to see you. This town needs its doctor."

"Ah, there you are!" a voice called out. It was Lord Ferndale. "Ready for lunch?"

Bernadette had the first pangs of hunger, and was mentally savouring the roasted potatoes the Ferndale Hall cook prepared so beautifully. Golden-crunchy on the outside and tender in the middle, she could almost taste them on her tongue already. She nodded eagerly.

"You too, Dr Williams, please join us. Cook keeps forgetting Mr Jackson and some of our staff are away, and makes far too much. We'd be grateful if you would accept." Lord Ferndale nodded in his usual amiable way.

Glynn said, "Well, in that case, I'd be glad to come."

Lord Ferndale beamed, and soon they were settled comfortably in the carriage, bowling along at a good place, the summer sun beaming down on them.

The potatoes were excellent and plentiful. Bernadette saw a glimmer of fun in her honorary grandfather's eye and wondered if he was up to his matchmaking tricks again. He insisted she sit by Dr Williams, and the direction of the conversation was decidedly medical, ensuring the two of them would have to talk to each other.

She didn't mind conversing with him at all; he was intelligent and well-educated, and she could definitely learn from him. But a romantic prospect? Attractive as he'd been with no shirt on, they were still too much at odds for her to consider that as a possibility. She did not want a husband who did not respect her skills. They would not get along, it would end in bickering and acrimony.

Glynn was all thumbs. If this were a medical examination instead, he would have passed with distinction. Alas, he'd never studied how to attend a lunch with a baron and his maiden sister, so he had no idea of the protocol. He'd just have to keep smiling and saying "thank you" and hope that would cover his lack of decorum.

"Relax, Dr Williams, you're among friends here," Lord Ferndale assured him.

"Be kind, brother, he's probably still recovering from the sermon," Miss Yates said. Then she passed a plate of string beans his way. "Do you like beans?"

"Thank you," Glynn said, spooning a few onto his plate. He'd watched the way Miss Yates had done it with the fork and spoon and copied her style.

He put the cutlery down on the plate. Nobody had started eating yet, so he didn't reach for his knife and fork. Bernadette was sitting opposite him, making a silent gesture with her eyes, looking to him, then back to the plate.

"Oh! Of course. Miss Bernadette, would you like some beans?"

"Thank you," she accepted the plate and served herself, then offered them to Louise.

Lord Ferndale said, "Let me know if your patient load

reduces at all after that blast from Millings. I hope it won't, for the health of the town."

"I am keeping good records, and the town is mostly healthy, aside from occasional farming and other accidents. I will let you know if patronage decreases."

Lord Ferndale picked up his knife and fork, and the rest of the table followed suit. Thank heavens he'd finally started, Glynn was famished and the food aromas were making his mouth water.

"And Bernadette, I hope you and the midwives can take a breath and rest, now that Dr Williams is in town?"

"He is a great boon to us all," she said.

Warmth engulfed Glynn at her praise.

"Excellent!" Lord Ferndale beamed. "You've ceased hostilities."

Glynn nearly choked on his roast chicken.

Accurate record keeping was something Glynn had established as soon as he'd arrived in Hatfield. It was something he'd begun in his early days in the army, a practice adopted from his father, and he had never stopped. On this quiet Saturday morning, as he completed some notekeeping from the patients he'd seen through the week, he couldn't help feeling frustrated at having to start from scratch with every patient. Usually a doctor would rely on the records kept by his predecessor, but whatever records Dr Rasley might have kept had burned in the fire. His trust of the midwives had increased after he'd attended the Hospital Committee meeting; their records had been excellent, although it was disheartening to learn of so many babes and their mothers who'd died in childbed or soon thereafter.

He looked across the street just as Bernadette returned to the bookshop from an errand with her herbs. Inspiration struck. Bernadette could help him.

Within a few minutes, he was across the street. The sign on the door said "Closed" so he knocked and opened it gently so as not to startle anyone inside.

A puffy-faced Louise greeted him behind the counter. The poor woman must have read the latest news arriving from France. It was ghastly.

"How are you bearing up?" he asked as gently as he could.

"It's all awful," she said, wiping her face. "Are you here for some books? I'll call Bernadette down to help."

"Thank you, although I'm not here to purchase, that can wait, but I'd be most grateful if I could speak to your sister. I'd ask after your health, but I trust Bernadette can offer better treatment?" The sister would have a much better tonic than anything he could offer - the warmth of comfort in a discomforting time.

Bernadette appeared cheerful as she came down the stairs. It warmed him to see her smile, although he tried very hard not to think about how much her smile affected him in a strange way.

"I've come to ask for your assistance with record keeping in the town. I'm keen to build some more knowledge about the town and the people. Injuries and illness and such."

"The hospital committee has good records," she suggested.

"Indeed they do. The reports at the last meeting were thorough and precise, and appear to go back several years. I also believe you excel at keeping good records, as you keep catalogues for the hundreds of books in the shop, and you keep the ledgers." He'd noticed her methodically working down the columns of accounts on several occasions.

Louise interrupted with a baleful, "I'm not that bad at it am I?"

"You're very good at other things," Bernadette reassured her.

Glynn tried not to chuckle. He was in a serious pursuit for accuracy. "Of course, Dr Rasley's records burned in the fire, so we've lost them. But I'm wondering, if we could work together to rebuild some reliable patient dossiers?"

She smiled at him and he felt those strange feelings again, which he tried very hard to ignore.

"The register of births, deaths and marriages at the churches will be a useful place to start."

"Of course!" he grinned with delight. He should have thought of that.

Then his smile dimmed. "Each church has their own?" He was sure the priest at the Catholic church would be very helpful, but the other…

"Yes, of course."

"Would this mean having to talk to Reverend Millings?"

Bernadette pressed her lips together in thought. She didn't appear too happy with the idea of having to speak to the man who so spitefully derided them from the pulpit. "He will likely be busy at the moment writing his sermon for tomorrow, but Mrs Millings and her helpers will be decorating with flowers for the service, and they won't mind us being there. The doors are always open."

His heart raced with excitement. "This will help so much. I will just collect my ledger so I can take notes!"

Within half an hour, they were in the church. He was glad he wasn't coming on his own, and admired Bernadette's bravery in accompanying him.

True to Bernadette's prediction, Mrs Millings and her helpers didn't mind them at all.

They set to work looking through the precious volumes, filled by dates and names of recent events. It felt like looking through time.

He took notes in his ledger of the recent births, so that he would visit the families and check on their health. "This is already helping so much. I'd be lost without you," he said.

She made a soft little, "Gosh," in response.

Had he gone too far? He really should keep their interactions as professional as possible.

But they weren't here alone, there were several women sweeping the floors and polishing the timbers.

The side doors opened and Reverend Millings walked in. The ladies and his wife greeted him almost silently and made deferential bobs.

Glynn gulped, but did not move. Any second now the reverend would see them.

He did.

His eyes rounded and his neck stiffened.

His skin had the same colour as a fresh dandelion flower, and his eyes showed yellow too in the whites. The man really wasn't well. Perhaps it was true that choler damaged the liver.

"You!" The vicar raised his hand and pointed at them. "What do you think you're doing?"

The man stomped towards them. Eyes wide with fury, puffy skin wobbling on his cheeks with rage.

Glynn grabbed Bernadette and shoved himself in front of

her to shield her. "This was my idea, Miss Baxter is blameless! I came to see the town recor…"

"Sinners in the house of God!" Millings screamed at them. "How dare you?"

Heart hammering behind his ribs, Glynn wondered whether Bernadette should flee while she still had the chance.

The young woman squeaked out, "We're doing this for the good of the town!"

Millings stomped closer, bearing down on them, spit flying from his mouth. "How! Dare! -"

Suddenly, his entire body stiffened.

No more words came out, despite his open mouth.

His eyes rolled back in his head.

Foam gathered and began to drip from his lips.

Nobody said a word as his entire body suddenly dropped to the floor with a tremendous thud.

A couple of the women screamed. Mrs Millings gasped and held onto the edge of a pew for support.

Glynn leaped forward and crouched beside the fallen man, reaching for the Reverend's neck and checking for a pulse. His own blood ran cold as he failed to find one.

"Wh-at's hap-pened?" Bernadette stammered from behind him.

Glynn shook his head, his fingers searching for any sign of life. "He's dead."

Mrs Millings collapsed onto the floor. The rest of the women rushed to her side.

Glynn turned to a pale Bernadette. "Probably for the best if you go home, and have some sweet tea." Their record keeping excursion was done, and she could not help anyone here. Best to get her out of the situation before a crowd arrived.

Wordlessly, she nodded and fled.

Glynn could not flee. He was a doctor, he'd just witnessed a man fall down dead in front of him and he had to do something.

He grabbed his ledger and began writing, noting the symptoms, the foamy spittle in his mouth, the distressing colour of his skin. There wasn't much he could do at this point but to make an accurate record of everything that had happened.

The women were comforting Mrs Millings, who would be in a great deal of shock no doubt. He went over and asked if anyone would make her a strong tea with plenty of honey. One of the helpers dashed away.

"Is he... gone?" Mrs Millings asked.

Glynn nodded in the affirmative. "I'm afraid so."

She slumped to the floor and a strange soft groan came out. It almost sounded like a sigh, but Mrs Millings was always so quiet, he assumed this was how she processed bad news.

Ruth rushed in from the door one of the helpers had only just exited. She looked to be in a complete state, still wearing a nightgown and bare feet from being abed, as she ran to embrace her mother.

"Oh Mama!" she cried, rocking her gently with comfort. "It's going to be all right."

Glynn stepped back and gave them some privacy in their

confusion and grief. "Let me know if you need anything. I shall contact the undertaker."

There wasn't a great distance between the church and the undertaker, Glynn mused. He spoke only briefly to Mr Barnstable, because his head was swirling with names of the people he should notify. He retrieved Canterbury from the livery yard behind the Red Lion and tried to work out in which direction he should set out. Every member of the town council should know. Well, Lord Ferndale first. He'd be the easiest person to speak to. He did not relish the thought of having to speak to Joshua Baxter or Mr Burton. They were already angry with him after he'd voted against them at the last meeting.

Then it struck him. There would be one less member of the town council holding back progress. Joshua Baxter had lost an ally. That made the thought of delivering the news to them just that little bit better.

Glynn wanted to punch Joshua Baxter with the way he'd taken control of the church service the next day. Not that there was a replacement yet, but the fact he'd assumed he was the most important person to deliver the news to the town stuck in Glynn's gullet.

"I urge all to treat this event with solemnity and lean on your faith. Now is not the time to engage in idle gossip." Then Baxter looked directly towards Bernadette and Louise, which was seriously unfair.

A replacement temporary curate arrived from the bishop a few days later. His first duty was to officiate at the funeral of Reverend Millings. Mrs Milling and Ruth looked weighed down by their black mourning dress. The widow had not come to see Glynn for any assistance, but she looked even more frail than usual. Perhaps he might suggest she start adding rich sauces to her food to restore her strength?

This vicar was so softly spoken they had to apply extra concentration to hear him. The people in the pews towards the rear of the church would have no chance.

The next day, Lord Ferndale convened an emergency town council meeting at the Red Lion. Glynn brought his records with him and had to deliver the unwelcome news.

"It's my belief this was not a natural death," he said. "Many people in the town observed that the late Reverend Millings had poor colour in his face for several weeks."

Lord Ferndale nodded.

Joshua bristled. "You're just making a cover story for yourself."

"Please, keep things civil," Lord Ferndale interrupted.

"He was the last person to see the vicar alive," Joshua complained. "He was fighting with him!"

Mr Burton sided with Joshua, of course. "You never said that when you told me he'd d- passed," the solicitor said pompously, glowering at Glynn.

"There were several women cleaning and decorating the church at the time I was there," Glynn said. "They will bear witness that I did not touch him. In fact, he was the one who saw me and started shouting on approach. I didn't even get close enough to touch him!"

Mr Burton scoffed and said, "Women." As if that dismissed any input they could make.

Lord Ferndale rescued the situation with some common sense. "I agree that this matter should be examined.

However, as my investigator is currently risking his life for King and Country, we shall have to wait for his return."

Joshua looked furious again at the mere mention of Mr Jackson, even though Lord Ferndale hadn't said his name. "I'm the magistrate," he said snappishly.

"Then perhaps you would care to do your job, Mr Baxter," Lord Ferndale said calmly. "If you know how."

That was quite a stinger, Glynn thought as the meeting broke up and a sputtering Joshua stormed out, Mr Burton the only man who followed immediately on his heels. Perhaps some of the other men were beginning to have second thoughts regarding which horse they'd chosen to back? About time, in Glynn's opinion. Baxter was a blowhard fool, Lord Ferndale a decent and honourable man, and anyone who couldn't see those things was blinder than the proverbial bat.

CHAPTER 9

Bad News and Worse Rumours

Bernadette returned to the bookshop from visiting the good women of Hatfield with a queasy stomach. Her dear customers had told her, in the most comforting tones possible, that Phoebe Baxter was spreading rumours about her being in some way responsible for the vicar's demise.

To a woman they swore their loyalty to Bernadette, and said they were passing it on so that she knew and could avoid Mrs Baxter.

They gave her even more goods to take home, which were increasingly heavy to carry back. She could use a really good sulking session with Louise, but as she made it into the shop, her sister's expression told her that wasn't an option.

Her own misery would have to wait until she could help Louise, who had fallen into another funk.

"Oh Lou, what's Joshua done now?" Bernadette asked with a sigh as she hefted her basket onto the counter.

"Not him," Louise sniffed, "It's the news. There's been a great and terrible battle and all I can do is pray that Shaun and Papa are somehow safe."

"I take it nothing's turned up from Papa?"

"Shaun either," Louise sniffed the words together in her glumness. "Honestly, why can't men write and tell us what's going on? Do they want us to think they're dead? Do they want us miserable?"

"I've visited the Alloms and they gave me pork pies. Why don't we stop early and have some food?"

"I'm not hungry," Louise muttered, reading through the news article again, as if reading it over and over would change the words to her liking.

"But they're Mrs Allom's pies!"

With a theatrical sigh, Louise said, "Maybe I'll have a bite of yours."

"I'll not have you wasting away, it will be bad for business," Bernadette said, trying to make light of it. "Actually, I heard some nasty rumours this morning. Phoebe Baxter is spreading lies that I poisoned Reverend Millings. Obviously, she hasn't directly said I did it, but she reminds people I know all about herbs and which ones are dangerous."

"That's the last thing we need," Louise said, wiping her face with one hand and scouting for her crowbar with the other. "I've a mind to teach her a lesson."

"So you hadn't heard yet?"

"I'm sure Rosie would have told me sooner or later," Louise said. "There will be plenty of gossip at the midsummer assembly, so if she hasn't heard it, she'll definitely hear it by then."

The Midsummer assembly was in three more days. It was the main social event of the summer, although this year the male dance partners would be greatly reduced. "Are you coming to the assembly?"

"I'm far too miserable to dance and talk politely with people. Who knows how awful the news will be by then?"

Bernadette was loath to go too. Especially at the thought of Phoebe spreading more lies about her. "Well then, I shall not go either. I'll stay home and look after you," she said firmly.

Louise sat up straight and her face dried almost instantly. "But you must, 'Dette. You must go and be merry and not have a care in the world! If you do not go, imagine how much worse Phoebe's rumours will become - and you not there to defend yourself? She'll say you're ashamed to show your face because you're guilty!"

Wonderful, Bernadette thought sarcastically. Pretending happiness she did not feel was the last thing she wanted to do, but Louise was right. She needed to put a brave face on things.

Nerves tense, stomach tight, Bernadette went to the assembly with Mrs Poole and Rosie. It was a very different crowd compared to the Midwinter assembly. Fewer people, and fewer gentlemen to go around. Her cousins were in attendance, including Benjamin. Last summer he'd had a flutter of eager young maidens gathering around him. This year he stayed close to his father Joshua. Both of them sneered when they saw her. She beamed with happiness in their direction, to show how unaffected she was.

It was all for show, but she maintained the pretence all the same. Joshua would never stop trying to get them out of the bookshop. Phoebe's petty rumour-spreading was yet one more attempt to destroy them. She couldn't help feeling frustrated all the same. Just when she thought they'd emptied their bag of tricks, they'd found a new one.

At least there hadn't been any more fires!

Grandfather and Miss Yates were so welcoming and lovely, she stayed close to them, smiling so much she started to feel slightly less upset by the nasty rumours.

"You seem a little anxious, Bernadette?" Miss Yates mentioned.

Bernadette gently told her the problem.

Miss Yates' eyes rounded in shock. "You help people, you never hurt them," she said defensively.

"Thank you," Bernadette said. They took it in turns to catch glimpses of Phoebe leaning in to speak to people. It was easy to see which people were easy to fool, and which others were shaking their heads and disagreeing with her. There were far too many people in the 'fool' side of the ledger for Bernadette's liking.

She would simply have to keep smiling and brave it out.

What brought a genuine smile to her face was seeing Dr Williams approach. He spoke briefly with a cheerful Lord Ferndale, then greeted Miss Yates and herself with a respectful bow.

"Miss Bernadette, I'd be honored to secure a dance with you this evening."

He was being so polite, she found herself grinning. "I wasn't aware you danced," she replied.

"The opportunity had not yet presented itself," he said. "Do you have any unclaimed dances on your card?"

"As it so happens, I do," she held up her completely blank card and a pencil. "You may claim two."

"Any more than that would be unseemly," he said, letting her know that he had either been asking somebody about the rules, or he knew dance etiquette far better than he knew table manners.

He'd claimed the very next dance, which began momentarily. She held her hand out for him to take. As her gloved fingers met his, warmth filled her hand and travelled up her arm.

"Did you know your cousin's wife is making merry stories about you?"

Chills replaced the warmth, but Bernadette beamed her fake smile and said, "Yes, isn't she *charming*?"

"They tried to claim I was a suspect too," he said as they reached their dance positions. "At a hastily convened town council meeting."

"I'm so glad the church women were there to bear witness." she said, as the music started up.

He kept their conversation going each time they passed each other, without missing a step.

"You dance very well," she complimented him as he executed a crossover perfectly.

"If you're wondering, Mrs Bell helped me refresh my skills."

Bernadette found herself laughing at his admission. As they danced, the fake smile she'd been using fell away and a very real one took its place.

She was having fun.

Later, when they were drinking lemonade and chatting with the Ferndales, a tall man approached and introduced himself.

"Miss Bernadette, I'm Stratforth, I was hoping your sister Miss Louise would be here."

"She sends her apologies, but she is …" what was it Louise had said? Her brain emptied and she ended up admitting the partial truth. "She is taking the news from France very badly. Our father has yet to return from those shores."

Only then did her nerves recover enough that she remembered Louise had given the excuse that she was looking after Brutus. But then she'd have to explain who Brutus was and ... that would only extend the conversation.

"Well, I might call in and see if she's feeling better on the morrow," he said, offering a respectful little bow. Then he walked over to where Joshua, Benjamin and Phoebe were holding their small court of friends and spoke briefly with Joshua.

Yes, it was probably for the best she hadn't mentioned Brutus, because Mr Stratforth had gone directly to his parents.

As she was watching Mr Stratforth, it was obvious to Bernadette that Phoebe and her friends were talking about her, whispering behind their hands.

She'd always had Louise to protect her in the past, but Louise wasn't here. For a little while she fought between two ideas; try her best to ignore them, or say something.

Saying something won out. Louise simply wasn't available the way she used to be. Bernadette knew it was long past time for her to step up.

She handed her empty glass to Glynn, excused herself and made a direct line to Phoebe. Her pulse pummelled in her neck with nerves, but she had to say something. "Dear cousin Phoebe, let us not hide behind our hands. My ears are burning and I know you are talking about me. Is there anything you would like to ask me directly?"

She scarcely believed those words had come out of her

mouth. Neither could Phoebe, judging by the shocked look on her face.

Phoebe quickly pulled herself together. "It's so unpleasant when people accuse you of a crime, isn't it?"

That stung, and for a moment Bernadette wondered if this rumour was in retaliation for the town keeping an eye on Benjamin. But then, Phoebe and Joshua had done their best to make all their lives miserable ever since their father had gone to France.

"I've done nothing. Dr Williams was there too, and he did nothing wrong either."

Phoebe crossed her arms over her chest with disbelief. "You have the herbs and the knowledge to poison the vicar."

"But I didn't do it. And … more to the point, why would I?"

"That's clear to all of Hatfield. He's been scathing about you and your sisters for a good while. We witnessed that each week in church. Nobody would blame you for wanting to shut him up, but you went too far."

Bile rose in Bernadette's throat and she thought she might disgrace herself. She gave a hard swallow and forced it back down. "I didn't touch him, and I didn't give him anything either. In fact," her memory suddenly came to her rescue, thank goodness, "I noticed a few weeks ago he was looking poorly and I offered him a tonic, but he refused. I doubt he would have accepted any medication from me, or indeed from Dr WIlliams, who also tried to offer him aid. Why, you heard his sermon last Sunday about it being God's will whether the sick recover or otherwise. He didn't believe in *any* medicines."

Phoebe opened and closed her mouth a few times, but

did not seem to be able to think of anything to say to refute Bernadette's truths. She turned her face away with a sniff.

That should at least make Phoebe's friends doubt the rumours; Bernadette had deliberately spoken as loudly as she dared without actually shouting. Yes, everyone had heard Old Brimstone hectoring them week after week, but there were plenty of people who'd seen her approach him outside church. Each time he would send her away with a flea in her ear, and any number of people from Hatfield could bear witness to that.

She made her way back to the comfort of Miss Yates' company. When it was time to dance with Dr Williams again, she enjoyed herself even more. He proved to be a charming dance partner and conversationalist.

When their second dance was over, she stayed only a little while longer before making excuses to head home.

Dr Williams quietly asked, "Are we allowed to leave early?"

"It's not really the done thing, but I need to rise early to prepare herb mixtures. You can stay and keep dancing if you wish."

He shrugged and made a rueful smile. "There's nobody else I'm interested in dancing with, and apparently we'd cause a scandal if we danced again."

Warm flurries filled her tummy and for a moment she forgot how to speak. A naughty thought popped into Bernadette's head. Should they cause a scandal? Common sense prevailed. She mustn't give cousin Joshua any more ammunition in his campaign against her, as tempting as that might be.

"Thank you for the dances. I must be getting home."

━━━━⚜━━━━

The music flowed into the night as she walked the few paces to the bookshop. Inside was dark, not even the glow of a candle upstairs. She felt her way through the shop and held the railing as she took the steps.

The curtains were back and the window was open. Muffled assembly music drifted in, and a little light from the moon. A shadow moved, surprising Bernadette, until she realised it was Louise, still sitting up, alone at the kitchen table.

"Lou!" Bernadette startled, hand to her chest. "I didn't see you there! Why no candle?"

"It went out. I was listening to the music."

Bernadette relit the candle and then put the tea-kettle on the banked stove. "I danced with Dr Williams, and he was very competent. Joshua, Phoebe and Benjamin were there, of course. She is spreading horrible lies about me. Oh, and Mr Stratforth asked after you."

It took a moment for Louise to respond. "Oh. The farmer?"

"Yes, he seemed very disappointed you weren't there."

Louise shrugged as if she didn't care. Well, how could Bernadette blame her?

Bernadette made tea and sat at the table, feeling the heavy weight of an uncertain future settle in the silence between them. The deadline to get the paperwork the Chancery Court had requested was only a few days away now, and they had nothing to send. What would happen next, neither of them knew.

"What are we going to do, Lou?"

"I don't know." Louise reached out, took Bernadette's

115

hand and held it tightly. "But I do know I'm not going to stop fighting. No matter what."

Bernadette puffed out a breath, then nodded, squeezing back. "No matter what."

Last night she had told Dr Williams the truth. Bernadette did need to get up early. She rose with the dawn, which was an incredibly early start at this time of year, to prepare herbs. Specifically herbs that would help bring on a woman's courses.

While she'd attended the midsummer assembly last night for the well-to-do, other gatherings had taken place across Hatfield with many of the remaining farmers and workers. There would be a great many young women who didn't want to marry the boys they'd lifted their skirts for after imbibing a little too heartily. The herbs weren't fool-proof, but they were the best available.

Then she stopped for a moment and wondered. There had been far fewer men than usual at the Red Lion last night, so that should be the case for the other gatherings. Perhaps the demand for herbs would not be so great this time?

Nevertheless, she measured the ingredients into sachets and added them to her basket between layers of rosemary and dense bouquets of parsley. She was extra careful with the front door to make sure the bell above it didn't ring and wake the others.

Roosters crowed in the back gardens. The golden morning sun shone across Hatfield as she went to meet two of the nearby midwives, Mrs Tristan and Mrs Leywood.

They too had been up with the sun, and each was happy to see her.

"As always, please remind the ladies that the herbs might not work," she cautioned, passing over her sachets.

"I always do," Mrs Leywood said. "But people can't help getting caught in the moment."

"Well, they shouldn't," Bernadette surprised herself with how judgemental she sounded. "Goodness, I didn't mean to be so blunt."

"You look tired," the midwife said, patting Bernadette's hand with affection. "I've heard the nasty things Mrs Baxter is saying about you, any wonder your nerves are strained."

She should rub some lavender on her sleeves to help restore calm. Then again, with the damages her cousins were inflicting, she would need all the lavender in Hertfordshire!

Her next stop was Mrs Bell, and she walked down the side of the house to the kitchen door instead of the front, so that she wouldn't wake Glynn.

Mrs Bell was always happy to see her, and they chatted quietly in the kitchen over tea and biscuits. They exchanged details about people's ailments and wrote them in Mrs Bell's notebook.

"I do like Dr Williams' ideas about record keeping, it is essential for the health of the town and I do believe he's approaching it from a position of altruism." Mrs Bell nodded in satisfaction. "I'm letting him copy anything he wants from my notebooks."

"I think it will be very useful too. It was a shame our timing was so bad at the church."

Mrs Bell sat up and reached over to Bernadette to deliver a warm embrace. "I know you had nothing to do with the reverend's demise. Nor Dr Williams. Nobody with a lick of sense is listening to Mrs Baxter."

A tear slipped out. Relief washed over Bernadette. "You have no idea how much I needed to hear that. Thank you, dear friend."

There was a knock at the front door. Mrs Bell said, "Goodness, we've lost track of time, Dr Williams has a patient already."

They listened out but there was no noise from Dr Williams in the hall. Instead, there was another knock.

"You get the door and I'll get Dr Williams up," Mrs Bell said.

Bernadette opened the door to see a young man standing there wearing a clerical collar. He took his hat off and bowed.

"You must be Miss Bernadette!" he said with a broad grin. "Lady Renwick draws an incredible likeness. I'm Mr Charles, your sister Miss Louise sent me over here to enquire about lodgings."

Shock and confusion swirled momentarily. Bernadette pulled herself together. "Come in, please, Mr Charles. You have indeed guessed correctly."

"I've come directly from your marvellous bookshop. I can see myself spending far too many hours there, it is a most wonderful emporium."

"Are you to be Hatfield's new vicar?"

"Temporarily at first, but I hope for a good while. Lord Renwick has recommended me to Lord Ferndale, who I shall need to meet with for approval."

Was this a dream? The last vicar despised everything about them. What a breath of fresh air this would be. Bernadette couldn't help grinning. *Grandfather is going to adore you.*

Mrs Bell was back in the hallway, which was becoming crowded, so they moved to Dr Williams' room at the front instead, where they could all take a seat.

"Mrs Bell, I don't need accommodation immediately. Lord Ferndale has seen to the first month at the Red Lion, where I'm sure I'll be most comfortable. But after that, all going well, I should need lodgings in town. I know there is a vicarage, but my predecessor's widow and daughter reside there, and I shouldn't want to inconvenience them until they are full ready to move on."

"I thank you most kindly for the advance notice. I shall certainly have a room ready by then," Mrs Bell said.

Dr Williams joined them a few moments later, stopping abruptly in the doorway as he saw Bernadette. Seeing him with tousled hair and still sleepy, she couldn't help blushing.

"Doctor Williams," she said, standing up to make introductions.

Mr Charles stood immediately as well, a welcome smile on his face. "What a fortuitous morning, to meet two Baxter sisters, a busy midwife and the town doctor."

They shook hands and exchanged more greetings.

Bernadette could not believe her good fortune, indeed, the town's good fortune, to have such a pleasant new vicar. She couldn't wait to tell Rosie about how nice he was and spread some good gossip about, for once.

After they'd had a short chat about the town itself, Mrs Bell said, "We shouldn't keep you any longer, Reverend, Lord Ferndale will be looking forward to meeting you. I have some letters to post at the Red Lion, so I can accompany you back if you like?"

"I thank you kindly, Mrs Bell," he said, grabbing his hat.

The moment the front door was closed, Bernadette made a noisy sigh of relief.

"Are you quite well?" Dr Williams asked.

"Oh yes, very well. What a wonderful young man."

"Are you… *swooning*?"

"Maybe a little?" Bernadette shook her head. "He is a little glimmer of hope in a dark world."

"Oh," Glynn said, looking out the window as the new vicar and Mrs Bell walked into the Red Lion across the street. "You're quite taken with him, then?"

A laugh escaped, but Bernadette immediately stopped herself at Glynn's baleful expression. "It is only with gladness that at last we have some good news. Phoebe has been telling such dreadful lies and we haven't heard from Father and Mr Jackson in so long. And… oh, never mind."

"What is it?" He reached for her hand, gave it a comforting little squeeze.

It felt right, her hand in his. It gave her a little strength. "Cousin Joshua is being even more beastly than ever. He's gone to the Chancery Court, and we are going to miss the deadline for providing evidence, and they'll declare him the inheritor of the bookshop."

Glynn swore, but it was in Welsh. The tone made it clear it was a strong profanity.

"I'm glad I don't know what that means," she teased, then added, "Dr Williams, respected member of the Hatfield community."

"I forget myself," he blushed.

He looked so adorable in his discomfort, she nearly laughed again. The good news of a new vicar was making her bubbly.

They were still holding hands, and neither of them seemed to have any inclination to let go.

Feeling almost as brave as she had been last night in confronting Phoebe, Bernadette dared to ask Glynn, "Did you think I was sweet on him after we only just met?" Had he been… *jealous*?

He shook his head with denial, but still didn't let her hand go. Eventually he made a bashful grin and said, "Yes, I did."

Her pulse made loud drumbeats in her ears to the point where she might have a little swoon. The doctor had feelings for her?

Goodness, that was a rather lovely development. She could use a few more of those in this dreadful world.

CHAPTER 10

A New Vicar And An Old Foe

It was lovely to see a carefree smile on Bernadette's face. The young woman he'd danced with the night before had appeared apprehensive and unsure of herself the whole evening. Yes, she had been polite, danced beautifully and smiled at the right times, but the worry lines on her forehead were ever-present. Today, they were gone, and a pang of jealousy caught him off guard. He should not feel that way. He had no claim or understanding. He also most likely had no rights to even attempt courting her; she was far too well-connected, even if her immediate family was in trade. One sister was a countess and another would eventually be a baroness!

So why was he thinking of the happy Mr Charles as some kind of … threat? Oh dear, that would never do.

"I am concerned for your well being," he managed to say. It was the truth, although not all of it. "Mrs Baxter has been spreading nasty lies. You were very brave to speak up to her last night."

"Thank you," she said, but her forehead creased again in worry.

It made his stomach flip to see those lines return.

"I don't mean to speak of bad things. No matter what your cousins say, I know you are not capable of harming people. It's not in your nature."

She rewarded him with a gasp and a broad smile that filled him with sunshine. "That does mean a lot to me, I thank you for it."

"I'll be happy to refute any such gossip with that sentiment, for I know it to be true."

They were still holding hands, and neither of them appeared to want to alter that arrangement. A sense of comfort nestled upon Glynn as they sat there with the sun shining brightly and the noise and bustle of Hatfield continued outside.

"I think," he started, knowing once he started he had to go on, "We did rather get off to a bad start, did we not?"

She nodded in agreement, then shrugged and added, "Just a little."

"I can see now what a valuable contribution you make in Hatfield, both with your herbs and your concern for people, and the bookshop for that matter. I find myself in your debt, I would not have been so easily accepted as the town doctor without your assistance and recommendations."

The words came as something of a surprise to him as he said them, but they were the truth. Calmness soothed him for having said them.

"That is generous of you," she said, her voice soft. "Thank you."

The air crackled with unspoken feelings. He summoned

his courage to ask if he might court her when Mrs Bell suddenly came through the front door with a gasp.

"Oh! You're still here, Bernadette!"

She slipped her hands out of his and the moment was lost.

Glynn much preferred the Hospital Committee meetings to the Town Council meetings. They were better run and far more congenial. As he waited for Lord Ferndale to arrive at the next Town Council, Joshua Baxter wasted no time in sidling up to him.

With a low voice dripping with threat, he said, "Everyone knows it was the youngest Baxter girl who had the tools, the opportunity and the motive to do the old reverend in."

Glynn bristled with indignation at Mr Baxter calling Bernadette a 'girl'. And the whole assumption that she was capable of murder.

"You are speaking of a member of your own family, your kin," Glynn said, trying to appeal to his humanity.

Joshua Baxter puffed himself up like an angry cat. "As the town magistrate, I must be objective in all things, even if it is a relative!"

Glynn pretended to sneeze to disguise the roll of his eyes. *Objective, my foot!*

When Mr Charles arrived, Glynn greeted him warmly and welcomed him to the council. It was a relief not to be the newest member any more. Mr Charles replaced the late Reverend Millings, altering the balance of power. It eased the pressure on Glynn, who'd previously had the deciding vote.

Joshua Baxter took his seat next to Mr Burton as the meeting came to order. They indicated Mr Charles should sit in the seat vacated by the reverend. The man smiled with good cheer and accepted it.

Lord Ferndale took his seat at the head of the table and welcomed all, then read through the list of items on the agenda.

"First order of business," Joshua volunteered, "Should be a moment's silence for the dear departed Reverend Millings."

Lord Ferndale said, "That is listed in the condolence motion farther down. We will get to it in good time."

"I object!" Joshua said. "I call for a vote to change the standing orders to allow a moment's silence for a valued man of the cloth and community faith leader, whose life was cut short so terribly!"

Glynn couldn't keep pretending to sneeze every time he rolled his eyes. A doctor sneezing wasn't exactly a subtle thing. They'd wonder if he'd caught a chill.

Lord Ferndale said, "Fine, we shall put it to the vote to change the standing orders. Those in favour show your hands."

Several hands rose, but as Glynn counted he realised they would not have enough.

"Those opposed?" Lord Ferndale asked, raising his own hand.

Glynn put his up, as did the others. They had enough votes even without Mr Charles, who appeared momentarily confused.

The new vicar turned to Lord Ferndale for clarification. "Does this mean there won't be a condolence motion at all?"

"Not in the least, we will have one in due course, it is the fourth item on the agenda," Ferndale confirmed.

"Well in that case," Mr Charles raised his hand, "Let's stick to the order of business."

Glynn approved of the new vicar's common sense already. He could see them becoming good friends before long.

Lord Ferndale counted and said, "Six Yeas, Eight Nays, the motion is dismissed. First item of business…"

Joshua leapt to his feet in anger, spittle flying from his lips. "This is a terrible state of affairs, not paying respects to such a bastion of the community as the late Reverend Millings."

"Sit down, Mister Baxter," Lord Ferndale did not raise his voice, but his tone was stern. "We will get to the item faster if you stop interrupting."

Joshua remained standing. "You're just protecting that spiteful herb girl. Everyone knows she had a hand in his demise."

"Now see here," Glynn rose to his feet. "That's slander! She did not lay a finger on him!"

"She didn't have to, she poisoned his food!"

"Steady on," Lord Ferndale said firmly. "This meeting shall come to order."

Glynn sat down and turned to Lord Ferndale. "The only way that's possible is if the reverend dined separately from his wife and daughter for every meal. That's highly unlikely."

"Are you blaming young Bernadette?" It was one of

126

Joshua's cronies asking that. Glynn thought it might be Mr Wellworth, but he couldn't remember their names as they usually all agreed with each other and voted as one. What an interesting development.

Joshua confirmed, "Yes, who else do you know who gets about town at all hours with poisonous herbs?"

"It's not like her, though," Mr Wellwood said as he scratched his chin in thought. "She helped my dear wife when her gout flared up. And she didn't need to, what with my wife and yours being such boon companions."

That started a few more of them talking about how Miss Baxter had helped them with various aches and injuries, with care and concern for their wellbeing instead of who they might be friends with.

Joshua slumped back into his chair, defeated from the voices on his own side.

"First order of business," Lord Ferndale resumed, after once more calling the meeting to order, "Welcoming the new member of council and new vicar of Hatfield, Mr Charles."

That earned a quick round of applause and Mr Charles thanked them. They reached the condolence motion in good time, and Joshua tried one more time to speak at length about the man of God, so cruelly cut down in his prime, but any time he tried to suggest a connection between Bernadette and his passing, he was shushed from his own supporters.

Glynn could not stop grinning.

As soon as the meeting finished, Joshua was up and out of the building. Lord Ferndale turned to Glynn and said, "That man has to go. Our town cannot have a magistrate who is so blinkered and holds grudges."

Glynn nodded. "Do you have anyone in mind?"

"I do, but first he must return safely from France before we can do anything."

He nodded again, realisation dawning. "You're thinking of Mr Jackson?"

"The same."

"He'd be excellent for the position," Glynn said. "Let's hope he returns in one piece."

It wasn't until he was back in Mrs Bell's house that Glynn began to chuckle. Mr Jackson would become the new magistrate, and he was Louise Baxter's sweetheart. Mr Ferndale was their self-appointed grandfather, owing to the eldest sister marrying his grandson. Mr Charles had arrived at the behest of another Baxter sister who'd married an earl.

It wasn't Lord Ferndale running Hatfield, it was the Baxter sisters!

And honestly, they were doing a mighty fine job of it.

Joy returned to Hatfield in the form of Mr Shaun Jackson, who arrived with another soldier who had a broken leg. Glynn was glad to be able to treat his injuries.

His patient went by the name of Sobriety Jones, and before they realised, the two of them were conversing in Welsh

"For some battlefield treatment, they did a good job resetting it," Glynn said. "There's no sign of infection either, which is excellent."

"Hurts like the devil though," Riot admitted as he stared through the front window to the bookshop across the street. "I need to stand tall at my wedding to Rosie."

"Let's measure you for crutches. Now that we have tradesmen back in town, it shouldn't take too long to make a set."

"I was hoping for just a cane."

"Crutches first, to help with the healing, then a cane for balance. All things in the right order."

They were both looking across to the bookshop. Bernadette walked out with her regular basket and set off down the street.

Riot looked at him and said, "From the look on your face, I see you two won't be far off standing up either."

His eyes widened. "Is it that obvious?"

Riot laughed. "I was only guessing, but you just gave it away!"

"I'm not… we're not… she doesn't much like me," Glynn prevaricated.

"Eh, don't think Rosie thought much of me at first, being a Welshman and not Catholic like her, but I won her over." Riot grinned. "Patience, man. Patience."

***

Shouts from the street roused Glynn in the middle of the night. Sleepy and confused, he thought about lifting his window sash and asking whoever it was to keep it down. People had been revelling and partying so much since the soldiers had returned. And there had been many more injuries from people falling down drunk and hurting themselves.

Looking out the window, he made out the shape of somebody banging on the bookshop door, urging them to wake up because of a fire. Definitely not revellers then!

Dressing quickly, he ran downstairs and out onto the High Street. It was hard to see much, and he had no idea what time it was. Noise came from the lane between the bookshop and the Inn. A clash of bodies and a fight of some kind. He might need to reset a bone or treat bruising.

There was Riot, with one of his new crutches at least - he truly refused to use both, which would set his recovery back. "Best check on the Baxters, there's been a fire upstairs," the Welshman called to him.

Glynn rushed back to his examination room and grabbed his travelling bag, then charged back across the street and into the bookshop. "Miss Bernadette, Miss Louise? Mrs Poole?"

He heard a young boy's voice, "Up here!"

It was Brutus. He was past the ability to keep up with how many people worked or lived upstairs any more, he only wanted to make sure Bernadette was all right.

Miss Louise presented herself first. "I've put it out," she said, "it was contained to my room."

"Well done," he said. "Did you breathe in any of the smoke?"

"Not much. My hands are starting to sting a little," she said, holding her palms out.

Bernadette came into the room and lit some candles. Mrs Poole and Rosie arrived, cinching dressing cloaks.

"I'll get some salve," Bernadette said.

She hadn't even seen her sister's hands, but upon examination, salve was precisely what Louise would need for her burns. They were not extensive, thankfully. "They should heal in a few days."

Miss Louise was impatient to get to Shaun, so he didn't keep her any longer. He tried really hard not to focus on

Bernadette first as he asked the rest of them, "Is the fire completely out?"

"I'll check," Brutus said, heading into one of the rooms. "No more smoke, but it smells like lantern oil in here."

"The fumes might make everyone dizzy. Best to close the door," he suggested.

"The window's broken," Brutus confirmed.

"That could help air it out somewhat? I suggest nobody stay in there or risk breathing in oil vapour or stepping on broken glass until daylight tomorrow."

They were startled and confused, but otherwise unharmed.

He had to check again with Miss Bernadette. "Will you be all right?"

"Thank you for your concern. I will be."

He nodded and grabbed his valise, making his way next door to the Red Lion, but nobody there was hurt. The arsonist had been caught, apparently, which was a huge relief. Hearing that it was Joshua Baxter's teenage son Benjamin was a shock, though. Had Joshua known? Sent the boy to target the bookshop and the Baxter girls? Rage rose up in Glynn's chest, and he didn't even ask if the boy had been injured. Shaun Jackson had the situation well in hand and the culprit locked in a coal-cellar. There was nothing for Glynn to do, so he made his way slowly back to Mrs Bell's.

He sat up all night in his room, watching the bookshop. Just to make sure nothing else happened. He could not stop thinking about Bernadette, about the way she had looked with her dark hair tumbling about her shoulders, a robe thrown on hastily over her nightgown and her feet bare.

She'd looked *fragile*. He'd never thought of her that way; although she did have a generally quiet demeanour and was physically quite small, the confidence with which she always expressed her opinions and the respect she commanded from the townsfolk made her seem larger than life.

Thinking of her trapped in a burning building made Glynn feel quite sick. Tired and gritty-eyed, he still kept vigil until morning came.

CHAPTER 11
Discoveries

Bernadette walked alongside Glynn to church on Saturday to resume their records search. Their gaits began to match, and he was an easy person to walk alongside - he didn't race ahead or dawdle.

"I appreciate your pace," she said. "My sisters tell me I walk too fast, although I find that ridiculous - I am the shortest of us, surely their longer legs should make it easy for them to keep up!"

"A brisk stroll is good for one's health," he said. "I'm not going too slowly, am I?"

They shared a smile as they turned the corner. The lilies and foxgloves growing on approach were in full bloom, as if they too had turned out to welcome the new vicar.

Like the previous time they visited, there were women sweeping the floor and decorating the altar with flowers. Mr Charles was in the vestry, a small room off to the side of the church. They made themselves known and he greeted them with a happy smile. But when they stated their purpose for their visit, his expression quickly turned glum.

CATHERINE BILSON & EBONY OATEN

He pointed to the large open volume on his desk. "Terribly sorry, I'm using them at present. What with all the banns and marriage licenses required of late. We can arrange another time, of course, but today is not very convenient."

"Ahh, of course," Dr Williams said.

Bernadette noticed Mr Charles was holding his wrist and rubbing it a little. "Is your arm giving you trouble?"

"Well, yes," he made a soft laugh as if it was nothing to worry about. "Rather a lot of writing of late."

Glynn offered, "As we're already here, would you like us to take a look?"

Bernadette hugged the knowledge to herself that he'd used the term 'we' instead of 'I'. As if he considered her a capable assistant or co-worker.

"House visits! How marvellous!" Mr Charles said. "And I could use a reprieve."

Glynn took a seat and ran through some tests. They were of the "Flex your fingers, does that hurt?" and "Turn your wrist to the left, then right, is there pain?" variety.

Meanwhile, Bernadette quickly looked at the pile of licences and had an idea.

"They're all the same?" she said to Mr Charles. "Except for the names and the dates, of course."

"Yes, and there's rather a lot that needs to be written out on each license. Please don't take this as a complaint. It's rather lovely to have the honour of joining people together under God."

"Why don't we save your arm from further injury by getting forms made at the printer instead?"

Glynn and Mr Charles looked up at her directly, both their faces beaming with approval.

"Capital idea!" Mr Charles said. "I should have thought of that!"

"That will reduce your muscle strain a great deal," Glynn confirmed.

Beaming with satisfaction, Bernadette grabbed a spare piece of paper and said, "I'll copy the requirements, and leave spaces for the names and dates, and your signature as well. I'm sure Mr Black will be only too happy to prioritise this job, considering how many people are in a rush to marry."

Mr Charles gave a good-natured laugh and said, "Then you'll have access to the records sooner!"

As they bid Mr Charles farewell, they walked to Mr Black's. He was delighted with the task and immediately grabbed his cases of cast metal letters to set the words onto their sticks, and began placing each stick into the frame.

They left him to it and began the walk back to the bookshop.

Bernadette said, "I was wondering whether we should try the Catholic church too, but they're probably just as busy as Mr Charles with marriage licenses."

"In which case," Glynn said, "Their priest may have the same injuries as Mr Charles. Shall we visit?"

"Excellent idea," Bernadette said, practically walking on air with happiness. He trusted her craft and her suggestions, in stark contrast to when they first met.

Later that day, they called in to Mr Black's with another printing job, this time for the Catholics. They paid him for the prints he'd already made for Mr Charles and Glynn accepted the bundle.

"I've had another idea," he said. "I could design a form

for my patients. No rush for those, but I'll definitely be back with a design for you."

Mr Black was delighted.

Bernadette asked whether she might have some copies as well. Then their records would be consistent. A place for name, address, date of birth and any previous major illnesses or injuries.

"That will be tremendously helpful. The midwives could use them too. We'll probably need a hundred copies, but I'm sure Lord Ferndale won't mind the bill."

"He'll be so happy to know the people of Hatfield are in such good hands," Bernadette agreed.

"We'll designate a place to keep the records in the hospital," Glynn said happily, "and then we'll all be able to look at them - you, me, the midwives, perhaps Mr Lennox too. All the health professionals of Hatfield working together." He caught the amused sidelong glance Bernadette was casting in his direction, and grinned back. "Yes, I'm well aware I'm singing a very different tune to when I first arrived. I'm a wise enough man to learn from my mistakes!"

***

Church on Sunday was a crowded event. Word had spread about the new vicar being kind, but more importantly, young and handsome. That explained the extra ribbons on the young ladies' dresses and their rapt attention when he spoke.

How much the mood had changed, too. Without Joshua or Phoebe, Bernadette didn't feel as if she were being examined and found lacking.

During the uplifting service, Mr Charles gave thanks for

those who had returned from the war and encouraged the congregation to pray for the families of those who had died or not yet come home.

Mr Charles read Louise and Shaun's banns for a third time, and a slew of others including for Rosie and Sobriety. Bernadette's brow wrinkled in confusion until Glynn leaned over and explained she probably knew him as Riot.

"Rosie's Catholic, though," Bernadette whispered. "Why is Mr Charles calling banns? They'll marry in the Catholic church…"

"Because Riot's not Catholic, he's Methodist. I think they're just covering all bases calling the banns in both places!"

Louise and Shaun would be getting married the following morning, and Bernadette was delighted for them. That meant their regular lunch at Ferndale Hall would be briefer than usual, as they needed to return home to get ready.

As they finished their light meal, Bernadette noticed Miss Yates having trouble standing up. In a heartbeat she was by her side.

"Stop fussing," Miss Yates said as Bernadette took her hand.

"I'm not fussing, I'm concerned."

Glynn was on the other side of Miss Yates a moment later, but he did not interrupt or take over.

"Is it a megrim?" Bernadette asked.

Miss Yates shook her head. "No no. I stood up too quickly. Little dizzy, but it's gone now. I'm fine, really."

Bernadette looked to Glynn and saw her own worry reflected in his face. "You need to drink more tea, Miss Yates," she said gently.

"I prefer sherry," the old lady complained.

"Nothing wrong with a little glass of an evening, Miss Yates. But I think it might be contributing to your discomfort. Tea will help."

"That's precisely what I would have said," Glynn said, bestowing a warm smile on them both. "You're lucky to have such a knowledgeable friend, Miss Yates."

In the carriage back to Hatfield, Shaun and Louise were lost in their own little bubble of happiness, and Mrs Poole and Brutus both dozed off to sleep, leaving Bernadette and Glynn to chat.

"Thank you for your confidence in my assessment of Miss Yates," Bernadette said, still brimming with pleasant feelings that he'd so readily agreed with her.

"Happy to. Lately, I have been reading about the work of Stephen Hales, and his observations on the pressure of blood in the body. I think it's a marvellous addition to medical knowledge. I wonder if Miss Yates has too much or too little."

"Blood *pressure*?" Bernadette was confused. "Does that play a part in people being thirsty?"

They became caught up in medical conversations, theorising about how strongly a heart pumped blood through the body, drinking tea or small beer to replace lost fluids, and concepts of people losing blood pressure perhaps as they aged. It fascinated Bernadette and filled Glynn with curiosity and wonder.

They didn't even notice when the carriage came to a stop outside the bookshop.

Shaun playfully kicked Glynn on the foot and said, "I thought we were in our own world, but you two even have your own language!"

They all burst into laughter as they climbed out of the carriage.

Shaun grabbed Glynn by the shoulder and said, "This way," as he took them across the street to Mrs Bell's.

"I shan't sleep tonight," Louise said, "I'm too excited about tomorrow."

That statement turned out to be a complete lie. Bernadette checked on her later and found Louise blissfully asleep in her room. The temporary boards were still over her window, but at least there was no more broken glass. No more arson attacks, either. Even better, no more impromptu visits from Joshua and Phoebe with their horrid demands, now that they'd been forced to leave for good with Benjamin after the little beast had been exposed as the arsonist.

Life was good, she thought with a sigh.

Now if only their father would come home, and they could prevail in the Chancery Court, life would be perfect.

Mrs Poole and Rosie fussed over Louise's hair. Bernadette sat Brutus on a chair and brushed his hair into a neat centre part. The doorbell to the shop tinkled and Bernadette had to leave Brutus to his own hair and see who it might be.

"Terribly sorry, we're closed this morning because we're going to a wedding," she called out as she descended the stairs.

There was nobody about. She checked the sign on the front door, but it was still turned to 'Closed'. Well then, who had rung the bell?

Someone sniffled between the shelves.

Following the sound, Bernadette suddenly stopped as

she found Ruth, hiding in a dark corner and crying. "Ruth? What's the matter?"

The girl sniffed miserably, her face pale and terrified as she looked up at Bernadette. "The herbs didn't work," she whimpered.

"Is this about your friend?" Confusion swirled. "The one you gave the herbs to?"

Ruth shook her head and sniffled some more, then pulled her jacket in tightly over her shoulders as if needing to comfort herself.

Bernadette knew that look. She stepped closer and wrapped her arms about the young girl. "Everyone is upstairs, nobody will hear us. How can I help?"

"I need more herbs," Ruth said. "I lied when I said it was for a friend. I took them as you said but it didn't work, so I need more. This can't happen."

She needed love and comfort, with no judgement, but surely Ruth couldn't mean what Bernadette thought? The girl was barely fourteen, and a young, sheltered fourteen at that! "Tell me all, Ruth, and I'll help as much as I can."

"Please don't tell anyone. But I'm with child."

Shock reverberated through Bernadette. The poor girl was still a child herself. She probably didn't even know what was happening. "Was it Benjamin? Did he make you do it?"

Ruth leaned back, her blotchy face still pale. She violently shook her head, and seemed a bit surprised that Bernadette had asked. "It wasn't him."

Bernadette had an uncharitable thought that nobody would be surprised if she said he *was* the father, because he wasn't around any more to defend himself. The horrible boy had pestered Ruth so much.

But now Bernadette thought of it, he couldn't have been

the one. He didn't come home for the Easter holidays and Ruth had needed the herbs before he'd returned for the summer.

"Who was it?"

"I cannot tell you, and please don't keep asking."

"You're right, I'll stop. But I do have to ask some more questions about your health. When was the last time you had your courses?"

Ruth sighed heavily. "I never got them. That's why I had to ask you about it."

That made estimating the timing very difficult.

"May I feel your stomach, through your dress? It might give me an indication?"

Ruth stretched the fabric around her middle, exposing her distended stomach.

Not a good sign. It was her first child which generally meant they showed a bit later, though Ruth was a thin girl. She had to be at least five months along, to Bernadette's experienced eye. One of the midwives would be able to make a more educated guess. Or perhaps Ruth would tell her exactly when, if Bernadette was able to get the girl to open up a little more.

"Would you mind unbuttoning your jacket at the top?"

Tentatively, Ruth flicked open the top two buttons, and Bernadette could clearly see her breasts had grown.

"I'm going to put a hand on your belly and have a gentle feel, is that all right?" She really needed a midwife here, like Mrs Bell, they knew so much more about the stages. Gently, she felt the shape of Ruth's belly, before stepping back with a sigh.

"Ruth, I'm not going to lie, I think you've already quickened."

"I don't know what that means," Ruth complained.

The poor girl knew so little of what was happening. "You're starting to show, and there might even be some movement. The herbs only work if you take them early enough, and even then there's no guarantee."

Ruth slumped to the floor and wept. "What am I going to do?"

Bernadette crouched down to try and comfort her, heart aching for the poor girl. "I'll think of something. You can stay here if you need to. We're off to church soon."

"But it's Monday?"

"Yes, and Louise is getting married."

"Oh! I forgot. I wasn't at church so I didn't hear the banns or the announcement."

"It's fine, but I do have to get back upstairs. You are welcome to stay here, and once we get back, we can work out what to do next."

"OK," she sniffled and nodded. "I can look after Crafty and the kittens while you're out."

"Kittens are the best medicine," Bernadette agreed, before heading upstairs and getting ready herself.

Bernadette couldn't stop thinking about Ruth's situation all through Louise's wedding, and the charming wedding party at Ferndale Hall afterwards. She danced twice with Dr Williams, enjoying herself because he was such a good dancer and being so friendly to her now, but her mind was far away. During their second dance Dr Williams must have noticed, because he led her off the dance floor and to a seat in an alcove. Fetching her a glass of lemonade, he handed it to her and stood looking at her thoughtfully.

"Will you tell me what is wrong, Miss Baxter?"

She took a sip and blinked at him. "Why, nothing," she said, trying to sound light and merry. "What could possibly be wrong? My sister is so happy, and I am truly overjoyed for her."

"That is obvious, but it is also clear to me that something is troubling you. Are we not friends? I should like to help you, if I can."

He was quite adorable, looking down at her with a little furrow between his brows. Bernadette sipped her lemonade again and looked around, checking that nobody was close enough to overhear them. "I will tell you, but it is important that you tell nobody else until I have more information, do you understand? It isn't my secret to share, but... I don't think I can give the help that's needed on my own."

"I understand," he said gravely, sitting down beside her and focusing his attention. "I will have to hear you out before I can promise my silence, however. If there is a possibility of someone being harmed, further action may be necessary."

"You'll at least agree to talk to me before you tell anyone else?" she pleaded.

"That I can do. I trust your judgment."

Her brows flew up in surprise at that, and he chuckled.

"We have come a long way, haven't we?" he said, echoing what she was thinking, and Bernadette had to smile.

"We certainly have. I trust your judgment too," she said, realising even as she said it that she'd trusted him almost from their first meeting. Definitely since he'd run out into the street and saved Ned Fellowes' life with a surgery

Bernadette had barely even comprehended was possible. She hadn't always liked him as she did now, but she had certainly respected his skills.

I started liking him when he *started respecting* my *skills*, she realised. And now... well this was no time to get into an examination of the more complicated feelings she was beginning to have for Doctor Glynn Williams. Ruth needed help, and soon, before it became impossible to hide the truth. Bernadette leaned in close, to speak very quietly into his ear.

"It's Ruth Millings," she said softly.

"The old vicar's daughter, who helps in your shop?" Glynn's brows furrowed, but he kept his voice down. "Is she unwell? She is a fragile-looking little thing."

"She's with child." Bernadette barely breathed it.

Glynn jerked back a little, shock spreading across his face. "She's a child herself!" he hissed.

"She's fourteen, but I agree with you."

"Who's the father?" Fury was beginning to enter into Glynn's expression.

"She won't say. By my estimate she's perhaps five months along, or a little more. I need to get Mrs Bell to look at her."

Glynn swore under his breath, shaking his head. "She needs to tell you who the father is, Bernadette."

She felt the strangest little glow inside as he used her first name. "And what if she doesn't want to marry him? What if he forced her?"

Glynn's mouth tightened. "What about the baby?" he fired back at her. "And what happens to Ruth afterwards?"

"Those questions are why I need help," Bernadette said quietly.

The anger seemed to go out of him, and he nodded.

Something else seemed to occur to him then, his eyes widening briefly. "We need to know who the father of the baby is, Bernadette." He said it very quietly, but deadly serious. "Not just to see if he's a possible marriage candidate. But because someone murdered Reverend Millings… and Ruth's lover would definitely have had motive."

Bernadette's mouth fell open. She stared at Glynn, wide-eyed.

"Get Ruth to tell you who the father is," Glynn said at last, after they'd sat in mutual troubled silence for a few minutes. "I need to talk to Shaun Jackson, I think. As the new magistrate he's responsible for investigating the reverend's death."

"Perhaps we could talk to him and Louise together?" Bernadette suggested, thinking that she'd be glad to have Louise's sensible counsel too. "Only, not today…"

"Not today." Glynn gave her a half-smile of agreement. "Not on their wedding day. This terrible development can wait a day or two. And… I think we perhaps shouldn't reveal Ruth's pregnancy until you've found out who the father is. I'll just persuade Mr Jackson that we need to do some more investigation."

"Good idea," Bernadette nodded in agreement.

"And what are the pair of you up to?" a teasing voice interrupted them. "Look at you, hiding away here with your heads together! Anyone would think the pair of you were courting!"

It was Miss Yates; Bernadette jumped to her feet, her face flushing red. "Indeed not, we were just discussing, ah, a patient, and wanted to preserve their privacy. No need to gossip." She gave Miss Yates a stern look, but the old lady just chuckled.

145

"Gossip is the lifeblood of Hatfield, dear girl. I doubt I'd understand your medical talk anyway. Now Mrs Poole is looking for you; time you headed home. Are you riding with them, Dr Williams?"

"I am indeed." Glynn made a gallant bow to Miss Yates. "Thank you for hosting such a wonderful wedding party, Miss Yates. You have done Mr and Mrs Jackson proud."

Miss Yates beamed happily, but the old lady wasn't done teasing yet. "As I shall for Miss Bernadette when her turn comes, Dr Williams."

Bernadette swallowed a retort, the fire in her cheeks burning even hotter. Dr Williams looked a little flushed too, she noted, as they made their escape and went to find Mrs Poole.

Did he think about her that way? She knew quite a number of unmarried young women in Hatfield had suddenly developed ailments that absolutely required the attention of a doctor, once they saw that Dr Williams was young and handsome. Glynn had professionally examined them and sent them to Bernadette with private notes that recommended particularly revolting, though healthful, tonics. He'd shown no interest in any of the young ladies keen to throw themselves at him. No inclination to spend time with any of them.

Except her, and she felt warm all over at the thought, even while she wondered if he was just maintaining a professional friendship with her because of their mutual patients.

CHAPTER 12

Investigations

The timing was terrible, but Glynn truly needed Mr Jackson's help to resolve the cause of Reverend Millings' death. He held off troubling Shaun and Louise for the best part of a week after their wedding, but he could wait no longer. Tomorrow, they would leave for their honeymoon in Eastbourne, which would create further delays.

To his delight, sensible Bernadette agreed, and she walked beside him to the Jackson residence.

"You're right to speak to him today, because they won't be returning to Hatfield directly. They're going to meet us in London for the hearing at the Chancery Court," she explained.

"Oh, goodness." He'd forgotten about that extra complication in the sisters' lives. "It must be weighing on your mind?"

"Somewhat," Bernadette said with a forced smile.

"How are you bearing up?"

"Keeping busy is providing a welcome distraction," she

said with a sigh. "And at least Cousin Joshua and Benjamin aren't here any more."

They arrived at the Jackson house just as Mrs Allom was walking out the garden gate.

"Must be the day for visitors," she said, as she held the gate for them.

They exchanged cheerful greetings and reached the door, just as Shaun opened it to farewell Mrs Lloyd.

"'Dette, it's so good to see you!" the newly-minted Mrs Jackson gushed from the hall. "Come in! Dr Williams, you're so kind to make a house visit!" her voice rose an octave, "Sean's broken fingers are healing so well!"

That sounded far too theatrical to Glynn, nodding to Mrs Lloyd as they passed each other.

There was another woman in the hallway fetching her hat. The haberdasher, he couldn't place her name as she hadn't come to see him for anything yet.

Mrs Jackson bustled their existing visitors out of their little house, then she directed Glynn and Bernadette into the sitting room.

Enough food for a week sat piled in bowls and on platters on the table.

"What's all this?" Bernadette asked as the same thought crossed Glynn's mind.

Shaun made a soft chuckle, "They say it's thanks for discovering the arsonist."

Louise stood beside him and wrapped her arms around her husband. "I think they want to check up on me." Then she gestured to Bernadette, "You must take this home with you, we'll be leaving tomorrow and we can't take it with us."

"I'm sure Brutus will gladly make sure nothing goes to waste," Bernadette said with a grin.

"Would you like me to check how your broken fingers are healing?" Glynn asked.

"They're good," Shaun held them out. The tips were a healthy colour. "Doesn't really hurt much except when I forget and rest them on the table the wrong way."

"We're sorry to break your idyll," Bernadette said. "But we need assistance before you leave tomorrow."

"Oh?" Shaun and Louise said in unison.

Glynn softly cleared his throat, "It's about the late Reverend Millings. I was hoping we could visit the vicarage and see if there is something we've missed?"

Shaun looked to the ground for a moment, then his head came up, his eyes bright. "I never checked the vicarage. Let's head over there now and see what we can find?"

"Excellent," Glynn stood and walked to the door.

"Gentlemen," Bernadette called out, "Aren't you forgetting that the vicarage is still occupied? Mrs Millings might not feel inclined to speak directly with the magistrate or doctor, but Louise and I can pay a visit and see how she's getting along."

Realisation dawned. "Thank you, ladies," Glynn said. "You're absolutely right."

Bernadette said, "Bring some of the food, I'm sure she'll be happy to take it."

When they reached the vicarage, Glynn stayed a few paces behind with Shaun as Louise and Bernadette spoke kindly with Mrs Millings. Their voices were soft and indistinct, but sounded kind and sincere.

The widow let them in and they sat in a modest receiving room.

During a pause in conversation, Glynn took his chance. "How is your health, Mrs Millings?"

She turned to him and shook her head. "Am I under investigation?"

Bernadette looked his way with an expression of frustration.

Shaun jumped in, "Not you, Mrs Millings, not at all. But would it be possible to search the house, just in case there's something we've missed?"

All colour drained from her face, her hand shot to her mouth and she stood up. "Are you, are you..?" she started, but then fled from the room without finishing.

Her footsteps vanished up the stairs and she shut herself in a room. Most likely her bedroom.

Louise and Bernadette slumped in their seats.

"I wasn't expecting that," Glynn said, "Should I go to her?"

Bernadette shook her head and sat up, "No, I will, and you come too, Louise. She'll feel easier talking with us."

Shaun shrugged at Glynn in the emptying sitting room and said, "Well, seeing as we're here, let's have a look around."

They found the Reverend's study behind a nearby door. The drapes were still open, with a view to the church entrance.

"I wonder if anyone's been in here since he died?" Glynn asked.

Shaun lifted a small waste basket, which had crumpled papers and a moulding apple core in it. "I'd say not."

Carefully and quietly, they checked cupboards and drawers for anything that might show a link between the late vicar and the person wanting to do him in. Letters would be handy, if anyone sent him threats of some kind.

Glynn checked the papers in the waste basket, but they were not drafts of letters, they were ideas for sermons.

"Wait up," Shaun said, reaching under the desk. "There's another drawer here, I think. I've seen a desk like this before and it had a secret drawer… there!" There was a sharp click, and a part of the desk that had appeared solid popped open slightly.

Pulling the previously hidden drawer open, Glynn gasped at the array of small bottles and packets.

Shaun held one up to the light to peer at the label.

"That's poison!" Glynn said.

"That doesn't make sense. Was he poisoning *himself*?" Shaun frowned, and Glynn shook his head in confusion.

Shaun set the bottles out on the desk so they could get a better look. "What are they for?"

"I'm not sure. Some of them could be from the last century; they look pretty old." Glynn scratched his chin thoughtfully. "I may need to consult with Mr Lennox. Even if they didn't come from his shop, he might know what they are."

Shaun found the latch to free the drawer, so they could carry the contents securely. The sitting room was still empty when they walked back.

"I'd say we wait for them outside," Shaun said. Then he called up the staircase, "Louise?"

No answer came. "Mrs Jackson?" he tried, with a smile in his voice.

Glynn called up, "We'll be in the garden, no rush."

"Speak for yourself," Shaun said, with a nudge to his shoulder.

As they waited for the Baxter sisters, Glynn and Shaun couldn't stop looking at the little jars of mixtures and poisons. There were so many, and they'd been hidden away so well.

Glynn caught a sudden flash of white in his peripheral vision as the figure of a young woman ran away from the property. "Is that …?"

"Looks like young Ruth," Shaun answered.

She was running in the opposite direction to town. He wondered aloud, "Should we give chase?"

"Two men chasing down a lass of fourteen?" Shaun said. "We're not ogres!"

It was on the tip of Glynn's tongue to mention she was moving at a decent speed for a pregnant woman. Just in time he held it back. Perhaps she was hoping to trip and fall, or in some other way solve her problem?

Bernadette and Louise exited the house with defeated expressions a few moments later.

"I offered her a tonic for her megrims, but she said they'd stopped," Bernadette shrugged. "She wouldn't tell us anything else."

Louise reached for Shaun's hand. "We tried to talk to Ruth, but she ran out of the house."

"Aye," Shaun pointed. "She went off that way."

They walked back to the Jackson's house, where Bernadette accepted a basket groaning with food. Glynn also balanced a bowl of pies and cold, cooked sausages on top of his drawer of poisons. They put a folded cloth between them, to make sure nothing broke.

"Keep investigating," Shaun encouraged, "We'll be back in a few weeks."

Glynn's arms began to ache before they reached the end of the lane. "You could give away a slice of cake with every book sold," he said.

"Brutus will make short work of this, he's a growing lad," Bernadette said with a laugh.

"My stomach was a bottomless pit at that age," he agreed, and they fell into polite silence for a little while.

"You mentioned Mrs Millings had megrims," Glynn ruminated. "Did she have them often? She never came to see me…"

"Oh don't worry, she never really came to me either. Ruth told me sometimes she was confined to bed for days with them, and I could see in the poor woman's expressions sometimes that she was about to get one," Bernadette said. "They can be so debilitating, but she kept it to herself and suffered in private. I doubt she said much to anyone."

A memory of the hospital committee meeting played in Glynn's mind; a woman scared of her own shadow. "I guess it's one consolation that she doesn't have to worry about *him* any more, at least."

Bernadette agreed. "We only had to listen to Brimstone's sermons once a week, I can't imagine what she put up with every day. Perhaps listening to him gave her the megrims!"

"We shouldn't laugh," Glynn said, then pressed his lips together to stop himself laughing.

"That would be wrong," Bernadette said as she looked away sharply, but he could hear the snicker in her tone.

When they reached the bookshop, they found Brutus at the counter. His eyes rounded with delight at the baskets of food.

Glynn was only too glad to put down the weight of his

153

burden on the counter. He shook his arms out to restore the blood flow, then took the bowl off the drawer of poisons and put it in front of Brutus.

"You can have as much as you like," Bernadette said to the eager boy. "But get a plate and a napkin so you don't make a mess."

He was off like a dart.

"Does Mrs Millings know about Ruth's condition?" Glynn asked once they no longer had an audience.

"I would think so," Bernadette said. "I would *hope* so." She looked worried.

The edges of a theory teased at Glynn's mind. "Don't you think that kind of worry would bring on megrims?"

"It probably would. She's so young and refusing to say…" Bernadette stopped as Brutus barrelled down the stairs with a plate and napkin.

Brutus lifted the towel off a basket and gleefully said, "Oh wow! Are these pies from Alloms?"

They both laughed at his enthusiasm. Bernadette said, "They are indeed. Save me one, and one for Mrs Poole too."

Glynn lifted his drawer of bottles. "Well, I'd best be off to see Mr Lennox about these." He kept the cloth on top. Nobody else needed to see what was in it as they walked past on the street.

Mr Lennox was delighted to see him. He walked up and down the aisle of his shop, showing off his smooth gait. "The heel lift was all I needed, Doctor. My hip pain has eased so much."

"But you're still experiencing some pain?"

The elderly apothecary nodded. "Aye, but it's not causing bother. Nothing like it used to, thank you very much for your clever thinking. I can help customers again rather than have to sit down all day and point to where Young Devon needs to find things."

"Wonderful news," Glynn said. Then he put the drawer down and lifted the cloth. "Today I am in need of assistance from you."

Mr Lennox clasped his hands together with glee at the sight of the bottles. "What do we have here?"

"I truly don't know. I was hoping you might be able to identify what they are."

"That one's poison," Mr Lennox pointed to the largest bottle, the one Shaun had looked at.

Glynn nodded. "That's exactly what I thought, but which one?"

"I wonder…" Mr Lennox picked up the bottle as he crinkled his lips to the side of his mouth in thought. "I'll be right back."

He walked through a door at the back of his shop. Glynn heard drawers opening and closing before Mr Lennox said, "Aha!" He arrived with a bottle that was almost identical, except this one had never been opened. "I'd say this is pretty close."

Excitement bubbled in Glynn. Perhaps the vicar was trying to treat himself for something and accidentally overdid it? "Would it damage your liver and turn your skin jaundiced?"

Mr Lennox frowned and shook his head. "No, but it would kill you. It's strychnine. This is added to baits in grain stores to kill rats and mice."

"Oh," the bubbles turned flat.

"Now this one, I know this one," Mr Lennox reached for

another vial. "Terrible stuff. Used for treating syphilis. Haven't sold these for a decade or more."

"Does it work?"

"If you survived the ferocious megrims it might," he gave a derisory chuckle. "I suppose it stopped people spreading it to others if they were bedridden for days with megrims."

Cogs ticked over in Glynn's brain. "Do you still sell any of these?"

"I have some out the back, but that's for farmers treating sheep for worms. I don't stock the rest of them. Where did you get these, by the way?"

"Er, patient confidentiality," Glynn said hastily.

"Of course."

"Mr Lennox, if you don't stock them, where would someone obtain them?"

He shook his head. "Haven't seen travelling snake oil salesmen for a fair while, they know better than to peddle their nonsense around here. Either I or Miss Bernadette would give them short shrift! Perhaps there was an advertisement in the news sheets? Placing an order in the mail is simple enough if you have the money to pay."

Glynn thought out loud, "And then nobody else knows about it."

Mr Lennox grinned. "I shan't enquire any further, but it seems you are in the depths of a mystery. Let me know if I can help in any way."

Glynn couldn't wait to speak to Bernadette again about his theory. He took the drawer back to his room at Mrs Bell and placed it under his bed for now. He'd need something far more secure to make sure nobody could harm themselves with these again.

Hunger pains gripped him as he woke the next morning. He could bother Mrs Bell for some vittles, but he also knew there would be plenty of food at the Baxters. He really should help them out with those piles of food. And he had to discuss his theory with Bernadette to see if she agreed with him. He'd spent the evening copying all the information he could read from the bottle labels in the reverend's secret drawer; he'd made two copies and would drop one off to Mr Lennox. The second, he put in his pocket.

"Good morning." Bernadette's bright smile from behind the counter lightened his heart.

"Good morning." As he approached, something small darted out from behind the counter and attacked a trailing boot lace; he looked down to see a black and white kitten with the end of the lace firmly gripped in its mouth.

"Hello, trouble!" Scooping the kitten up, he held it up with a laugh. "A born hunter, are we?"

"Too small to join his mother in depositing mouse entrails in inconvenient places. As yet, that is," Bernadette said dryly.

The kitten's face was mostly white, with one black ear and a smudge of black on its nose that looked rather like a moustache. Glynn tried not to melt as it mewed pathetically at him.

"Is he spoken for yet?"

"No… Louise and Shaun plan to take one of his sisters, but he's available." She looked hopeful. "Would you like him?"

"Once my cottage is ready, yes, I would. I'll need a

mouser. And I did promise to take one, since it's my fault they are here at all."

"Then he is yours! What shall you name him?"

He thought about it for a moment before grinning. "Well, a cat with a proud literary heritage deserves a literary name. What about Byron?"

"Perfection!"

Another customer came into the shop, and Bernadette had to turn her attention away. Quietly, she said to Glynn, "Pop upstairs and see Mrs Poole. She'll make you a cup of tea. We have so many cakes and biscuits, please eat something!"

"Be delighted to help." Since that was exactly what he'd hoped for, he nodded and made his way upstairs, trying to fight off a pang of disappointment that she couldn't come with him.

Mrs Poole was more than happy to see him and make him a cup of tea, and put out more cakes and biscuits than he could ever possibly eat. Brutus appeared out of nowhere to assist, though, and the pair of them sat and munched in companionable silence.

As Glynn ate, he found his eyes drawn to the dresser against the kitchen wall, and its neat rows of jars, tins and packets, all carefully labelled. So many different herbs and teas!

It occurred to him then that perhaps he was approaching the poisoning question from the wrong direction. Making his way back down the stairs after thanking Mrs Poole, he checked that nobody was in the bookshop before going to Bernadette.

"You're a skilled herb woman. If you wanted to cause the

symptoms that killed Reverend Millings, what would you use to do it?"

Her mouth opened with shock, and she blinked at him several times. "I… I don't know. I've never… I don't *hurt* people!"

"I know. Please don't think for a moment that I am implying you had anything to do with the reverend's death! But you know what herbs and drugs can do. Would an over-dose of something have caused those symptoms?" He took the folded sheet of paper from his pocket and spread it out on the counter. "Would a dose of any of these have caused them?"

Bernadette picked up the paper and read it closely, chewing on her lower lip. "I don't know what some of these are," she admitted. "I don't think any of them would…" she paused, blinking. "Not his symptoms," she said slowly. "Hers."

"I beg your pardon?"

"Belladonna. Drops of belladonna." She tapped her finger on the paper. "You've inventoried two bottles here, one full and one almost empty. It's a sedative, but it's very strong. Not as addictive as laudanum. But… it can cause severe headaches. Megrims that can last days."

Glynn rocked back on his heels. "You think the reverend was giving it to his wife…?"

"To make her sleep."

"Because…?"

"She annoyed him? I don't know, I'm just guessing!"

"But if he was poisoning her, who poisoned him? Did he accidentally take some himself?"

"Belladonna wouldn't cause his jaundice, nor kill him in the way it did." Bernadette sounded completely confident about that. "He'd just have gone to sleep and never woken up." She looked back on the list. "I don't know what some of these are, but of those I recognise… none of them would have done that."

"I'm going to ask Mr Lennox about the others. But again, Bernadette… if you did want to cause those symptoms. What would you use? I looked at that dresser with all those herbs upstairs… if you found out someone had hurt one of your sisters maybe and you had to be rid of them… what would you use?"

She chewed on her lower lip again, and he found himself watching the gesture closely.

"I'd need to think about it," she said finally. "Let me know what Mr Lennox says?"

"I will. But I do think we might be looking in the wrong place. Wherever he got the knowledge, the reverend knew his poisons. I don't think he poisoned himself by accident. Someone else did it, and it must have been deliberate."

"So we're back to the question of who is the father of Ruth's baby?" Bernadette sighed. "He must have been completely unsuitable for him to not allow them to marry."

Glynn nodded slowly, puzzling it over.

Bernadette added, "She's not come into the bookshop today."

"We saw her running off, Shaun and I, away from town. I hope she's returned home. Perhaps we should visit again, try and see her together?" Glynn suggested. "And I should like to ask Mrs Millings some more questions about her headaches, including whether her husband used to give her anything."

"I could come after closing this afternoon," Bernadette

suggested. "Four o'clock? And come with you. I think she'd be more likely to talk to me."

"Four o'clock it is, then," Glynn agreed. As he left the bookshop to make his way back to the apothecary's shop, he tried to tamp down the pleasure he was feeling at the prospect of spending more time in Bernadette's company. It really wasn't right to be feeling so happy when they were investigating a horrid murder!

CHAPTER 13

Co-operation

Glynn had shocked her with his questions about how she would murder someone if she needed to. Bernadette spent the rest of the day wracking her brain and consulting her mother's herbal journals trying to work out what the answer might be. By the time he tapped on the bookshop door at five minutes past four, she had developed a few theories.

"Bear in mind," she said to him as they walked together towards the vicarage, "that I would not dare risk any of these. It would be far too easy to give too large a dose, and that could cause death immediately. But I thought of a few things that, in small regular doses, could have caused the reverend's jaundice."

"Such as?" Glynn looked at her with interest. They were speaking very quietly, of course, her arm linked through his and their heads bent close together, and it occurred to Bernadette that to onlookers they might look like a courting couple whispering sweet nothings to each other. She caught a sidelong glance from Mrs Freebody, passing by, and blushed scarlet.

"Arsenic," she whispered quickly, fixing her eyes on the path in front of her. "Was there any in that drawer of poisons?"

"Not that we could identify."

"Hm." She chewed her lip. "The others are more... natural poisons. More in my line than Mr Lennox's, if you catch my drift."

"I do indeed. What might they be?"

"There are some mushrooms. Galerina, or Amanita virosa."

"Amanita... I thought that was immediately fatal?" He recalled reading about a case of poisoning from the lethal fungi known more commonly as Death Caps.

"You're thinking of Amanita phalloides, and yes. It would be. Amanita virosa is a relative. Not quite as danger-ous." They had reached the edge of the vicarage garden, and Bernadette slowed her step, looking at a plant in the hedge. "There are other plants... not mushrooms. Hemlock, monks-hood, hellebore." She pointed. "Foxglove."

They both looked at the tubular flowers, pink with white spots inside. And then Bernadette pointed to another plant, small and yellow, which looked rather like a dandelion but with less petals. "Celandine, too."

"You're telling me there are two plants right in this garden which could have caused jaundice?" Glynn said slowly.

"Three." She pointed at another. "That's tansy." She hesi-tated, but then decided if she was going to trust him, she might as well trust him completely. "I use tansy, Doctor. It's an ingredient in a tea which I give to young women who've missed their courses. It was in the tea I gave Ruth, which didn't work. I use it in very small amounts, and I allow no more than two doses."

"What else is in that tea?" Glynn asked.

"Pennyroyal, rue… a few other things." She gave him an innocent look when he raised an eyebrow at her. "A trade secret, Doctor. Or do you wish to train as a herbalist as well as a doctor?"

He laughed, shaking his head. "You know what you're doing, Miss Baxter. I'll leave that to you."

His compliment filled her with confidence. She tried not to glow with happiness as they made their way up the path to visit the widow.

Mrs Millings did not appear particularly happy to see them, but she invited them in for tea all the same.

"We want to make sure you're all right," Bernadette began, hoping the timid woman might not run away to her room this time. "And if there's anything we can do for you, let us know."

"Thank you for the food yesterday, it made an excellent repast for Ruth and I," she said.

Relief spread through Bernadette that Ruth had come home in time for dinner.

Mrs Millings poured tea and they waited for her to speak, giving her all the time she needed. After a fair while of nothing, she made a strange laugh and said, "Isn't it funny what you remember? He used to make me a tea blend for my megrims. When he… left, my first thought was, "How will I get my tea?" but then… I never had another megrim."

Bernadette and Glynn looked at each other. This was going to require a great deal of tact.

"Mrs Millings," Glynn said slowly, "we've had some new information, and it paints a bad light on your late husband. We believe he might have been causing your headaches."

She balked and put her teacup down, shock on her face. "He *caused* them?"

"Perhaps with some drops of belladonna in your tea," Bernadette said, very gently.

Again they waited for her to think about what their words might mean. It seemed she would say nothing until she eventually muttered, "I'd sleep for so long."

The awkwardness grew, and it was so tempting to reach out to Mrs Millings and embrace her.

Glynn's voice was low and kind. "What reason would he have for wanting you asleep?"

Her face paled and her lips pressed together in a thin line of fear.

Bernadette rushed in, "He can't hurt you now, Mrs Millings."

The frightened woman shook her head, her hand flying to her mouth as she began to weep. "Yes he can," she sobbed.

Soft footsteps came from upstairs. Bernadette hoped they belonged to Ruth.

"Perhaps you should get some rest, ma'am," Glynn said kindly. "Are you having any trouble sleeping?"

"No… no." Mrs Millings shook her head. "Perhaps you'd best go," she added.

Bernadette wanted to ask more questions. Wanted to find out if Mrs Millings knew about Ruth's pregnancy; it was becoming urgent that something be done. Ruth needed to be out of Hatfield. Without her mother's support, that might be impossible.

Glynn's hand under her elbow encouraged her gently out of the vicarage, though, and Bernadette tried not to grind her teeth together.

"She's hiding something," she hissed at Glynn as they began to walk.

"I know. But we can't force it out of her. She trusts you, I think... but she's not ready to talk."

"Ruth doesn't have much time!" In her mind's eye, Bernadette saw Ruth's swelling belly. In just a few more weeks, if not even sooner, Ruth would have to leave or go into hiding. "One of them is going to have to talk to me!"

"Try to be patient," Glynn advised. "Let's go and see Mr Lennox again. He was looking over that list and consulting some catalogues he has, trying to discover if any of the poisons might have been the one that killed the reverend."

Bernadette sighed, frustrated. "I don't think I'm cut out to be an investigator. However does Shaun do it? People don't tell you the truth!"

Glynn was grinning. "What, and you've never had a patient lie to you?"

"Not usually. People come to me when they need help, and when I explain that I can't help unless I know what's actually wrong, they tell me." She looked at him curiously. "Do they lie to you?"

"All the time. Many of Hatfield's young women have an imaginative array of maladies." He grinned at her. "I send them across to you for your special tonic."

"Indeed." She tried not to laugh at the memory of Miss Burton's expression after she took a sip from the small bottle of tonic Bernadette had given her. "I told them very firmly that they must take a teaspoon every morning and night until the bottle is empty."

He burst out laughing, and Bernadette began to giggle too.

"It won't hurt them, of course!" she snickered. "Quite the opposite, it's very healthful. It's just absolutely disgusting."

Glynn wiped at his eyes. "Oh, you are marvellous, Bernadette. I shall be sure to keep sending you any more young ladies who develop mysterious maladies in the presence of a man they think is eligible!"

"You *are* eligible, what are you talking about?" She looked at him curiously. "Don't you want a wife?"

They had arrived at the apothecary's door, however, and there was no time for him to answer, because Mr Lennox was hurrying over to greet them and welcome them inside.

"Come in, come in. What excellent timing." He turned the sign on the door over to Closed. "Young Devon can finish tidying in here. Do come into the back and sit down."

He offered them tea, but having just drunk a cup at the vicarage they each declined politely, taking seats at the scrubbed pine table in the back room.

"I went through your list," Mr Lennox said. "And though there is some rubbish there, and we will need to consult on how to carefully dispose of it, I must say that there is nothing at all which could have caused the symptoms you observed in the Reverend. Either the jaundice or the foaming mouth when he passed away."

"Thank you for confirmation of what we'd been thinking." Glynn said. He glanced at Bernadette, and she gave a little nod, trusting him to draw Mr Lennox into their confidence without betraying Ruth's secret.

"Well." Mr Lennox took a handkerchief out of his pocket and mopped his brow after Glynn explained they thought the reverend might have been drugging his wife with belladonna. "That's a dreadful thing, indeed. Why?"

"Perhaps he thought he was helping," Glynn said. "No matter his motive, however, it is at an end."

"And a good thing too!" Mr Lennox said indignantly, before shaking his head. "Still. This does not solve the problem at hand, does it? What did the reverend take that killed him?"

"And who gave it to him? It seems apparent that he had some knowledge of these matters," Bernadette put in. "Neither Dr Williams nor I think he would have taken something in error."

"A fascinating conundrum," Mr Lennox said, and all three of them sat in silence for a moment, before Mr Lennox finally shook his head. "Well, it is possible we will never know, but I do hope the murderer has no intentions on anyone else. Certainly we will be looking closely at anyone who appears a little jaundiced, won't we?"

All of them agreed to that, and Glynn pulled a notebook out and said "Talking of which. I have been consulting with the printer and designing a form which I intend to use for all patients. Perhaps eventually I will have one for every soul in Hatfield; that is certainly the intention. Whether they come to me, or here to you, Mr Lennox, or to the midwives or Miss Baxter. I'd like your opinions on my design."

He opened the notebook to show them the sample form, neatly drawn and labelled. They bent their heads over it, commencing a lively discussion.

Bernadette appreciated that both men not only listened when she made suggestions, but actively solicited her opinions. It was rewarding to be respected in her field by men and not just women, she thought. She could see herself working with Glynn and Mr Lennox in the future, using their combined knowledge to better the lot of all their patients and clients. Happiness welled up inside her at the thought, and she couldn't stop smiling.

"Crate arrived for you, Miss Bernadette!" Mr Thomas from the Red Lion shouldered the door open the following morning and set the crate down in his usual delivery spot on the floor.

"Thank you, Mr Thomas," Bernadette said, rushing around the counter to look. It was a much taller crate than they usually received. Was this from her father? It would be the first crate from him in eight months, if so! But no; she frowned at the handwritten label pasted on the side. It had come from London, from… a cabinetmaker?

"Where's Lou's crowbar?" she muttered, going back around the counter. Finding the tool, she pried unsuccessfully at the lid for a moment.

"Let me help!" Brutus begged as he arrived, and Bernadette handed him the heavy tool. Brutus did very well in levering off the lid, and they both stared in puzzlement at the contents.

"That's not books," Brutus said.

"Indeed it's not." She stared at the cabinet with its tiny drawers. "It looks just like the one Dr Williams has, only newer. Perhaps it was sent here by mistake?"

"That's your name on the label," Brutus pointed out.

"It's beautiful!" It was a stunning piece of furniture. Little drawers with brass handles that opened with a smooth slide. There were delicate glass doors over the cupboards. The entire cabinet was so beautifully crafted, she caressed its polished surface.

"Ah, it arrived." Dr Williams entered the shop and smiled at her, as she bent over the open crate.

"You ordered this?" Bernadette straightened up, even as her fingers lingered wistfully on the silky wood. "Why did you have it delivered here, instead of to Mrs Bell's?"

"Because it's not for me. It's for you. Do you need help to carry it upstairs?"

She stared at him incredulously. "I beg your pardon?"

He had the grace to look a little abashed. "I thought you could make use of it. I remembered you admiring mine... and your herbs and bottles are organised upstairs but don't have a cabinet in which to reside. It also has a lock. To keep secure the more, ah," he cast a glance at Brutus, who was listening with apparent fascination, "hazardous of the medications you work with."

That... was a wonderful idea. But this would have cost a pretty penny. "Did you charge it to Lord Ferndale's account?" she asked.

"No."

"I cannot possibly accept, Dr Williams, it is too valuable a gift!" She shook her head.

He shrugged and softly said, "Please understand. You have given me a far more valuable gift in this town. Your acceptance of me - despite my behaving like a foolish prig initially - and your generous sharing of knowledge has eased my path to acceptance by the whole town. Please, accept this as a small token of my appreciation."

Tempted, she hesitated, began to shake her head. "It is not a small thing."

"I can't return it," he said. "And I can't use two of them."

"Maybe you should have the new one…"

"Oh goodness, I can't even think of emptying out my old one. And it has such sentimental value. No, no, this one is for you. Let me carry it upstairs, where would you like it?"

It was by far the nicest gift anyone had ever given her. She wanted to sit and spend her time sorting and filling it, organising the tools of her trade, but she had no choice but to sit at the bookshop counter. Brutus couldn't manage alone.

"Thank you," she said fervently as Dr Williams left again, with a tilt of his hat. "Thank you so much."

"You're very welcome. I hope you find it of use!"

She certainly would. She could barely focus, happily thinking about what she would store in which drawer and how she would make labels - perhaps Brutus could make her some stinky glue to paste the labels on to the front of the drawers.

The door bell tinkled, and Bernadette glanced up with an absent smile for the incoming customer, which disappeared instantly as she saw Ruth slip in.

"Ruth!" Bernadette forced herself to stay sitting, not appear too eager. She didn't want Ruth to flee again. "How are you feeling?" she asked, cautiously.

Ruth lifted a shoulder in a half-shrug. "All right. Not sick," she said quietly.

"Are you coming back to work?"

"If you'll let me."

Brutus was out on an errand; Bernadette made a decision. "Will you sit and talk with me a little, Ruth?" she asked as gently as she could. "I'll lock the door so we won't be interrupted."

Ruth hesitated, but then she nodded.

They sat down in the alcove near the fire stove at the back of the shop, and Bernadette reached out to take Ruth's hands in hers, noting how cold they felt.

"Do you have any plans for what to do?" she asked.

"Plans?" Ruth's voice shook even on the single word.

"You can't stay in Hatfield unless you marry the father of the baby," Bernadette said, as kindly as she could. "You must see that, Ruth. Your reputation will be ruined, and you, your mother and your baby will all suffer for it."

"Oh." A tear trembled on Ruth's lower lashes.

Bernadette hated how innocent Ruth was, and how she was going to have to do a lot of growing up, very quickly.

"If you want to keep the baby, you need to go somewhere you're not known. It would be easy enough to pose as the wife of a soldier who fell at Waterloo…" Bernadette stopped. Ruth was shaking her head violently.

"I don't want it. I don't! I tried to get rid of it, it's *his*…"

"Whose?"

Ruth clammed up again.

Silently Bernadette counted to ten, but the girl stubbornly wouldn't talk. "Ruth, you need to tell me. We're concerned, Dr Williams and I, that the man might have had something to do with your father's death. I know you said it wasn't Benjamin…"

"It wasn't! He was a pest, but he never touched me."

"Then who was it?" Bernadette said, doing her best to remain patient even while a part of her wanted to shake Ruth.

Ruth's mouth set in a thin, stubborn line. "It doesn't matter. There's no possibility of marriage."

The way she said it was so flat, so final. *Had* it been a soldier who'd died at Waterloo? Bernadette supposed it was possible. More possible than Benjamin Baxter, given the timeframes involved. She sighed, and tried another tack.

"You can't do this alone, Ruth. Does your mother know?"

Every bit of colour that remained in Ruth's face leached from her. She snatched her hands out of Bernadette's and leaped to her feet.

"Ruth, no!" Bernadette tried to grab at the girl, but Ruth was too quick. She fled from the shop as though the hounds of hell were on her heels, the door slamming behind her.

Eventually the girl would have to stop running and face her problems, but if she refused to talk to even a trusted friend, how in heaven's name could they help her?

CHAPTER 14

Revelations

Tempted as he was to invite himself to dinner at the Baxters, Glynn walked past the bookshop and onwards to the Red Lion. Mrs Bell was out tending to a mother in childbed, and although there was plenty of food in her kitchen, it would be a cold repast otherwise.

Tonight, as the cool summer air danced around his neck, his stomach required a hot meal. A wall of noise assailed his ears as he walked through the front door; the inn was certainly doing a roaring trade this evening.

"Doctor Williams!" a familiar accent sang out. Riot Jones and some of the patrol men were at a table, and Riot waved Glynn over welcomingly. He joined them, pleased to be invited into the fold.

They shifted down the bench seat to make room for him.

"Riot, what's occurring?" Glynn asked as he joined them.

"No fires at all," Riot said with a happy grin, and the rest of the team clinked their tankards with merry agreement.

Another of the men mentioned they'd helped a few

174

others to get home and keep them out of fights. "Otherwise they'd be seeing you for black eyes and broken teeth."

"That could be fun," Glynn joked. "Don't rob me of business."

Riot was in charge of patrols while Shaun Jackson was on his honeymoon, but as nobody else had taken up the habit of setting fires, they were finding life in Hatfield had returned to a sedate rhythm.

"We had some dairy cows escape from a field," Riot said. "That kept us busy, herding them back in."

As Glynn tucked into his baked trout with mashed potatoes and green beans, he said, "I hope your skills haven't rusted, because I am in need of you tomorrow."

The rest of the men looked interested, but Glynn had to disappoint them. "Sorry, lads, just Riot, I'm afraid."

They groaned and returned to their meals.

Riot asked, "What do you need?"

"Can you visit my rooms at Mrs Bell's in the morning? Wave at the window rather than knock. She's out delivering a baby this evening and will no doubt need her sleep tomorrow." Glynn hoped Riot would agree to come to the vicarage with him and search again. Glynn wondered if Riot might spot something they'd previously missed. Even if he did not, he would at least be an objective party to offer fresh ideas.

Most of all he could trust the man to be prudent.

"Done," his countryman said cheerfully. "I'm exercising the privilege of command tonight and letting the lads patrol without me."

"Are you able to patrol, now?" Glynn asked. Riot had broken a leg at Waterloo, barely eight weeks earlier, and Shaun Jackson had been badly delayed getting home as he'd refused to leave the loyal Welshman behind. Riot had been walking on crutches lately, though, and now Glynn couldn't see them anywhere.

"Not for long," Riot admitted. "But I can walk short distances without my leg getting tired. Happy to come and see what you need tomorrow."

Saturday morning dawned brightly. Despite the 'closed' sign on the bookshop door, it opened when Glynn tried the handle. Glynn poked his head in, careful not to let the cat or her kittens out.

To his delight, Bernadette readily agreed to his plan for the day. "Ruth came in yesterday," Bernadette said as they walked back to his consulting room. They quietly took seats, so they didn't disturb Mrs Bell upstairs.

Perhaps, when he became better known, and he'd studied some more books, the Hatfield mothers might allow him to attend their births and offer assistance.

A doctor could dream!

"Did she confide who the father was?" he asked Bernadette

"No," she shook her head and appeared to be in genuine pain for her young friend. "Only that it would be impossible to marry him. I'm wondering if it was a soldier who didn't return?"

"Would explain a lot," he ruminated.

Bernadette sighed with confusion. "She ran off again when I pressed her."

"Poor lass must be terrified."

Riot arrived and waved at them through the window as

agreed. They met him on the street and made quiet greetings.

"Where to now?" Riot asked.

"The apothecary, and then the four of us shall visit the vicarage and see what else we might have missed."

They soon had Mr Lennox join them, and they walked together to the Millings residence.

Riot asked, "This is about Old Brimstone?"

Bernadette quietly snorted into her hand.

"The late Reverend Millings, yes," Glynn gently corrected him.

Mr Lennox chuckled. "Brimstone."

Riot sighed noisily, then added, "The new lad's a breath of fresh air, isn't he?"

"Definitely," Mr Lennox agreed. "He's far too nice for a nickname to stick at all, unless it's something like Charming Charles!"

"Agreed," Bernadette said. To Glynn, her sigh sounded wistful, rather than relieved.

A strange feeling took hold again, and he recognised it as jealousy. This shocked and annoyed him in equal measure. He had no right, no right at all to be jealous. He wasn't anywhere close to Bernadette's social status, so what business was it if she and the amiable, eligible Mr Charles might make a match of it?

None, he reminded himself sternly.

Mrs Millings gave a wary smile to Bernadette as she opened the door. The moment she noticed three men behind her, the widow made to close it again.

"We're here for your welfare, Mrs Millings," Glynn promised.

Reluctantly, she let them in.

Bernadette kept Mrs Millings distracted in the sitting room while he, Mr Lennox and Riot examined the kitchen and the pantry, looking for herbs or spices that might be mislabeled. Anything that might offer a clue of some kind.

After a thorough search, Mr Lennox had several samples he wanted to take back to his shop to test. Riot was keen to learn more from Mr Lennox, so he left with the apothecary, thanking Mrs Millings most kindly on their way out.

Glynn felt he should leave too. They'd disturbed Mrs Millings' peace too many times. On the positive side of the ledger, she at least wasn't suffering from megrims any more.

Wringing her hands together, Mrs Millings suddenly said, "I'd like you to stay, Dr Williams, Miss Baxter. My conscience can't bear it any more."

Frozen to the spot, Glynn readily agreed. So did Bernadette, though she gave him a wide-eyed look, obviously wondering what the widow was about to admit to them.

"Shall we move to the sitting room?" Bernadette asked.

"No, no, the kitchen is fine. I'll get Ruth down, she needs to hear this as well."

The minutes moved slowly as Glynn and Bernadette looked to each other, waiting for the daughter to arrive. He was sure Mrs Millings was about to confess something. It took all his concentration to remain patient and wait in silence.

Mrs Millings then fussed over making more tea and poured four cups.

A nervous-looking Ruth came downstairs. Glynn sipped his tea to make sure he couldn't interrupt.

Mrs Millings started talking. "Ruth, darling, you need to hear this from me instead of town gossip. For a long time…"

To Glynn's surprise, it was Ruth who interrupted with a strangled voice.

"He did horrible things to me."

Dread filled Glynn. "Who?"

"I'm so sorry," Mrs Millings said, embracing her daughter. "I begged him to stop."

"He didn't," Ruth sobbed. "He'd come for me when you had megrims. He'd say the devil was in me and he had to cast it out."

She's talking about her father!

Horror flooded through Glynn as he realised what the poor girl was confessing to. Even worse, if that were possible, it made her a prime suspect in her father's death.

All the same, he listened to the broken sobs of young Ruth. Every now and then his gaze caught Bernadette's stricken face.

Ruth was so brave, divulging what had taken place. What stuck in Glynn's throat was the reverend having posed as a bastion of the community, lecturing everybody else on morals and behaviour, while he was doing such depraved things to his own daughter.

It was a completely uncharitable thought, but Glynn hoped Old Brimstone was rotting in hell somewhere.

"I am so dreadfully sorry," he said, after a long, shocked silence.

"This is not your fault," Bernadette added. "I'm not surprised you wanted to poison him. I would have done it myself if I'd known."

Ruth frowned and wiped her face. "I didn't, though!"

Glynn tried to keep a softness in his voice. "Nobody would blame you for it. It never need leave these four walls."

CATHERINE BILSON & EBONY OATEN

"I didn't do anything," Ruth said. "Was he poisoned? I thought maybe he just had an apoplexy. Or that God finally answered my prayers and smote him down!"

"He appeared to be poisoned," Glynn confirmed. "But we're not sure what h…"

"I did it," Mrs Millings said.

The room fell to silence, all eyes turning to the widow, who sat very straight in her chair, her face calm.

"I poisoned him because he wouldn't leave Ruth alone. I was so relieved when she was at your bookshop, Miss Baxter, because I knew she was safe with you. I'm glad he's dead. It means she can live the rest of her life in peace."

Glynn and Bernadette looked nervously at each other, then Bernadette looked to Ruth, giving her an encouraging little nod.

The girl gulped and said, "Mama, I can't."

She pulled back her dressing gown, showing the expanding belly on her tiny frame.

Tears spilled down Mrs Millings' face as she took in the fact her daughter was already with child. "I should have killed him sooner. This is all my fault."

"It wasn't your fault, Mama. It was his."

The two embraced in mutual sorrow and support, tears flowing freely.

"I should have done more," Mrs Millings sniffed through the tears.

"But your megrims were so severe," Ruth said. "And what could you have done, really?"

Mrs Milling spat out, "Those stupid bloody megrims!"

Her curse surprised Glynn, but under the circumstances, he didn't blame her.

He took another sip of tea, waiting silently as the mother and daughter began to come to terms with their deeds.

Mrs Millings turned to Glynn and said, "He was bringing on the megrims, with belladonna or such like, didn't you say? Trying to make me sleep so I'd be out of the way. All the while I was poisoning his tea in the hope it would slow him down."

"What did you use?" Bernadette asked, and Mrs Millings looked at her.

"Celandine, from the garden."

Bernadette glanced at Glynn, nodding. It was one of the plants she'd pointed out to him, the one that looked a bit like a dandelion.

"I made a tea of it, but it didn't work. He wasn't well, he turned yellow, but he still wouldn't leave Ruth alone. So then I used tansy. My mother always said it was very dangerous and she was right."

Suddenly freezing mid-sip, Glynn put his tea down and looked in horror to Bernadette, who pushed her cup away.

"No! You don't have to worry," Mrs Millings said. "I would never harm you. Or anyone else. But, I would do it again to protect Ruth. I just wish I'd been better at it. Oh Ruth, I'm so sorry."

There was a great deal of sniffling and tears, not just from Mrs Millings and Ruth. Bernadette dabbed at her eyes and Glynn's throat constricted.

After some more tears, Mrs Millings turned to Glynn and said, "You may as well call Mr Jones back so he can arrest me."

"We'll do no such thing," Glynn blurted. Then he realised it was true. He had no intention at all of turning her in. He didn't for a moment believe that she was a danger to anyone else, and the reverend had received exactly what he'd deserved.

"How would that be justice?" Bernadette said. "Ruth needs you."

"But I've confessed to killing my husband."

"Patient confidentiality," Glynn said, feeling pleased with the thought. "And he was subjecting you to debilitating megrims that altered your common sense."

"But whatever will we do now?" Ruth appeared ready to panic as she looked at her mother.

Bernadette reassured both of them. "We can find somewhere for you to go, somewhere quiet where you can have the babe away from Hatfield gossip."

"We simply up and leave? That will set tongues wagging," Mrs Millings said.

"Not in the slightest." Bernadette had more answers, deeply impressing Glynn. She'd obviously been thinking things through and creating plans, despite Ruth's unwillingness to cooperate earlier. "You're in deep mourning, and at some point you will need to vacate the vicarage anyway. We'll mention you're staying with family and that will be enough."

He wondered if she had some plan. He wished he had relatives left in Wales; that would surely be far enough to send Ruth and her mother, but there was nobody left there that he could trust. He wracked his brain. He'd not made many close friends at medical school; they all knew he was common-born, only there because of his wealthy patron, and it had been much the same with the other surgeons he'd served with in the army.

"I do so wish I'd done more," Bernadette said a little later, as they walked away from the vicarage.

He nodded, feeling as if he'd also let the poor girl down. "You did a great deal," he realised. "You gave her a place to go each day where he couldn't reach her."

She nodded, as if thinking it over.

"And you also bore the brunt of his anger," he added. "Perhaps keeping Ruth away from him is why he targeted you so ferociously in his sermons?"

She sighed heavily, his ideas not relieving her sadness by much.

"Do you have an idea, for where they could go?"

"Indeed I do." She had wiped her face, but her eyes were still red-rimmed from crying. It didn't make her any less beautiful, as the warm summer sun touched her face with a golden glow. "My sister Marie married the Earl of Renwick, who has a grand castle in Cumbria. A very, *very* long way away. Marie knows and loves Ruth already, of course. It's the perfect place for Ruth and her mother to hide away until the baby is born, and I'm sure Renwick will help them resettle."

Must be nice, Glynn thought a little wistfully, to have wealthy and influential relatives with castles at their disposal. "Better than the remote Welsh fishing village I was thinking of, where I grew up. I've no family left there, besides."

"Thank you for thinking of it, but I'm sure Cumbria is the answer. I'll write to Marie straight away."

CHAPTER 15

Predicaments

B ernadette thought sending Ruth and her mother to Marie would be the perfect option. From her sister's letters, Alston Castle sounded vast. A girl and her mother could easily be absorbed into the staff. Perhaps in time Ruth could become a companion to Marie? And there must be some local farming families who could be paid to take in the babe if Ruth didn't want to keep it, which Bernadette suspected she wouldn't; the child would be a permanent reminder of what Ruth had suffered.

Dr Williams came into the bookshop soon after she opened up on Monday morning, which immediately brought a smile to her face. Mr Thomas followed straight after.

"Don't let the cats out!" she called out.

They hastily shut the door and breathed relief that they had not let Crafty out, nor any of her rambunctious offspring.

They were both well-dressed, as it was Rosie and Riot's

wedding day today. There had been a great many weddings of late.

"Post arrived, Miss Baxter," Mr Thomas said, handing over some sealed notes. Then he looked a little sheepish and said, "Is Mrs Poole about by any chance?"

"Of course," Bernadette readily agreed. "She's upstairs. Don't keep her long, she's busy getting Rosie ready."

Glynn put his hat down on the counter, and he looked about his feet for the kitten he'd christened Byron. The cute little devil was already after his bootlaces; he stooped to catch it, laughing as the kitten attempted to dive inside his trouser leg and hide. "Little scamp! Don't you rip my good clothes! I can hardly stand up next to Riot if my legs are shredded!"

One of the letters that had just arrived was written in Marie's hand, so Bernadette opened that one first. It was lovely to hear from her, but the contents made her sigh with frustration.

"I don't mean to pry, but, is anything the matter?" Glynn asked, watching her expression.

"Bother," she said, scanning the details. "Double bother."

"Bad news?"

"Not exactly, but it's rather a complication." Her mind started spinning with ways around this, but no solutions presented themselves. "It's from my sister, and she sent this on ahead, express. I will be delighted to see her, but she's already on her way to us."

Glynn looked confused.

She kept her voice low in case Mr Thomas should re-appear. "It means we can't send Ruth to Marie because Marie's already half-way here."

CATHERINE BILSON & EBONY OATEN

"Oh!" Glynn agreed, looking crestfallen. "Bother indeed."

"Yes. And we must find somewhere soon. There's only so long before people start to talk. Mr Charles has been so patient, but he should be moving into the vicarage."

"Mrs Bell has a room for him now that Shaun has moved to his new house," Glynn said, then brightened. "We can sound Mr Charles out later today, after the wedding."

"About whether he is happy to hold off moving into his residence? Would he wonder why we were asking such a thing?"

Glynn looked thoughtful and nearly said something, but Mr Thomas came down the stairs. He doffed his hat and said, "See you soon, at church."

They bid him goodbye and Bernadette walked out from the counter and turned the door sign to "closed".

"You were going to suggest something?" Bernadette asked.

"I was wondering whether we sound out Mr Charles to see if he might know anybody to take in Ruth and Mrs Millings?"

"That's brilliant!" She beamed at him. "And I know he won't talk, he's terribly discreet. Haven't heard anything at all from Rosie or Mrs Poole about him, only that some of the younger ladies are wanting their hair done for Sunday mornings!"

Dr Williams really was such a thoughtful man to suggest they speak to Mr Charles. And so kind. He'd taken to the people of Hatfield with such care and consideration. Not just for their medical ailments, but their overall wellbeing. Nothing at all like her first impressions, of a man who ranked his education higher than people's experiences.

She had badly misjudged him.

Watching him play with Byron was delightful. His whole face came alive and his voice rose into a childish tone as he talked to the playful kitten. "You're going to love your new home. The cottage is almost ready!"

For a little while, it was so much fun just to watch him being incredibly silly and gentle with the baby animal.

After a few minutes he seemed to remember he had an audience. He looked at her, startled.

They both laughed their nervousness away.

"I wanted to thank you again for the gift of the cabinet," she started. A kitten leapt on her foot - the one set aside to accompany Mr Charles into the vicarage - and she picked her up. The little thing was all purrs and softness; then the little fluffball kicked her feeble legs into Bernadette's palm slaying an imaginary dragon. Her fight was all play for now, but as the kitten grew into cathood, rodents wouldn't stand a chance.

"I'm glad you're happy with it," he said, as Byron leapt in and out of his hat on the counter. "Have you filled it already?"

"Not yet," she placed her kitten safely on the floor so it didn't accidentally fall off the counter. Then she moved to do the same for Bryon but he dashed away from her, scarpering up Glynn's arm and stopping at his shoulder.

"Ease up!" Glynn laughed.

Bernadette laughed too and she reached for the kitten the same time as he moved his hand to grab him. Their hands somehow both had the kitten, sending warmth through her whole being. Together they moved the kitten down to the floor before letting him go.

Glynn removed his hand and the warmth vanished,

"The cabinet was a beautiful gift," she said as they both straightened and then leaned on the counter. So personal. A courting gift? If so, it was perfect.

Glynn gulped but said nothing.

Gently, she reached for his hand. The shop was closed, Rosie and Mrs Poole were still getting ready; nobody would interrupt them.

His hand firmly in hers, she took her chance. Stepping in closer, she tilted her head up. Her eyelids lowered a little, and her lips moved closer to his. It felt so natural, so right.

Momentum closed the distance as their lips met with a gentle, natural touch. Her heart thrummed in her chest. Light danced along her skin. Her hand came to rest on the lapel of his coat, and she drew him closer.

The kiss gained imperceptible pressure, then her lips parted on a soft sigh. This was everything she had hoped it would be.

Then it was more. A soft groan escaped from his throat and he reached for her waist, pulling her closer in.

The beautiful moment transformed into bliss as she revelled in the sensations.

"Oh yuk! Not you two as well?"

She broke away from Glynn and turned to see Brutus standing on the stairs. He was completely disgusted with them, his young face screwed up with distaste.

She must be blushing furiously, but Bernadette didn't care. "Dear Brutus, you'll change your mind when you're older."

"I will not!" he insisted, turning around and heading back up the stairs.

A nervous laugh escaped, and as she turned back to

Glynn, in the hope of picking up where they had left off, she read only deep dread in his expression.

Why did he look despondent? It didn't make sense, their kiss was lovely!

To her continued confusion, Glynn backed away and would not look her in the face.

"I should not have…" he began but failed to complete. "That was not…" another thought remained unfinished. He kept backing away.

"I thought you enjoyed that as much as I?"

He'd responded so positively, but now he was running away. Nothing made sense. Moments ago she was losing herself to the sensation of a kiss and now she appeared to be losing him entirely as he made haste for the door and let himself out.

Confused and speechless, Bernadette moved to the other side of the counter and found the seat. Here she sat, head in her hands, wondering what had just happened and how it had ended so poorly.

All the gossip she'd heard from Rosie, and a fair few of her customers, especially those who needed her after a seasonal assembly, had talked about how wonderful kisses were. That men wanted kisses so much, they often couldn't stop.

Had she found the only man in Hatfield who didn't like kissing?

The door jingled and it was Glynn again. He still didn't make eye contact and he marched forward, grabbed his forgotten hat off the counter and marched straight out again without so much as a word to her.

"You can't ignore me like that for the rest of the day," she said to the closed door. "We'll both be at Rosie and Riot's wedding."

As the words left her mouth, something cold flipped in her belly. Bernadette had agreed to be Rosie's maid of honour, and Dr Williams was Riot's best man. It probably would have been Mr Jackson, but they didn't want to wait for him to get back from his honeymoon.

At least it would be easy to get Mr Charles' attention after the ceremony, as they'd have ample opportunity to bend his ear once the paperwork was signed.

She sighed unhappily. *What did I do wrong? Was it because I instigated the kiss? Did he think me too forward? But after he gave me such a lovely courting gift of the cabinet, it felt so natural!*

Somehow, she'd made a mistake. How she wished one of her sisters was here, to ask for advice!

Rosie and Riot's wedding was delightful. A smaller affair than Louise's and Shaun's of course, but Rosie looked beautiful in a new dress, and Riot quite handsome in his best suit with a wide smile on his face as he watched his bride make her way up the aisle towards him. Because Rosie was Catholic, they were in the Catholic church, not a place Bernadette had ever frequented. The priest seemed kindly, though, and very welcoming, and most of the ceremony was familiar.

Mr Charles had attended to show support, and stood chatting with many of the congregation in the churchyard afterwards. Bernadette waited until he had finished exchanging pleasantries with the priest before sidling up, seeing from the corner of her eye Glynn coming to join them.

He hadn't looked at her even once during the ceremony, keeping his gaze focused on either the bridal couple or the priest, and Bernadette tried to push away the hurt.

"Could we talk, Mr Charles?" She indicated Glynn with a nod of her head.

Mr Charles looked from one to the other of them, his cheerful expression sobering as he took in their serious looks. "Of course, Miss Baxter. Shall we walk together?"

The Catholic church wasn't in the centre of Hatfield; they had about a half-mile walk back to the bookshop. Bernadette nodded, accepting Mr Charles' politely offered arm. Glynn walked along behind them in silence, and she remembered that she had once thought he might be a little jealous of Mr Charles. Peeping back at him, she caught him looking at her with his jaw clenched, though he quickly looked away when he caught her gaze.

I don't understand him at all. Tears pricked at the back of her eyes, but she blinked them away determinedly. She needed to focus on Ruth's urgent predicament right now, not mooning over a man giving her such mixed signals.

"What did you need to talk to me about, Miss Baxter?" Mr Charles asked. "I collect from your expression that the matter is somewhat serious, and from the presence of Dr Williams that it might be perhaps of a medical nature. I do assure you that anything you tell me will go no further - I may not be bound by the seal of the confessional like my Catholic colleague, but I know how to be discreet."

There were too many people about; even now someone was stopping Glynn to ask him a question, and she could see another woman walking towards them purposefully, eyes fixed on Mr Charles. Bernadette didn't dare let Ruth's name slip from her lips at this moment. "Would it be possible to meet privately, Mr Charles, with myself and Dr Williams?"

"Of course." Mr Charles had clearly noticed the privacy issue too. "Perhaps in Dr Williams' consulting rooms? I have an appointment at four… but after that?"

Bernadette wanted to suggest somewhere else, but Mrs Poole and Brutus would be at the bookshop, the Red Lion would be busy with everyone celebrating the wedding, and she could not ask Mr Charles to open the church just for this. Glynn's rooms made sense, as even if Mrs Bell was home, they could trust her to be discreet. Bernadette still planned to ask the experienced midwife to examine Ruth at some point.

"Very well," she said reluctantly.

"I shall see you at five, then," Mr Charles said, then raised his voice as the woman approached. "Good afternoon, Mrs Frakes! And how are you today?"

Bernadette disengaged from the young vicar and turned back to find that Glynn had just managed to escape from the man who had stopped him.

"No time to talk right now," Bernadette said. "He'll meet us in your consulting rooms at five o'clock."

Glynn nodded abruptly, not meeting her gaze. "I'll see you there. I need to go visit Mr Hawley. Excuse me." He walked away without a backward glance, and Bernadette was left to make her way home to the bookshop alone, wondering again what she had done wrong.

CHAPTER 16
Planning

Mr Charles arrived a minute or two before Bernadette that evening, for which Glynn was grateful. He didn't want to be alone with Bernadette; if she'd arrived first, he might lose his mind and kiss her again. Their kiss was all he'd been able to think about since that morning, though he hated himself for it.

He had no business encouraging it, let alone enjoying it so thoroughly.

When she did arrive, she looked at him with those beautiful hazel eyes full of hurt and confusion and he couldn't even make himself meet her gaze, utterly drowning in guilt.

"What is it you needed to talk to me about?" Mr Charles said, and Glynn turned to him gratefully. What his heart wanted didn't matter in the grand scheme of things. "Mr Charles…" he hesitated. "If I may be frank?"

"Please, do." Mr Charles smiled encouragingly. "I promise, I will not be offended by anything you might say, and for the two of you to come to me, it's obviously a serious matter. Best not to beat around the bush."

"Very well." He cast a sidelong look at Bernadette, but she was sitting silently looking at her hands, obviously content to let him take the lead for now. "You never met your predecessor, Reverend Millings. I did not know him well, as I am a recent arrival to Hatfield. But frankly, he was one of the most unChristian men I have ever had the misfortune to encounter. That he was a clergyman made him even worse, for he was most unsuited to the task."

Mr Charles grimaced. "You are not the first person to make that observation to me, Doctor. I suspect I will be long years undoing the damage Reverend Millings did to many souls here in Hatfield."

Encouraged that they understood each other, Glynn nodded. "There is one soul he caused more damage to than any, and that is the one Miss Baxter and I are eager to seek your counsel regarding. The reverend's daughter, Miss Ruth Millings."

Mr Charles blinked, and then looked sorrowful. "That poor wee lass? She seems like a scared little mouse. I've barely had the opportunity to speak to her."

"Her father abused her cruelly," Glynn said. "And when I say abused…" He paused, trying to think of a way to phrase it tactfully. It was so unspeakable.

Mr Charles' expression grew more horrified. "You are not implying…"

"She's pregnant," Bernadette said bluntly.

"Her own father!" Mr Charles looked aghast, covering his mouth. "No. Oh, no." He closed his eyes and put his hands together for a moment, obviously praying for guidance. When he opened his eyes, his expression was resolute. "What can I do to help?"

"Ruth needs to leave Hatfield, as soon as possible. She is

supported by her mother," Bernadette said. "I wrote to my sister Lady Renwick…"

"An excellent choice!" Mr Charles nodded at once. "Lord and Lady Renwick are generous souls who would discreetly assist Miss Millings, and Alston is a long way from Hatfield gossip."

Bernadette had to interrupt his praise. "They are already on their way here at the present time, and our letters will have crossed in transit. Ruth needs to leave now. Before the signs are unmistakable."

"Oh, I see." Mr Charles tapped a finger on his lips with one hand, while the other strayed behind his back, as if he was about to begin pacing the room. He remained seated and nodded his head. "You are aware, of course, that I am from Alston also? My parents have a large farm, and my brother is lately married to a young Scotswoman. They have plenty of room and would happily take in the Millings women… in fact, if Ruth does not want to keep the child, I'm sure Morag would love to have a wee bairn of her own to raise. I shall write ahead, but I think we can safely send Ruth and Mrs Millings north at the earliest opportunity, without waiting for Lord and Lady Renwick. I assure you they will be safe with my family until Lord Renwick is able to make a more permanent place for them."

"That is very good of you!" Bernadette's face was alight with happiness as she and the young vicar worked out the logistics of their plan, and Glynn couldn't stop looking at her.

It was agony being so close, yet so far out of reach.

He should never have touched her, as much as his heart ached to hold her close.

Come to think of it, he shouldn't have given her the

medicine cabinet. What kind of hopeless fool bought something so personal for an unmarried woman?

If he wanted the answer to that, he need only look in the mirror.

As Bernadette - for his sanity he really should think of her as Miss Baxter - and Mr Charles spoke of the logistics involved in removing Miss Millings and her mother from town, Glynn further chastised himself for his juvenile behaviour. It had taken that kiss earlier today for reality to come crashing down upon his shoulders. He'd crossed the line, that much was obvious. His only option was to beat a hasty retreat back to his side of it.

And stay there.

He brought his thoughts back to the issue at hand, as Mr Charles told them he would write a letter immediately and send it that very day so that his mother could prepare for guests. "Shouldn't take but a moment. It will arrive before they do. All will be well."

"I will visit Ruth and her mother and help them pack," Bernadette said, "and ensure they have adequate funds for the journey. They can tell friends that they are going to live with relatives."

"Which is true!" Mr Charles said. "As long as we don't specify precisely *whose* relatives."

He and Bernadette both laughed merrily, and it twisted Glynn's gut. This was the kind of man Ber- Miss Baxter should marry. A gentleman to the core, closer to her own age, kind and charming... Mr Charles was everything Glynn knew he could never be.

"Goodness," Mr Charles said, "I feel guilty that this will resolve my accommodation issues as well. The Red Lion is a comfortable inn, but it will be a boon to have a residence of one's own. I look forward to claiming my kitten!"

Glynn too would soon have a residence of his own. It would do him good to not be so close to Miss Baxter every day.

To not be so tempted by her kind nature, clever mind and helpful ways. That had to be the cause of his heart pain. Simple proximity.

They saw each other every day, that's why he'd leaned into familiarity with her. A woman whose sister was a countess! It was sheer madness that he'd even allowed himself to think of her romantically.

They bid Mr Charles farewell. Glynn fully expected Bernadette to walk to the vicarage and deliver the news, but instead she closed the door.

And stayed on his side of it, much to his discomfort.

"Why did you kiss me this morning?" she asked.

He wasn't expecting such a blunt question. "Er," his brain seized up as he looked at her soft, pink lips. *Bad idea!* "I think you kissed me."

"And? You kissed me back. You returned the gesture."

Did she have to run her tongue over her bottom lip at that moment?

True, he'd enjoyed it. He'd more than enjoyed it. He'd *revelled* in it. Guilt plagued him because he'd not stopped her or stepped back. He'd joined in gleefully and encouraged more. Goodness knows where it would have ended had Brutus not interrupted them!

"I thought you liked me?" Bernadette said, her expression full of hurt, those beautiful hazel eyes shimmering with unshed tears. "I thought this was a… a natural progression of events. The cabinet was so personal and thoughtful, and

197

you said you'd bought it with your own funds, not charged it to Lord Ferndale. I could only interpret it as a courting gift. Tell me how I misread the situation so badly?"

That was the trouble. She had not. She'd read the situation completely correctly, except that he was the one in the wrong. He'd been in the wrong from the beginning.

As the granddaughter of his employer, it was wrong. Yes, it was an honorary connection, but still, she had that close connection and he should not have encouraged her.

One sister would one day be a baroness, and another was already a countess. That elevated Bernadette into the clouds, and far, far out of his reach no matter how much he desired her.

If only she were merely in trade, they could be together.

The words, "It's the trade," slipped out.

"What?" She jumped in before he could get his thoughts to line up in the right order. "You don't like that I'm in trade?"

"No, wait, I didn't mean that." Sensible words fled from his mind. He tried to catch them but they tumbled like autumn leaves and slipped away.

"But you said it," Bernadette accused when he didn't give her an adequate reply. "Have you not noticed, you're in trade yourself? As a doctor, you're barely a gentleman."

His voice leapt out of him. "I know that!"

She recoiled.

His heart cracked. "I didn't mean to snap, I didn't mean it like that..."

"That's the problem with you. How am I supposed to know what you mean when *you* don't even know what you mean yourself?"

She was behaving like a jilted lover. Surely it hadn't gone

that far. Had it? It didn't matter about his own heart, but he did need to protect hers before she developed any more feelings for him. Which was such a strange thought; that a woman like Bernadette Baxter would give her heart to a man from a Welsh fishing village.

"You are young," he began, hating how pompous he sounded, but he had to carry on, had to somehow persuade her that she was wrong. "In time you will realise you've mistaken friendship for more. In a few months there will be someone else far more suitable."

She stood there, mouth open in shock.

His stomach clenched at how he'd hurt her, but how else was he to create a respectable distance between them?

"A few months? Do you really expect my affections to be so fleeting?" she gasped out finally.

Her eyes filled with tears, but they didn't spill over. It shredded his heart to see her like this. That he'd caused this.

Glynn didn't say anything, terrified that whatever might come out of his mouth would be wrong. Would reveal how desperately he loved her. She must never know.

"So be it," she said when he did not speak, turning and leaving.

He let her have the last word. His own throat was too constricted to speak.

An annoyed sigh erupted from him as she closed the door behind her. He staggered up to his room and collapsed on his bed with a groan. Then he got up and closed the curtains so he wouldn't be tempted to look out across the street at Baxter's Bookshop, and properly collapsed this time.

CHAPTER 17
Farewell and Welcome Home

The next morning, Bernadette wrapped some novels up in a piece of brown paper, tied some string around it, and walked around to the Red Lion, where the first coaches would soon depart. The coach going north would take Ruth and her mother far from Hatfield. They crossed the street holding a carpet bag each, Ruth holding hers with both arms so the bag blocked the view of her belly. Both were dressed in black mourning clothes, that made their pale skin look all the more lifeless. Mr Thomas was there loading travel crates and bags onto the top of the coach, while the rest of the passengers took their seats. Mrs Millings smiled a little stiffly at Bernadette.

"We shall write when we reach my sister," she said, maintaining the facade for the benefit of anyone else's ears.

"Please take these, they might help pass the time," Bernadette said, trying not to burst into tears as she gave Ruth a last hug. She could hear the girl's quick breaths in her ear as Ruth clung to her briefly before letting go. "I will miss you. Take care," she whispered in Ruth's ear.

"Thank you," Mrs Millings said, keeping her face steady as she accepted the parcel.

"Thank you for everything," Ruth whispered, clasping Bernadette's hands tightly one more time before she turned at her mother's urging and climbed into the carriage.

To Bernadette's immense relief, there were no Hatfield residents travelling in the same carriage, further reducing any chance of gossip.

Mr Thomas checked the door was securely closed once Mrs Millings had settled herself beside her daughter. He performed a quick count of passengers and appeared satisfied that it matched his list. A moment later, he waved to the driver that they were ready to leave, and the coachman cracked his whip and called to the horses.

As much as Bernadette wished she could stay and watch the carriage leave town, there were simply far too many things for her to do to allow the luxury. Or perhaps it was that she'd watched too many carriages leave town in the last year, carrying her sisters on far adventures while she was left behind. She blinked back tears and resolutely did not watch.

As she walked back to the bookshop door, she glanced at Dr Williams' room across the street. She hadn't spoken to him since they'd joined forces with Mr Charles to resolve Ruth's predicament. Then he'd so callously rejected her. Something looked different; she stopped and stared for a moment. Fresh pain stung her as she took in his new sitting position through the window. He'd moved the furniture around so that he had his back to the street - and with it, her!

Was she such a horrible distraction he could no longer stand the sight of her?

Making haste, Bernadette charged into the bookshop and shut the door quickly behind her. She should turn the

'Closed' sign around to 'Open' but she needed to compose herself first.

The timing of Glynn's rejection could not have come at a worse time. If Louise were here, she could unburden herself, but Louise was on her honeymoon. When her sister returned, there was a crate of binding and repair jobs waiting for her.

Mrs Poole and Brutus were still here, but the latter would not be any help at all. He seemed disgusted with the entire concept of love. She had to remain behind the counter in case a customer came in, so she couldn't go upstairs at the moment and have a good cry with Mrs Poole.

Bernadette gave herself two minutes to compose herself, pulling her handkerchief from her pocket and blowing her nose. She took a steadying breath, turned the sign to 'Open' and fixed on a smile.

Rosie came in a short while later, with a beaming grin and a young woman with her. "Miss Baxter, I brought my cousin Mary, to see if she'd be suitable to take my place."

"Oh Rosie, you're so kind," Bernadette wiped her eyes and made up the excuse that she missed Louise, when Rosie looked at her sharply and asked if she was crying. "It's lovely to meet you, Mary, are you any good with ledgers?"

The girl looked shocked and said, "I thought I'd be cleaning, not doing numbers? I can't read!"

"It's all right," she tried not to giggle. "My sister Marie was the best at it, but she doesn't live here any more, so it's something I have to do."

"If Mary's no good," Rosie said, "I have plenty more cousins who'd be glad of the work. But she's a good cleaner and washer…"

Bernadette reassured both women. "If Rosie vouches for

you, Mary, then that's all I need. Thank you for coming. Rosie, would you like to take her upstairs to meet Mrs Poole? She can show you around. Do you need a room to stay in? We have plenty of spares."

The residence, and the bookshop, felt so empty without her sisters. Bernadette's feet itched to walk around Hatfield, as she used to. Taking herbs and tonics to people all over town. But there was nobody else to stay behind the counter, so it fell on her to do that.

It dawned on her then that for the first time in her life, she had to do everything. Everything that her father and her sisters had used to share between them. The responsibility weighed heavy on her shoulders; even though there was no longer a risk of losing the shop if they closed the doors for a few days, she somehow couldn't bring herself to do that. Her father had trusted his daughters to keep the shop running, and even though it was only Bernadette left, run it she would.

A slow trickle of customers came into the shop during the day. Some wanted books, while others said Dr Williams had sent them over as she had more expertise about their issue.

It was a lovely compliment. If she wasn't so infuriated with him, she might almost think he admired her. That was back when she was misreading every signal he'd sent her way. Now she knew it wasn't admiration. It was probably something far more prosaic, like the patients probably were 'beneath him' as they only needed remedies rather than medicinal compounds from Mr Lennox.

Mrs Bell visited in the afternoon, bringing with her a confused scowl on her face. "I don't like engaging in idle gossip, but it was impossible not to notice a change in Dr

Williams. I've seen men disappointed in love often enough to read the signs. You've rejected his suit, haven't you?"

"Is he miserable?" Delight infused Bernadette better than one of her own tonics.

"He is, and he made me assist in shifting the furniture about so he doesn't have to look over here, so I knew something was wrong. For the maintenance of peace under my roof, please tell me what happened."

"Very well, I will." Bernadette stood up, placed her hands on the counter and leaned forward. "This is the fact of the matter. I did not reject Dr Williams. *He* rejected *me*."

The midwife's jaw dropped open and stuck there.

Bernadette would have laughed if she wasn't suffering so much heartache. It was obvious Mrs Bell hadn't expected that at all.

"He is an idiot," Mrs Bell said, closing her mouth at last. "I… I most sincerely apologise. Have your ears been burning of late? I have been saying your name far too much under my breath… I'm dreadfully sorry. I completely misread the situation."

With a sigh, Bernadette confessed, "So did I."

"Oh my dear girl," Mrs Bell came around the counter, her arms out for a hug.

She took one more step, Bernadette thrust her hand out and said, "wait!"

Mrs Bell leapt back.

On the floor, between them, was a pile of mouse entrails.

"I've been so busy I forgot to check this morning," Bernadette grabbed the rags and the dustpan, then took the mess out to the courtyard.

When she came back in, Mrs Bell was ready with open arms again and she took full advantage of the motherly hug.

"I haven't had time to get out and see my usual customers either. I know you're busy too, but if I gave you a list would you be able to get around to seeing some of them?" Bernadette asked hopefully.

"It's the least I can do," Mrs Bell said. "Would you like me to poison his dinner?"

"No, no," the thought of poisons was a little too close to home for the time being. "Don't need to go that far. Hatfield needs its doctor."

"It's a pity Hatfield's doctor doesn't realise how much he needs you," the midwife countered. "Men can be such idiots!"

Bernadette revelled in the sympathy, and she realised that even if her sisters weren't here at this moment, she did have good friends all around her.

Bernadette also explained that Mr Charles wouldn't be needing a room after all, as - and she phrased this very carefully - Mrs Millings and Ruth were off to stay with relatives. There'd been no time for Mrs Bell to examine Ruth, but Mr Charles had assured them that his mother was experienced in midwifery. She'd know what to do to help Ruth.

"And the doctor's house will be ready soon as well," Mrs Bell said. "It will be just me in the house again. I won't know myself."

"Will you be all right?"

"Well, I was feeling sorry for Dr Williams, but now I know the truth I'm almost looking forward to seeing him off. Perhaps I'll talk to Riot Jones, see if some of the patrollers are looking for rooms. Nice law-abiding men who don't mind my strange hours!"

They hugged some more and Mrs Bell consoled Bernadette further, before Bernadette reached for a sheet of paper and her pen. It wasn't long before Bernadette had a short list of the patients she was most concerned about. She furnished Mrs Bell with a basket of carefully selected herbs and they parted on the best of terms.

It hurt so much to see the back of Dr Williams through the front windows at Mrs Bell's as Bernadette waved the midwife off.

Returning to her seat at the counter, she couldn't hold back the tears as Byron, the kitten Glynn had chosen for himself, pounced on her shoes.

"Why?" she sniffled unhappily, picking up the kitten and cuddling him, pressing her face into his soft fur. "Why won't he even talk to me any more? I miss him!"

Little Byron rubbed his cheek against hers and purred, almost as though he knew she were upset and trying to comfort her. The tears flowed harder.

The bell tinkled, and Bernadette took a great gulping breath, trying to prepare herself to face customers. Did she have a handkerchief in her pocket? She attempted to dry her tears on Byron's fur, unsuccessfully.

"Well, this is a fine welcome," a laughing voice said. "Where is everybody?"

Bernadette's eyes flew wide, and she shot to her feet, almost dropping Byron, who sank his claws into her arm to hold on. She didn't even notice as she stared at the beautiful, very pregnant woman standing in front of her.

"*Estelle?*"

"Dear sister." Estelle, eldest of the Baxter sisters and now Mrs Yates, stepped forward with a beaming smile, deftly scooped the kitten from Bernadette's hands and presented him to her husband, before seizing Bernadette in a loving embrace.

"When… when did you get back?" Bernadette stuttered, utterly shocked, as she returned Estelle's hug. Or tried to, because Estelle's stomach was very much in the way. Knowing her sister was pregnant was one thing; having the evidence of it pressed firmly against you was quite another!

"Just now! We sent a letter when the ship docked in Bristol, but we've travelled fast and directly here. I daresay we might have come ahead of it."

"You have! It is so good to see you."

Released from Estelle's embrace, Bernadette looked past her to her husband, who was holding Byron in the air and cooing at him. "And you, Mr Yates!"

"Don't you dare call me that, my name is Felix, as you well know." Felix Yates beamed happily at her, before coming forward and bending to kiss her cheek. Finding it wet, he blinked in confusion. "Are you… crying?"

"I'm happy to see you," Bernadette lied, brushing her hand over her cheek.

"Which, of course, is why you were crying when we walked in," Estelle said dryly. "Felix, dearest, I know we had planned to go on to Ferndale Hall, but it is getting quite late. Perhaps we'll stay here tonight and go in the morning?"

"I'll pop over to the Red Lion and get someone to ride out there and tell Grandfather," Felix said good-naturedly.

"Don't…"

"… let the cat out, I know." He put Byron down on the counter and left, with an adoring look at Estelle that Bernadette did not miss seeing.

"Look at you, you're glowing," Bernadette said hastily, not wanting Estelle to pursue the reasons for Bernadette's tears. "When do you think you are due? Have you seen a midwife?"

CATHERINE BILSON & EBONY OATEN

"Oh yes, of course. At the end of October, or early November." Estelle cradled her stomach with an expression Bernadette had never seen on her face before, soft and wonderingly loving. "I was absolutely determined to be home by then, but dear me, I have never been so dreadfully sick. They call it morning sickness, but it would last all day!"

"You poor thing! Were you able to get any ginger? It definitely helps - the Ferndale glass houses have produced lots this year, I have been able to make an excellent tea. Come on upstairs and have some, Mrs Poole will be delighted to see you!"

"And Louise?"

Bernadette blinked at Estelle. "When did you last receive a letter from us?"

"The end of July. The one you wrote, with details of what Joshua is trying to do in Chancery Court, the blackguard!" Estelle's eyes shone with righteous fury. "So I told Felix that we must come home, no matter if I was sick every mile of the journey."

That was the letter she'd sent at the beginning of July... Shaun Jackson had still been missing then. And they hadn't caught Benjamin as the arsonist, and Bernadette had been at odds with Dr Williams. Well, she was at odds with him again, now. Her hand flew to her mouth. "Oh, sister. How much I have to tell you!"

"Perhaps you should start with where Louise is!" Estelle said, as Bernadette went to the door and turned the sign over to Closed. She did not lock it, so Felix would be able to come back in, but she certainly did not want to deal with any more customers this afternoon.

"Eastbourne. On her honeymoon, with Mr Jackson."

Bernadette had the satisfaction of seeing Estelle look quite flabbergasted.

"And you don't need to worry about Joshua any more. Benjamin turned out to be the arsonist, and when Mr Jackson caught him trying to burn down the bookshop, he and Lord Ferndale made Joshua and Phoebe leave for the Americas in exchange for not forcing a prosecution."

"Benjamin was the…" Estelle clutched at the edge of the counter for support. "The WHAT?"

Bernadette suddenly recalled that she and Louise had decided long ago that they were not going to worry Estelle with details of the arson attacks. They had, in fact, gone out of their way to paint a rosy picture of life in Hatfield, right up until they'd been forced to admit that with the upcoming Chancery Court hearing, matters had gone beyond what they could cope with alone.

"Let's go upstairs and sit down and I shall make you a lovely cup of ginger tea," Bernadette said quickly. "I really do have a lot to tell you."

Mrs Poole welcomed Estelle back with cries of delight, and Felix too when he came upstairs to join them with his hands full of kittens. Brutus slipped in a few moments later, grinning broadly, and Bernadette started off by explaining that Brutus was now living with them and the bookshop was safe as Brutus was its heir apparent, with his property held in trust until he came of age.

Estelle had a hundred questions, but it soon became apparent that she was not content merely to hear the details of Louise's romance and Joshua and Phoebe's fall from grace

"And let's return to the matter of why you were crying on a kitten when we came in, 'Dette," Estelle said, her hazel eyes sharp over the rim of her cup as she sipped her ginger tea.

Mrs Poole snorted. "Because of a fool man who doesn't know what's good for him!"

"Oh?" Estelle raised an interrogative eyebrow.

Bernadette clamped her lips together. Mrs Poole, however, was not about to let Estelle go uninformed.

"It's the new doctor, Doctor Williams. A clever young man he is, knows far more about medicine than Doctor Rasley ever learned, but not much about how to court a young lady."

"I see." Estelle's gaze returned to Bernadette's face, and Bernadette looked at the floor. Her sister saw far too much.

"Felix, dearest." Estelle looked at her husband. "Perhaps you should go and meet this Doctor Williams."

"An excellent notion! I could do with stretching my legs after spending most of the day in a coach."

"You'll not have to stretch them far. Just across the street to Mrs Bell's. He's living there, and has a consulting room, while the doctor's house is being rebuilt. You'll see him through the downstairs window," Mrs Poole said helpfully, and Felix took himself off.

"Now, darling." Estelle set down her teacup and took Bernadette's hand. "Tell me everything."

Bernadette dissolved into tears again, and Estelle at once pulled her closer.

"There, there," Estelle whispered against her hair. "It's all right. I'm home, and we'll solve it all. I promise."

Bernadette didn't know how that could even be possible, but she desperately wanted to believe it. She clung to Estelle like a drowning man to a rope, hoping that somehow, her older sister would know what to do to make everything all right again.

CHAPTER 18
An Elegant Evisceration

Glynn hated having his back to the street, but the rearrangement of his consulting room served its purpose in that he no longer suffered the torment of regularly seeing Bernadette Baxter. Or looking at the bookshop door in the hope of seeing Bernadette Baxter. He sat at his desk, the sun behind him causing his body to cast a shadow over the papers he wrote on.

The other issue of facing away from the street was that he could not see patients approach Mrs Bell's door. A customer knocked, which caught him off guard and he smudged ink on the paper.

Sighing impatiently, he put his quill in the ink pot and walked to the front door. An elegantly-dressed man stood there, with curls of golden hair that shone like a halo in the late afternoon sun.

He smiled broadly and said, "Dr Williams, I take it?"

"Yes," he said. "Is this a medical emergency? I'm finishing up my paperwork for the day."

"Not at all," the man said and stepped in anyway,

placing his hat on the hat rack beside the door. "Well, yes, it is an emergency, but far from medical. Wait, I am wrong," he kept on talking as he walked into the consulting room, "This is all fine and modern! It's good to see Hatfield has a modern medicine man."

Glynn scratched his head in confusion and said, "Come in," even though the man was already in the room and looking about.

He carried the energy of a curious puppy. Broad smiles, bright shining eyes and a sense that something valuable might suddenly break if he weren't careful.

"How can I help you, Mr…?"

"I am Felix Yates," he stated, then stood there.

Was he waiting for applause?

"I'm terribly sorry, Mr Yates, the name doesn't ring a bell. I'm still rather new to Hatfield."

"Give it a moment. I'm sure you know Miss Florence Yates, who's on all the committees."

"I do, yes." But she was a spinster.

"And my grandfather, Lord…"

"Ferndale!" The pieces clicked together in Glynn's head. Then he suddenly wanted to be copiously sick. "You're married to…"

"Estelle, Bernadette Baxter's sister. Yes." He sat on the edge of Glynn's desk, grinning with glee. "And Bernadette Baxter is at this moment weeping copiously on my wife's shoulder, after a failed attempt to use a kitten as a handker-chief. I adore my wife and do whatever I can to keep her happy, Dr Williams. Alas, we arrived in Hatfield barely half an hour hence and my wife is already dreadfully *un*happy."

Glynn stood there not sure how to proceed. Did he take a seat? He would be far lower than Mr Yates… which, of course he was. Mr Yates would one day inherit the Ferndale Barony, and also be his future employer.

"Do sit down," Mr Yates said, and Glynn's behind found his chair.

"Honoured to meet you at last, Mr Yates." He finally managed to say something coherent and sensible.

"You should probably call me Felix. And what's your first name?"

"Glynn," he said, before blinking. "But I couldn't possibly..."

"Well, perhaps it can wait until we are brothers-by-marriage."

Glynn choked.

"Or have I got quite the wrong end of the stick?" Mr Yates' cheery blue eyes hardened, becoming suddenly quite icy. "Would you care to enlighten me as to exactly why Bernadette was crying into a kitten about you when we arrived?"

He absolutely should not feel even the slightest bit happy that Bernadette cared enough to cry over him. Glynn firmed his jaw and looked Mr Yates in the eye. "Regrettably, Miss Baxter has mistaken a professional respect from myself for stronger emotions. I'm afraid she fancies herself in love with me."

"Dear me." Felix's eyes were still rather icy. "Fancies herself in love with you. And you are not available to return her feelings because you are... already married?"

"No!" Glynn flinched. "What do you take me for? I'd never have ki..." he caught himself just in time.

"Kissed her, I see," Felix said, just as though he hadn't stopped at all.

"I didn't kiss her, I kissed her *back*," Glynn said mulishly, aware even as the words left his mouth that they made abso-lutely no sense.

"Bernadette." Felix's lips twitched. "I should not have thought it of her. And following this episode where you did not instigate the kissing, but kissing nonetheless occurred?" He raised a golden eyebrow.

"I came to my senses," Glynn said bluntly. "With respect, Mr Yates. I'm barely a gentleman - I certainly wasn't born one. I have little except my salary; not even my own home. I'll be living in a house provided by my employer. I have nothing to offer a wife, and certainly not a lady like Miss Baxter." He stared at Felix. "A lady who has one sister a countess, and another a future baroness. Miss Baxter can look far higher than a man who works for a living."

Felix nodded slowly. "I see, indeed. I suppose I should have thought of it earlier; Grandfather and I really should have set up something to provide dowries for the other sisters after I married Estelle…"

Glynn saw red. Jumping to his feet, he snapped "I am not going to live off my wife's money. I've worked hard for everything I have, I'm not an *aristocrat*."

Immediately he wanted to bite his tongue. Mr Yates was the epitome of a born aristocrat, for all he didn't yet have a 'Lord' in front of his name. The golden-haired man didn't seem to take offence, though, letting out a hearty laugh.

"Well, I dare say I deserved that, Glynn! You have your pride, I see. But let me caution you." Felix slipped off the desk and walked over to the door, a loose-limbed, utterly confident stride. "Pride is not a dish that tastes too pleasant. I trust you'll discover that soon enough."

Glynn wanted to punch the smirk off Felix's too-handsome face, but somehow, he kept his seat. *He's going to be my employer,* was all he could think. *I can't.*

"Good evening, Glynn," Felix said cheerfully. "I'm sure we'll meet again. Soon."

Dear Lord, I hope not.

"You'll be being invited to Sunday dinners at Ferndale Hall as one of the family before you know it, I'm sure!"

Glynn blinked at Felix's parting shot. Sunday dinners at Ferndale Hall had been a regular event almost since he arrived in Hatfield. Did that mean he was... *already* accepted as one of the family? He'd come to be extremely fond of Lord Ferndale and Miss Yates. The kindly old gentleman and his sweet sister had filled a hole in Glynn's life he hadn't even realised was there.

Would he ever be invited back to dinner after apparently breaking Bernadette's heart? How could he go anyway, even if he was invited, and look at Bernadette across the dining table?

"This is a fine mess you've made of things, boyo," he muttered to himself, hearing his late father's voice in his head as he slumped back into his chair and stared at the floor.

The door closing heralded Mrs Bell's arrival home. She looked through the open door of his consulting room - Felix hadn't closed it on his way out - and saw Glynn sitting alone.

"What an idiot," she said scornfully, and the honest truth was that Glynn was beginning to agree with her.

"You as well?" Glynn looked up at his landlady and winced. He should have stayed mute and let her pass, but now that he'd responded, she marched into the consulting room and stood by the desk.

"Come on, let's move this furniture back to the way it should be."

The woman was right that the furniture was much less conveniently placed now, but fixing it was the last thing he wanted to do at the moment. All he really wanted to do was sulk about how unfortunate he was to have such misdirected affections when there was nothing he could offer Miss Baxter.

Thinking about her as Miss Baxter instead of Bernadette helped. marginally. In the same way that it marginally helped to bang one's head against a timber wall instead of brick.

Apparently, however, it was entirely futile to resist. Mrs Bell wasn't taking no for an answer, and Glynn sighed and got up, grasping hold of one end of the desk.

As they shifted the desk back into its old position, Mrs Bell said, "Now you will be able to see your patients on approach."

He clearly took the hint. She wanted him to see Miss Baxter when she walked in and out of the bookshop.

"You clearly want to give me a piece of your mind, Mrs Bell?"

She may as well flay him, he'd already been so cheerfully put in his place by Mr Yates. Which also added to his pain. His place was so far beneath Miss Baxter, how could an aristocrat like Mr Yates not see how poor the match would be? Yet he seemed to encourage it? He'd heard the nobility were a little batty, even eccentric, but Felix Yates took the biscuit.

"I don't need to tell you anything you don't already know to be true. You and Miss Bernadette are made for each other. Now get over yourself and apologise and beg her to take you back."

He wasn't going to argue how impossible that would be. He let her have her triumph.

"I'll take dinner at the Red Lion tonight," he said, suspecting that if he was silly enough to eat at home, Mrs Bell's usually excellent cooking might turn out to be less so tonight. Burned or over-salted would likely be his lot.

"How very sensible of you," Mrs Bell said.

From the glint in her eye, Glynn suspected she might even have had something worse planned! And since he didn't want to spend the night becoming more closely acquainted with his chamber-pot, he very wisely took himself off until her temper cooled.

Glynn would far rather have avoided Felix Yates for the rest of eternity, but fate saw fit for the next town council meeting to be scheduled just two days later, and when Glynn entered the assembly room at the Red Lion, Felix Yates was seated in Lord Ferndale's place at the head of the table.

Everyone else already knew Mr Yates, it seemed, including Mr Charles and Riot Jones, who must have made his acquaintance in the last couple of days. They were all shaking his hand with great cheer, before inquiring anxiously about Lord Ferndale's health.

"Grandfather is in the very best of health, it's kind of you to ask," Mr Yates said in his annoyingly cheerful way. "But he has been expressing for some time that he would like me to take on a greater role in the running of the barony, and, supported by my estimable wife, I am delighted to follow his instructions and do whatever is necessary. Starting with standing in for him today."

"Congratulations are to be offered to you and Mrs Yates, I understand," Riot Jones said. He was standing in for Shaun Jackson; Glynn had rather hoped that his fellow Welshman, a very down-to-earth man, would share Glynn's opinion of the ridiculous young aristocrat, but Riot seemed quite impressed by Mr Yates.

Glynn wanted to growl under his breath at how irritatingly likable Mr Yates truly was. He slumped into his chair and tried not to sulk, doing his best to ignore the proceedings unless he was called upon to vote.

Unfortunately, Glynn could not pretend he wasn't there for the entire meeting, as the matter of the hospital was soon raised for the council's attention, and Mr Yates seemed exceedingly interested. Mr Charles was happy to tell the council that the bishop had accepted his recommendation that the large piece of vacant land beside the vicarage be used for construction of the hospital.

"Most excellent news," Mr Yates said. "And do we have the workmen and materials available?"

"Soon," Riot said. "The men are completing work on the doctor's cottage this week, but harvest is beginning and all hands will be needed. By the time the crops are in, the materials we've ordered will have been delivered, and it shouldn't take long to clear the ground and get the building up."

"And for the furnishings?" Mr Yates looked at Glynn. "Doctor?"

"I have a list," he said ungraciously. "I can place the orders at any time, if we have somewhere to store everything until the building is completed."

"Stacks of room at Ferndale Hall." Mr Yates made a note in a book in front of him. "Please go ahead and order everything delivered to the Hall, Doctor. I'll make arrangements to have it transported into town when you're ready for it. Better to have everything on hand than be waiting for things that take an unexpectedly long time to arrive."

He was right; and that was generous of him. Glynn clenched his teeth, trying very hard not to like Felix Yates, but realising that it was impossible. The man was too nice. He was handsome, generous, sensible... he was exactly the sort of man a Baxter sister deserved. No wonder he'd married one of them. He probably had a dozen friends just like him he would be ready to introduce Bernadette to.

Glynn didn't realise he was clenching his fist until his pencil snapped between his fingers.

CHAPTER 19
Another Reunion

It was so reassuring to have Estelle home again. Her sister glowed with happiness in between looking a little uncomfortable. The ginger tea helped a great deal with her queasiness, which in turn helped Bernadette feel useful. Still, it was hard to see her sister and Felix so obviously, blissfully in love and happy when she was so personally miserable.

Also, there was so much to tell Estelle about events, but at the same time she had to hold back a great many details so that she didn't overwhelm her, or fill her with worry. Their main issue was the Chancery Court hearing; best focus their energies on that.

In the grand scheme of things, what was a disappointment in love when a judge was about to preside over her entire future?

At least Estelle and Felix only stayed the one night before going on to Ferndale Hall, and Estelle was in no fit state to be travelling back and forth to Hatfield. Bernadette would have to go to her.

Brutus, bless his heart, rose early and checked the floor

for entrails. He even replaced the hessian at the bottom of the stairs for Crafty to sharpen her claws. The kittens were bouncing about, copying their mother's actions. Mr Thomas came in with some letters and Bernadette smiled and tilted her head toward the stairs to let him know Mrs Poole was in.

It seemed as if everyone else around her was in love. If they were any happier, she'd need to drink some ginger tea herself to stop from becoming bilious.

In the afternoon, more happy people arrived, and they gladdened her heart.

Two schoolboys tumbled into the shop, eyes wide with delight. "Hello Auntie Bernadette!" they called out.

"George and Richard!" She melted at the sight of her new nephews. It could only mean her sister and the Earl were not far behind.

Despite now being a countess, Marie bounced in and gleefully ran to Bernadette, her arms wrapping around her so tightly she lost her breath.

They held each other and cried with joy. Bernadette confessed, "I've missed you so. Louise was terrible at accounts!"

"Do you need me to look them over?"

She laughed and said, "You're allowed to come in and rest from your journey first." Then she turned to her brother in law and said, "Lord Renwick, it is a delight to see you, and the boys."

George and Richard had found the kittens already and were at the bottom of the stairs playing with them.

Brutus came downstairs and the boys immediately remembered each other. They sat together and the twins bragged of how big and ferocious The Pied Piper had become at Alston, while Brutus relayed the Hatfield tales, including the arson attack on the bookshop itself.

Marie did not appear to have changed at all, except her clothes were more distinguished. Renwick was happy to step back and let the sisters catch up, provided they showed him any more rare books they might have. Bernadette laughed and opened the locked cabinets for him to peruse, and he settled himself happily at the counter to search through the shelves.

Nothing more had come from father since January and the lack of new arrivals caused Bernadette to wince when Marie asked.

"Still nothing?" Marie asked, her expression deeply concerned.

"I would have written straight away if it had." Bernadette shook her head, pressing her hands to her stomach, willing away the sick feeling which always came over her now when she thought of the long silence from their father.

Mrs Poole came down the stairs and noticed the new arrivals, coming forward to embrace Marie. She made a quick greeting to all and promised to return soon with tea and vittles for the weary travellers.

"We have plenty of room, if the boys want to stay upstairs with us?" Bernadette offered.

"They are keen to see Mr Charles," Marie chewed her bottom lip. "And we rather hoped he might have moved into the vicarage by now?"

"He's recently taken up residence," Bernadette said, and now was as good a time as any to have a very quiet word with her sister about how exactly that had come about.

"Brutus, dear, would you mind the shop while Marie and I reminisce?"

They moved to the shelves of the lending library. Keeping her voice low, Bernadette relayed the pertinent events while Marie made first shocked and then soothing noises, and nodded understanding.

"You've done exactly the right thing," Marie said. "Morag will be so happy to have a young friend, even though Ruth might have a little difficulty understanding her at first. I shall write as well to offer full support for when we return, and ask our housekeeper Mrs Ellwood to look in on them too."

"Thank you," Bernadette thought she had no more tears, but the relief at knowing Ruth and her mother would be looked after released a fresh reserve of them.

Marie and Renwick would be staying at Ferndale Hall, but the boys were delighted to be staying with Mr Charles to catch up with their old tutor. It meant they could come and go to the bookshop whenever they liked, and have adventures with Brutus and the kittens. They would remain in Hatfield while the Baxter family attended Chancery Court, and then Renwick would come back and take them off to Eton for the Autumn term.

After tea and shortbread, Marie almost had to drag her husband away while he added "just one more" book onto his stack, and bundled the boys into the Renwick carriage.

"They're great fun!" Brutus said. "Are they staying in Hatfield?"

"For about another two weeks, then they're off to school until Christmastide I'm afraid," Bernadette replied.

Brutus pursed his lips together in thought. "I should like to go to school with them."

It was on the tip of Bernadette's tongue to say Brutus attending Eton might be impossible. But then again, her sister had married an Earl. And surely there was sufficient money from the half of Joshua's estate in trust for Brutus.

Nothing was impossible, really.

Then the glums came back with a vengeance. If only the dimwitted doctor across the street who held her heart knew that. Felix had told her what Glynn said, and Bernadette wanted to march across the street and slap some sense into him! She didn't care about Glynn not owning his own home, or that he wasn't born a gentleman. Those things didn't matter! She cared that he was kind and clever, and most importantly of all, supportive of her interest in medicine and the health of her fellow man. Or, mostly women. Glynn could look after the men, as far as she was concerned. It would be a most sensible division of labour between them!

They already had an excellent working partnership, or had, before he'd stopped speaking to her. Why wouldn't he see that they could be partners in love, too? She wiped away frustrated tears. Stupid, stupid man!

With his grandson and wife returned safely to Hatfield, Lord Ferndale and Miss Yates held a celebratory dinner at Ferndale Hall. It was to welcome people home, but also for some last-minute strategy before they travelled to London for the Chancery Court hearing. Bernadette and Brutus closed the shop for the day, as Mrs Poole came with them. They travelled in the Renwick carriage to the vicarage, where they made room for Mr Charles, George and Richard. Brutus and Richard stood on the back of the carriage where footmen would usually stand. They cheered and laughed into the wind. George sat beside the driver, with the promise that he could ride at the back on the return journey. The three boys were already fast friends, and George and Richard were eager to help in the bookshop. They were truly a pleasure to have around.

The late summer sun beamed into Glynn's consulting room as he filled in another patient record. Mr Black and his staff had created the stationery he wrote upon, and a surge of pride filled him as he wrote in the details of his most recent patient's medical complaint. It was, by coincidence, a man who worked for Mr Black who was having shoulder pain. It wasn't a surprise, given the man's age, that he suffered. Perhaps he would pay a visit to the print shop to see how the man worked, and whether it might be possible to alleviate the pain with a different work technique.

There was a report he'd been reading looking into the field of worker injuries and repeated actions. It was fascinating (and a little upsetting) to him, as he read about poultry workers plucking feathers for hours on end one day, and then not being able to move their hands the next. He also had to be careful that he didn't immediately start looking for similar injuries in Hatfield just because he'd read about something being investigated as far off as Manchester.

He'd seen the fancy carriage pull up outside the bookshop, but it covered the door of the shop. He could only assume the owner was a nobleman, judging by the crest on the door, the liveried driver and beautiful horses.

It only reinforced how completely wrong he was for Bernadette, that she moved in these high circles, while he studied reports on chicken pluckers hurting their wrists.

He completed his patient record and filed it alphabetically.

Resuming his seat, Glynn took up reading another medical report. Soon after, the Ferndale carriage parked in front of his window, completely blocking the view.

That cheerfully annoying Mr Yates was back.

"Glynn!" he called out as he walked in without even knocking this time.

"Mr Yates," he looked up from his desk. Again, he was low while the other man towered above him.

"Mr Yates was my wastrel father. Call me Felix. Everybody does." The emphasis was that if Glynn didn't call him by that name, he would therefore be a nobody.

He kept his voice as neutral as possible, "To what do I owe… the pleasure, Felix?"

"Remember I said before long you'd be dining at Ferndale Hall?"

He remembered the encounter. Every excruciatingly proper moment of it. He nodded.

"Well, you're invited. My darling wife is in the carriage, let's not keep her waiting."

"I… wait. I can't," he looked around for excuses, but his room was empty of other patients and everything looked far too neat to even pretend he needed to tidy things.

"One does not simply turn down an invitation to a magnificent repast at Ferndale Hall!" Felix said, in that delightfully threatening way he had about him.

The man knew how to flay someone alive and have them smiling at the same time.

But it was impossible. Simply impossible. Not after he'd treated Bernadette so poorly, even if it was for her own good.

"I can't face her," he admitted.

Dammit, what was it about Felix Yates that made him confess that?

"Well, I'm afraid it's not up to you. As your employer," Felix indicated the carriage outside, "I'm ordering you to get in."

There was absolutely nothing Glynn could say to that apart from "Yes, sir."

"Felix. And this is my wife Estelle," Felix added as Glynn got into the carriage.

"Did the two of you drive all the way from Ferndale Hall to Hatfield just to collect me?" Glynn asked grumpily, looking at Mrs Yates' swollen stomach. "You really shouldn't be bumping about like this, ma'am."

"I needed to get out of the house," Estelle said. "And yes, Felix insisted we come and get you."

"Absolutely," Felix said sunnily. "As I was fairly sure you'd refuse anyone else attempting to order you to attend."

It was like being disembowelled by an adorable bunny rabbit. Glynn's stomach hurt, yet he couldn't look away. "You've married a very annoying man, Mrs Yates," Glynn couldn't help but say to Estelle, who laughed, clearly not offended.

"You have already spent enough time with Felix to sum him up well, I see." Sitting back, hands folded over her belly, she cast her husband a look of adoration. "However, somehow with time, the annoyance seems to transform to affection. I don't know quite how he does it, but he grows on one."

"Like mould," Glynn muttered.

"I'm still right here," Felix said in tones of mock indignation, "where I can hear the two of you insulting me."

"I don't doubt you have both been insulting *me* where I cannot hear you," Glynn decided to go on the offensive.

"Well, you have been an absolute idiot, from what I hear," Estelle said cheerfully. "Have you come to your senses yet?"

"Nothing has changed!" Glynn insisted. "You are all trying to make a match which is unsuitable in every way, and it seems I am the only person who can see sense!"

"All these months with Bernadette, and you do not know *her* at all," Estelle said, sounding a little sad.

"I know she deserves better than a man who cannot give her the life she should have."

"Who are you to judge that?" Estelle raised a brow at him, and he saw the echo of Bernadette in the expression. It was that exact same look Bernadette always gave him when she was challenging him in some way, making him think beyond the boundaries of his education and experience.

"What Bernadette *needs*," Estelle said firmly, "is someone who will support her in her calling. Which, despite how well she's been running our family business entirely on her own, is helping others medically. And from what Bernadette has told me, she has found that support from you. Or do you deny regularly sending patients to her that you believe she is better skilled to help than you are?"

"You are as annoyingly determined to be right as Bernadette is," Glynn grumbled, unable to meet that challenging look, and staring out of the window instead.

Estelle sighed. "And you are determined to be stubborn. Well. We shall see. Perhaps the Chancery Court will take the decision out of your hands."

"What about the Chancery Court?" Glynn frowned, but

the carriage was drawing up in front of Ferndale Hall and Felix and Estelle got out without answering the question.

Glynn dragged his feet in behind them. Miss Yates came up and spoke as kindly to him as ever, before introducing him to Lord and Lady Renwick and their sons.

Lord Renwick was not as intimidating as Glynn had expected. Yes, he was tall, and dark, and Glynn suspected he could look quite forbidding if he wished, but the wide smile that never left his face made him seem very approachable

Lady Renwick was also not what he'd expected. Having met three of the four Baxter sisters already, Glynn had expected the physical resemblance of brown hair and hazel eyes, but Lady Renwick wore glasses and had a much more quiet manner. Finding himself seated between Miss Yates and the countess at lunch, however, Glynn soon realised that Marie was a very clever woman. She asked a few pene-trating questions and he found himself telling her something of his background.

They were so enchanting and engaging, he didn't realise how out of his depth he was until he was already drowning. Estelle Yates made what sounded like a polite comment on the surface, but carried with it strong undercurrents. "Bernadette, that new cabinet is stunning. I would love something similar for Ferndale Hall."

Bernadette swallowed hard and her eyes darted toward Glynn, then back to her sister. "Yes, it is lovely."

"Is it from a local cabinetmaker?"

"Ah, I'm not sure, it was a gift."

Estelle looked at the Baron. "Oh, did you give it to her, Grandfather?"

"I am innocent!" Lord Ferndale exclaimed, expression guileless.

Glynn coughed. "I, er, I gave it to Ber- Miss Baxter."

Silence fell across the table faster than a guillotine blade, everyone staring at him.

Lord Ferndale said, "What a thoughtful, *personal* gift that is."

Glynn closed his eyes and wished he could sink through the floor.

Agonisingly later, the ladies removed themselves so the men could remain and discuss tactics.

Glynn was desperate to get away, but had no idea what he should do. If he removed himself, would he insult his hosts? If he remained, would he be outstaying his unwelcome?

He simply had no clue.

One more reason why he and Bernadette were so unsuited.

"Dr Williams, I'm glad you're here," Lord Ferndale said.

Glynn remained rooted to the spot.

"Now, let's talk brass tacks. You're a good man, and a good match for Bernadette. I'm too old to wait for you to catch up to good sense. Do you hear me?"

"I think so," he said, wondering exactly what was going on.

"Good. I thought Felix had the matter in hand, but apparently not, since I am not yet advised of good tidings."

"I did try, Grandfather," Felix said. "But I truly think he needed to hear it from you."

The family patriarch spoke as if Glynn wasn't even in the room. "That's a shame. But I'll let this lapse slide as I've heard excellent reports back from the town council meeting. Can you believe he gave Bernadette a medical cabinet? I could not imagine anything more perfect for my youngest granddaughter."

"I haven't yet seen it myself, but Estelle was in raptures and as you heard, she is keen for one."

"Yes, so give that doctor a good knock on the bonce and get him to contact the maker." The old man shook his head. "Any wonder Bernadette thought it was a courting gift."

If the gates of hell themselves had opened, Glynn would have gladly stepped through rather than sit here being flayed so politely.

"The Chancery Court," Renwick said, in a blissful change of subject. "Marie and I prepared a speech, if it's needed."

"Good man," Lord Ferndale said.

They talked for a little more with plans of who might say what. They would stay at Renwick's London house and meet the barrister who would represent them to the court.

"And the Jacksons will meet us at the house as well," Renwick said.

As things were winding down, Glynn dared to say, "I'm sure I won't be needed."

"My good man, you're the most important one," Felix said.

"I am?" Surely they were having a lend?

Felix sighed, but looked so pleasant about it. "My wife is in a delicate condition. She will need a medical professional with her at all times."

"She still has about eight weeks, does she not?" Felix was making feeble excuses. They were going to London, not the wilderness. There were doctors and midwives aplenty if Mrs Yates should need help, not to mention Bernadette travelling with them.

Renwick looked at Lord Ferndale, and then back at Glynn, before leaning forward and imparting further information. "Three of the Baxter sisters are already wed, and well taken care of. Bernadette is not. She is not even promised to anyone. She is the one in the most peril, without her father here to represent her. As much as we prepare, there's no guarantee of success at Court. For all we know, the judge may take it upon himself to solve the situation by marrying Bernadette, or he might marry her off to one of his cronies!"

"Anything but that!" Glynn swallowed through sudden dryness in his throat as reality came crashing down upon his head. Could he really lose Bernadette, to some complete stranger? The very concept left him short of breath.

Three noble sets of foreheads creased in his direction as he realised what a fool he'd been.

"I... have rather made a dreadful hash of things, have I not?"

Three sets of foreheads unfurled, then the gentlemen they belonged to burst into laughter.

"About time you came to your senses!" Lord Ferndale said.

Glynn thought about it for a moment. "But... if things don't go our way at the Chancery Court... I would rather not raise Bernadette's hopes, only to be unable to fulfil them for reasons out of our control. I will come with you to London, but please don't say anything to her beforehand."

The gentlemen looked at each other, and then Felix shrugged. "I suppose it's only a few more days. Very well. But please stop ignoring her, it's making her miserable, and if one of those sisters is miserable..."

"They are *all* miserable!" Renwick said.

Felix said, "And that makes their husbands miserable, so please stop!"

Glynn smiled despite himself. Estelle was right. Annoying though Felix could be, he definitely did grow on one.

CHAPTER 20

The Chancery Court

S ince Bernadette hadn't seen Marie's new home at
Alston Castle, it hadn't quite sunk in yet that Marie
was a countess. Seeing her magnificent London townhouse
in the heart of Mayfair really brought it home, however.
Bernadette fairly gaped as she made her way up the steps to
the wide double doors, promptly opened by a butler.

"Goodness me." Estelle caught Bernadette's arm in hers.
"This is very grand!"

"Do you think Alston Castle is this grand? Marie seems
completely at home!"

Marie was just stripping off her gloves and handing them
to the butler, apparently accepting the deep bows and curt-
sies the staff were offering as her due.

"*Lady* Renwick," Estelle said, then gave an odd little
laugh. "It's too strange to think that one day I shall be Lady
Ferndale. I cannot come to terms with it."

A shriek greeted them as they entered the hall, and
Louise came running from a parlour to the left, trying to hug
both Estelle and Marie at once. Shaun Jackson followed with

a grin on his face, stooping to kiss Bernadette's cheek. He looked curiously at Mr Yates, and Bernadette realised that of course they had never met.

"Shaun, please allow me to introduce your brother-by-marriage - Felix Yates. Felix, Shaun Jackson."

"A great pleasure," Felix said, enthusiastically pumping Shaun's hand. "My word, everyone told me you were a great tall fellow, but you really are a veritable giant! How admirably well suited you are for our dear Louise!"

Shaun looked pleased by that, and disposed to like Felix. They all progressed into the parlour where Estelle promptly sat down with a sigh and said "I've been sitting in a carriage all morning, why do I feel like all I want to do is sit some more?"

"Is that a rhetorical question?" Bernadette said dryly, "or do we need to once more go over the reasons why a seven-months-pregnant woman needs to rest a great deal?"

"Ugh." Estelle smiled at her, and then beckoned her to come and sit down close. "All four of us together again," she said with a happy sigh as Louise and Marie sat down too.

"And three of us married!" Louise said joyously.

Marriage was obviously agreeing with Louise just as well as with both her other sisters. Bernadette shoved down a pang of jealousy, glancing towards the other side of the room, where the gentlemen had congregated by the window. Glynn seemed to be on better terms with Felix now, and at least he was no longer ignoring Bernadette, though he did not seem to be actively seeking her out either. He was just being perfectly polite, as though they were mere acquaintances rather than the closeness she had come to enjoy.

She wasn't entirely sure why he'd come to London with them. She was probably more capable of looking after Estelle at the moment than he was, despite Felix's loud declarations that his wife must have her doctor in attendance. Glynn was far too intelligent to fall for that.

Realising she was staring at him as he talked animatedly with Shaun, Bernadette made herself look away, grinding her teeth. He did not return her affections, it was as simple as that. She needed to make herself move on!

"Marie, dearest." Renwick came over and interrupted the sisters' reunion. "Let the maids show everyone to their rooms, so that we can all wash up and change for dinner. My barrister is coming, so that you can all meet him before tomorrow."

"Very well," Marie said with a little sigh. "I suppose we can talk to our hearts' content later."

Bernadette hoped so. She had the sinking worry that everything would turn out exactly as planned for everyone but herself at the Chancery Court. What if they gave her guardianship to someone she'd never even met, who turned out to be an absolute ogre? It was very possible she wouldn't even be allowed to go home to Hatfield. She might never see her sisters, or Glynn, again for years!

The barrister, a Mr Sears, did little to calm her fears. Deferential to Renwick, polite to the other men, he barely acknowledged the sisters if one of them chanced to ask a question.

"Well, I did not care for him overmuch," Louise said bluntly as the ladies retired to the parlour after dinner, leaving the gentlemen in the dining-room with their port.

"Too late to get someone else, I'm afraid!" Marie made a face. "I could see Renwick was not pleased when Mr Sears ignored my question and Renwick had to ask it again, but the hearing is tomorrow. We shall just have to let him do his job."

"That's all very well for you to say," Bernadette said, twisting her fingers together nervously and trying to remember if she had packed any chamomile tea. She desperately needed something to help her feel calm. "You're safely married and needn't fear your future being handed off to some random stranger!"

"I'm sure that won't happen," Marie said, but Bernadette could hear the lack of confidence in her voice. The countess then tilted her head and changed tactics. "On the other hand, perhaps this will drag out for so long you'll come of age before it's over. Then the entire point will be moot."

"If you're trying to cheer me up, it's not working," Bernadette said.

Bernadette held Estelle's hand as they travelled to the Inns of Court. She was supposed to be supporting her sister in her time of need, but Estelle was the one who exuded calm and provided comfort to her instead. Bernadette felt absolutely sick. She'd drunk Estelle's ginger tea instead when her sister claimed she did not feel nauseous that morning, but it didn't seem to have helped.

Men in wigs strolled about as Bernadette and Felix helped Estelle out of the carriage. Having Felix's smiling, confident demeanor gave Bernadette a sense that everything would be all right. But oh, how her stomach roiled and rolled with uncertainty! She pressed her hands against her belly and silently ordered herself to breathe.

"Are you all right?" a quiet voice said, and she looked

around to see Glynn standing nearby, his brow furrowed with concern.

"Yes," she said automatically, trying to summon up a smile. It felt thin and weak, and she sighed, deciding to be honest. "I'm nervous."

He hesitated, and she wondered if he was going to throw out some silly platitude, telling her everything would be all right. Instead, he said "You have a lot of good people in your corner, Bernadette. I don't think they'll let anything bad happen to you. If the worst outcome should come to pass… well, there are options. I have a plan."

"What kind of plan?" she wanted to ask, but there was no time; they were being called inside and separated.

At least he called me Bernadette again. It was a small thing to feel happy about, but somehow Glynn using her name had settled the worst of her stomach's uneasiness. Bernadette linked her arm through Estelle's, and they followed Marie and Louise inside.

Chancery Court was an imposing stone building with high panelled windows. If it was designed to make attendees feel small, it certainly fulfilled that duty.

A solicitor guided the sisters to the back of the court, where they could sit in the gallery. They were under strict instructions not to speak, which suited Bernadette as she fretted away.

The judge in black robes and a long wig that would not have been out of place in the times of the Cavaliers, sat on the King's Bench at the other end of the hall, while the gentlemen sat at the long table with the solicitors and barrister as they began reading the details of the petition. The sun beamed through the tall windows, casting colour and spots of light as it passed through the stained glass, illuminating the dust motes floating in the air. A lot of dust. Bernadette sniffed in disapproval. Did the silly men even let maids in here to clean? Rosie, or Mary, would never have allowed a room to get so dusty!

Lord Renwick and his barrister did most of the talking during the hearing. The judge paid attention to the earl, and Bernadette had never been so grateful to have that kind of connection. They thought they were fortunate to have Lord Ferndale as a benefactor, but an earl was somebody even court judges were happy to listen to.

An earl and a baron and his heir, a town magistrate and a town doctor - eminent members of the community were joining forces to provide guardianship for one young woman who ran a bookshop, safeguarding the Baxter family's legacy for Brutus.

The judge shook his head. Bernadette's ears strained to hear his comments.

"You're willing to vouch for a woman operating a business?"

Renwick's barrister stepped up and explained further.

"It is not her business, it is her cousin's, by the name of Brutus Baxter. He is heir to the bookshop and the residence above in the event of Mr Matthew Baxter's demise, and is running it as a going concern at the present time, ably assisted by experienced personnel hired by his guardians. There is no further issue of women running a business. Brutus Baxter is the ward of Lord Ferndale and Mr Jackson, the town magistrate. He is the Baxter of *Baxter's Fine Books*, m'lud."

The 'lud' nodded. Bernadette grinned to herself. The 'experienced personnel' were herself and her sisters, but it would hardly be helpful to explain that to the judge. The barrister had listened, then, at least to Renwick's barrister.

"If, when Brutus Baxter comes of age in nine years, it is the case that Matthew Baxter has not returned, we shall then return to the court to have Matthew declared dead, m'lud."

The words hurt Bernadette's ears. She did not want to hear anything referring to her father as no longer being of this earth. Her father had to be alive, somewhere. He simply had to be. Estelle's hand tightened around hers, and Bernadette glanced at her sister's face. Estelle had always been the best of them at putting on a brave face, but their father had been gone more than a year, and eight full months had passed since they last heard from him. Estelle's other hand rested on the swell of her belly. Bernadette could guess what she was thinking. Would Matthew ever get to meet his grandchild?

As the day wore on, the light changed angles and the barrister's voice droned on. More men in wigs came in and sat in the rows between the main table and the gallery at the back. It made it difficult to see what was going on with so many more bodies in front of them.

Bernadette's ears strained to hear Renwick's barrister over the murmuring, whispering crowd.

"And so, you see, m'lud, we have come not to prosecute the petition lodged by a Mr Joshua Baxter, who has since left England permanently for the Americas, with his wife and two remaining sons, but to declare it moot, since Mr Brutus Baxter is the heir to Mr Matthew Baxter's estates. All we should like to do is declare Lord Ferndale, Lord Renwick, Mr Jackson and Dr Williams as the rightful guardians of Miss Bernadette Baxter until her father returns to these shores, or until she comes of age, whichever happens first."

CATHERINE BILSON & EBONY OATEN

There was a little movement at the table. It was hard to see what was going on. It might have been Glynn standing up.

But why would he be standing?

"My Lord," he said. Yes, it was definitely Glynn's voice. "I seek to have my name removed from the board of guardians for Miss Bernadette Baxter."

Her heart could have stopped with shock. Could he be more cruel? Why would he request such a thing unless he was planning on leaving Hatfield altogether?

"For what reason, er, Mister…" the judge said, searching for his name.

"Doctor Williams," Glynn provided. "For the reason that I'm not a suitable guardian, because I wish to marry her."

The court erupted.

Bernadette sat in mute shock.

Had he just said he wanted to marry her?

He could have asked me first! But a smile was beginning to spread across her face, warmth flushing her cheeks.

He wants to marry me.

Another shock came hot on the heels of the first, even as the judge was banging his fist on his desk and called the court to come to order.

A man's voice rang out from the doorway, loudly saying, "Then perhaps you should ask me?"

Whoever could that be? Bernadette couldn't see past her sisters. It was Louise, taller than the others, who caught sight of the man in the doorway, and shot to her feet.

"Father?"

242

CHAPTER 21

Order In The Court

Chaos erupted. Bernadette felt a little faint, but she didn't want to miss a second of this. She and Marie scrambled up from their seats, peering past Louise to see if it was really true. Estelle was a little slower, but she too got to her feet.

Their father stood there in a beam of light, large as life!

But also… Glynn had just told the court he wanted to marry her. They'd shared one kiss, which was beautiful and everything she'd ever wanted in a kiss, and then he'd rejected her. Well, she'd make him wait a long time for an answer if that was the case. He had some explaining to do first!

The judge shouted for order and a man in a wig walked to the gallery to remind the women to be quiet. He might as well ask a bird not to fly. Their father had returned! Louise waved frantically and Matthew saw them all together. His hands covered his heart and he bowed to them.

He was alive!

As the court finally quieted a little, the judge called out, "You claim to be Matthew Baxter?"

"I am he," their father said firmly, walking towards the front of the court.

Bernadette drank him in with her eyes, relieved beyond belief to see him. His coat looked travel-worn, he seemed a little thin, and his hair was longer than she remembered, tied back in a queue, but he was clean-shaven, tanned, and looked healthy enough.

"Is there anyone in the court who can vouch for your identity?" the judge said, peering at Matthew over his glasses.

Lord Ferndale rose and cleared his throat. "I can easily do that; we have been acquainted these thirty years. That is indeed Matthew Baxter, of Baxter's Fine Books, and I am jolly well delighted to see him again, hale and hearty!"

"It is very good to see you too, Arthur." Matthew grinned at Lord Ferndale. "And I look forward to being introduced to all these fine sons-in-law my girls have managed to find in my absence."

The judge said, "In that case, I daresay the court can rest. I declare the original petition void as the reasons for it no longer apply. As Brutus Baxter's father completed the appropriate legal steps to appoint his guardians, that matter is not in question. You are dismissed from the court."

The solicitors at the table groaned with disappointment. They'd probably been counting on this to run for a year at least.

"Now will you please get those women out of my courtroom?" the judge barked.

"Crotchety old man!" Estelle laughed, but she was already pushing at Marie to get out of their row of seats.

Matthew had spun around as soon as the judge dismissed the case, and rushed back towards them. They met him in the aisleway and flung their arms around him, clinging tightly and all talking at once. Bernadette could hardly believe her father was really here!

"What *happened*?" she chorused along with the others. "Where have you been?"

"I promise I'll tell you everything," Matthew said, half-laughing as Louise squeezed his ribs hard. "And it seems you all have a great deal to tell me, but come. Let us get out of this court before the judge has us charged with disturbing the peace. Are you staying in a hotel somewhere, Arthur?" He looked at Lord Ferndale, who had come to join them.

"No, no, Renwick has put his townhouse at our disposal," Lord Ferndale said cheerfully. "A good thing too, with such a crowd!"

Matthew had a horse, which was being held by a street urchin outside the court, and Bernadette realised that he had ridden right up to the doors and raced into the hearing.

"You've been home to Hatfield," she said as they all gathered in the large drawing-room at Renwick's townhouse.

"Indeed, I arrived this morning, spoke briefly with Mrs Poole, and realised I was urgently required here. Hired a horse and rode straight to London, to arrive just as you were receiving a very dramatic proposal." Matthew grinned, enveloping her in a great hug. "You'd better introduce me to your young man, 'Dette. Did someone say he is a doctor?"

"He's not my young man," she said, even as she flushed to the roots of her hair.

"Well, not yet, since I haven't given my consent." Matthew looked at her closely. "And I'm not in a hurry to do so, either, so we have plenty of time to talk about it. Unlike Estelle! How soon am I to be a grandfather?"

"You are already a grandfather," Estelle laughed, which made Matthew's eyes fly wide.

"What?" he gasped.

"She is teasing you, Papa." Marie shook her head at Estelle. "I have two stepsons, is what she means, Renwick's boys. They are fine lads; I cannot wait for you to meet them!"

"Well." Matthew laughed, and then he looked around at them all with a mischievous twinkle in his eye. "I am glad to hear you have all been busily expanding the family, and I must tell you, I have also done my part."

They all stared at him, and he grinned, obviously enjoying himself. "Do you recall your mama's cousin, Céline Fenouillart? You never met, of course, but they exchanged letters for many years."

"Of course," Marie said at once. She had taken over the shop's correspondence once their mother passed. "She's the one who wrote to you telling you about all the books being looted and burned from French châteaux!"

"Indeed." Matthew's smile was fond. "I found her, after an extensive search, in Limoges, at the end of February. Just days before Napoleon landed at Cannes and chaos erupted."

"We thought it must have been something like that." Louise nodded. They were all hanging on his every word. "And you had to go into hiding?"

"Yes... if it was just me, I might have been all right. Thanks to conversing with your mother in French all those years, I could pass for a native and I had excellent forged papers. But Céline had her two sons with her, Philippe and Pierre, and Philippe is sixteen - the recruiters tried repeatedly to get him to sign up, to the point of force. We went into

246

hiding and tried to make our way to the western coast when things quietened down as Napoleon headed north, but there was not a boat to be had." Matthew spread his hands. "I could not leave them, nor the books."

"Books?" all four sisters chorused, and they were joined by Renwick and Ferndale this time.

Matthew chuckled. "Indeed. I sent some of what I found home, but some of the books were so rare and valuable I did not trust anyone to take them. By the time I found Céline and her boys I had a whole cart full."

"And do you have them with you still?" Renwick asked eagerly.

"You have found a husband after my own heart, I see," Matthew said to Marie. To Renwick he replied, "Yes, they are safe in Hatfield, along with my wife."

"Your wife!"

"I married Céline... I had to, in order to bring her and the boys across the border into Spain with me, and from Bilbao we were finally able to take a ship for England." Matthew's smile was almost sheepish. "I married Céline out of necessity, but... I do also love her a great deal, and she loves me. I hope you are not upset with me, girls..."

"Never!" Bernadette said firmly, and her sisters agreed with her. "Mama has been gone a long time, Papa. I know she would have wanted you to be happy, and she loved Céline. She would be delighted that you have found happiness in each other."

"And now we have brothers!" Louise exclaimed. "Oh, I cannot wait to meet them. What an adventure you have had, Papa!"

"Tell me more about these books," Renwick said, and Marie started laughing.

"I apologise, Father, he is very single-minded about books…"

"And he is not the only interested party. Have you a catalogue, Matthew?" Lord Ferndale butted in.

Matthew grinned. "I had a little time aboard ship to begin one, but it might simply be easiest for the two of you to go through the collection with me, now I have it safely at the bookshop."

"An excellent notion," Lord Ferndale approved. He eyed Renwick. "I suppose we shall have to civilly negotiate who can buy what, hm?"

"At least we will have first look, before any advertisements are sent to the newspapers," Renwick consoled.

"And I regret to advise you that I will not be giving friends and family discounts," Matthew said. "I did not smuggle these books through war-torn France and risk my life for them more than once for nothing! I planned to sell them to raise enough to richly dower all four of my girls - though from the brief information Mrs Poole passed on, it seems as though only Bernadette might still need a dowry?"

Bernadette sneaked a glance at Glynn, who stood at the edge of the group hanging on Matthew's every word. Glynn's expression turned blank and wooden as Matthew mentioned her dowry, and then he turned and walked stiffly away.

Matthew noticed, and Bernadette felt his eyes on her, but they could not speak of it at that moment, not with everyone clamouring to ask him more questions. Renwick, Mr Yates and Mr Jackson were all eager for a private audience to assure Matthew of how happy they were in their marriages to his daughters, and how well they would provide for their wives without any need of a dowry. Any conversation with or about Glynn would have to wait.

After a hearty meal and much carousing and many tales of shared adventures - although they didn't talk much of the fires because Bernadette, Louise and Marie had decided not to worry poor Estelle too much - Bernadette slipped out into the back garden to breathe the crisp autumn air.

She coughed with the amount of soot and smoke that came with it, and couldn't wait to return to Hatfield in the morning. What an incredible, emotional and exhausting day they'd all had. What a sensational entrance on the part of their father. And a step-mother and brothers waiting to meet them in Hatfield.

No wonder Papa looked so happy and healthy despite his adventures - he had the love of a good woman by his side.

Of course she missed her mother, but in some ways this was a second chance for all of them. Perhaps Céline might also be interested in herbs? She might have some extra knowledge that Bernadette's own mother had not passed down to her.

Footsteps sounded behind her. When she turned, there was Glynn.

"I'd be happy to leave you be if you want a little serenity. It was all a bit raucous today," he said, his expression diffident.

"It was at that, but you can come and sit," she shifted over on the stone bench to make room.

The moment he sat, she let her displeasure be known. "You're hopeless."

"I am?" He sounded offended, but he had no right to be, in her opinion! It was she who had every reason to be cross!

"Very."

"May as well let me have it then. Just about everyone else in your extended family has given me a set down, so I suppose it's your turn." He smiled wryly.

"You asked my father before you even asked me. You asked the *court* before you asked me!" That was the bit that hurt. Actually, no, there was more. "I know you enjoyed our kiss. And then you pretended I didn't even exist. How was that supposed to make me feel?"

"Well I…"

"… And then you stand up in court saying you want to marry me, without even asking me first?"

"That's…"

"You asked my father? He's barely been back in the country a day! I'm glad he hasn't given permission."

Silence.

Bernadette stood up and started pacing, trying to keep her temper in check.

"I thought it was what you wanted?" Glynn said softly.

"What I wanted?" Bernadette repeated, incredulous. "I want to be wooed!" She stamped her foot. "I want to be wooed and… and be loved and not spoken about like some parcel to be handed over from one person to another."

He drew in a sharp, shocked breath and said, "You're absolutely right."

"Good," she sat back down on the bench, satisfied he was finally listening to her.

"I am hopeless," he said, echoing her earlier statement.

"Hopeless at love, and… I find myself hopelessly *in love* with you."

"Now, you see?" she exclaimed triumphantly. "Was that so hard? More of that, if you please."

"That's just it. It is rather difficult. And your father talking about a dowry just now makes it even more difficult than before."

"That's silly. A dowry will help enormously!"

"Difficult for *me*. I want you to be happy and comfortable, but what can I offer? I work at the grace and favour of Lord Ferndale, and later, if I am so lucky to still be employed, for Felix… who is also your brother in law."

Bernadette tapped her foot impatiently, but held her tongue.

He sighed and said, "It hurts my pride not to be able to offer you a good house and a future of comfort that I have made. Everything I have is more or less borrowed and bestowed by others."

Bernadette rolled her eyes. "I am in a great deal of discomfort and annoyance right now, because of your pride. Have you not noticed how much you are already part of this family?"

Glynn slumped with the realisation. "I want you to keep your dowry, though. I cannot accept it. There must be a way we can put it in a family trust so that if I fall out of favour and lose what I have, you will not suffer?"

"This is not wooing," Bernadette snapped. "This is making excuses. Woo me. Now!"

"I love you," he blurted hastily.

"Good. I love you as well, you silly goose. Now stop making me miserable and kiss me."

He did as she commanded, and it was even better than

their earlier kiss. This one had privacy, a cool autumn night and no interruptions. They both gave in to the kiss, matching each other's enthusiasm and tenderness. Warmth spread through her whole body as he held her in his arms.

When they came up for air, Bernadette said with a giggle, "That's an excellent start. In time, I'm confident you'll convince me to marry you."

He quietly laughed, and promised, "I will work on my pride."

"Good," she kissed him again and it was a complete delight.

A little later, she asked him, "So, what did you mean outside the courthouse about a plan, if things didn't end up going our way?"

"Renwick offered me his carriage, and I was going to ask you to elope with me to Gretna Green."

"You definitely would have asked me first, would you? You wouldn't have just bundled me in?"

He laughed a little louder this time, and she joined in. Soon they were kissing again, and it felt perfect.

CHAPTER 22
Home to Hatfield

C éline Fenouillart, now Céline Baxter, was a slender woman of around forty years of age with silken black hair and laughing blue eyes. She embraced all of Matthew's daughters as though they were her own long-lost children, and they could not help but warm to her at once. Her two sons, Philippe and Pierre, were sturdy handsome lads with surprisingly good English, or perhaps not so surprising since they had been travelling with Matthew for the best part of six months. He would have worked hard on improving their English to ready them for their new lives in England. Philippe was sixteen and Pierre thirteen, and they had already taken Brutus and Renwick's two sons under their wing. The bookshop was full of boys and kittens, an uproar Bernadette found rather delightful, though she noticed Marie putting on ear mufflers and beating a hasty retreat.

"I feel as though I know you all already, after so many years of letters," Céline said, embracing Bernadette, "but I am so glad to have the chance to know you properly at last! I want to learn everything about running the bookshop, your father has told me all about it, and it is high time you all had some time to relax. You have worked so hard!"

They had. They really had, and as Bernadette looked around the bookshop, it all came crashing down on her; the last year of work and worry, of her sisters one by one falling in love and marrying and leaving her behind. Her face crumpled and her breath began to come quickly, and suddenly strong arms went around her.

"Bernadette," Glynn said softly, and she turned into his arms, buried her face against his shoulder, and burst into tears.

"She's a little overwrought," she vaguely heard him say over her head, and then he was leading her outside and across the street to Mrs Bell's, to the consulting room where they had spent so many hours talking.

Glynn didn't say anything. He just sat down on the couch, pulled Bernadette into his lap and let her cry it out.

"Need a tonic?" he whispered into her hair when her sobs finally subsided to shuddering breaths.

She hiccupped a half-laugh and shook her head. "I'll be all right."

"Of course you will. You're one of the brilliant, beautiful Baxter women. But I just wanted you to know," he nuzzled at her ear, making her catch her breath, "that if you ever do need to fall apart for a little while, I'll be here to catch you."

"Wow," she murmured. "You're getting the hang of this wooing thing quite nicely, Doctor Williams."

He kissed her most satisfactorily, and half an hour later Bernadette returned to the bookshop with a smile on her face feeling a great deal more composed. Céline took in her kiss-swollen lips and mussed hair with an amused smile but said nothing, just tucked her arm through Bernadette's and said;

"I have something you particularly would like, I think. Did you know that your mother came from a long line of keen herbalists?"

"Mama did always say that," Bernadette agreed.

"She left for England before our mutual grandmother passed away, otherwise I am sure the family treasure would have been left to her, but as it happened, it came to me instead. Now, I think you should have it."

"The family treasure?" Bernadette said, wide-eyed. "But… that came from your husband, didn't it?"

Céline's first husband had been very wealthy, though not titled, and left her extremely well provided for at his death ten years ago. The property had all been seized, unfortunately, but Céline was nothing if not resourceful. She had converted every asset she could manage into jewellery and smuggled quite a fortune out of France sewn into the hems of her gowns.

"Oh, not the jewels." Céline waved a graceful hand. "That's just money, though I am sure there are a few little pieces you would like, I will gift them to you for your trousseau. No, this is a treasure come down from the women in our family." She was leading Bernadette up the stairs as she spoke, away from the crowded bookshop; it seemed half of Hatfield wanted to come in to welcome Matthew home, even though it was Saturday and the shop wasn't officially open.

Céline fetched a small leather satchel, set it on the kitchen table and opened it, taking out a package wrapped in linen and oilcloth. She opened it almost reverently and took out a book, before placing it into Bernadette's hands.

Wondering what the book could be, Bernadette opened the plain leather cover, frowning when she found not a printed frontispiece, but a prettily done drawing of some lavender stalks. "What…" she began, turning a page, and finding the next page full of delicate handwriting, in French. "Oh. Wait!" Translating the first few lines in her head, she turned wide eyes on Céline. "This is a herbal!"

"My grandmother's. Your great-grandmother's." Céline shrugged. "I have a little interest, but not nearly so much as you. You are the rightful heiress to it, I believe."

"Oh, I think I am going to cry again," Bernadette said, and Céline laughed and embraced her.

"We will all have some tears, I think, before we settle into happy lives together, but your troubles are over, Bernadette. I promise."

They dined in the assembly room at The Red Lion, as there was nowhere else to immediately accommodate the expanded Baxter family. Lord Ferndale and Miss Yates joined them, as did Riot Jones and Rosie and Mrs Poole. Mrs Bell also came over and made a firm friend in the new Mrs Baxter. Every twenty minutes or so, Lord Ferndale rang a small bell and declared everyone should swap seats so that others could have a turn to sit and talk with Matthew.

The five boys had their own table, and they made enough noise for treble their number. There were gasps as Philippe and Pierre regaled the English boys with their adventures and their own terrors. Bernadette's heart soared as she saw Brutus's delighted face. The isolated lad who had been so put upon by his own family and older brother, was now surrounded with the warmth of new friends and family. George and Richard were enthralled with how daring Pierre and Philippe's lives were, and clung on to every word. Later, they called out to their father, "Pa, can we stay in Hatfield instead of going back to school?"

"Nice try," Lord Renwick said with a laugh. "But perhaps we can look into Brutus, and Philippe and Pierre, joining you at Eton in the New Year?"

That brought loud huzzahs from all the boys. The sight of their collective grins, laughing faces - and by turns worried expressions (as Pierre told a particularly frightful tale) warmed Bernadette to her soul.

Word spread around town like a hot summer wind, and soon there were even more townsfolk pouring in to the Red Lion to see Matthew Baxter with their own eyes.

Bernadette's father was once again the centre of her world.

Well, perhaps slightly off centre, as she caught Glynn's grin from across the table. The past year had been so difficult, but she knew now, as she savoured the potato and leek soup - which Céline declared superb - that no matter what else happened in the future, she would get through it with her family.

Slowly, life settled into a steady routine. Marie and Renwick stayed another week after Renwick took his sons to Eton, before departing for their Cumbria home with a carriage stuffed full of enough books to keep even the Earl of Demanding happy, as the girls had laughed together. Lord Ferndale bought a massive pile of books too, and happily told Felix that he intended to spend all winter reading them and Felix would have to manage the Ferndale estates in the meantime. Felix protested, but not too much; he seemed to be thoroughly enjoying his new role, especially with a town council that voted with him far more often than not.

Louise and Shaun Jackson settled into their house, and though they invited Brutus to come and live with them, Brutus decided he would rather live at the bookshop. Matthew was delighted that the entail would eventually make Brutus his heir; as he and Céline did not expect to have any more children, Matthew planned to finish raising Brutus as his own son. Céline had sold some of her jewels for quite a sizeable fortune, certainly enough to set Philippe and Pierre up in whatever professions they desired to pursue in the future, and the three boys were already close and affectionate. Brutus finally had the brothers he deserved, and he could not have been happier.

They would need a tutor to get them ready for attending Eton after Christmas, Matthew determined, and set about the search. Mr Charles was qualified, but he had a very busy parish to minister to now that Lord Ferndale had awarded him the living permanently. Instead, Mr Charles recommended a former classmate of his from Cambridge and a man by the name of Mr Eldar soon arrived in response to Matthew's letter inviting him to Hatfield.

Mrs Bell was delighted to have a tenant again in her spare room, which suited all, and her front room changed from being a consulting room to a classroom.

Glynn's cottage was finished, and he moved in happily with the kitten he'd named Byron, and another cousin of Rosie's who came in daily to clean and cook his meals. He set up a consulting room there for the moment, though he told Bernadette she would have the room for her herbs once the hospital was completed.

Glynn made a great effort to court Bernadette without putting any pressure on her, and they soon fell comfortably back into the excellent working relationship they had begun to develop before he'd momentarily turned into an idiot. Bernadette was the one who ended up moving in with Louise and Shaun, as the apartment over the bookshop was really quite crowded these days, as well as noisy with three young boys living there!

Bernadette was not the only one who moved out of the bookshop; saying that her job was now done now that there was a new Mrs Baxter, Mrs Poole finally accepted the admiration of Mr Thomas, the ostler from the Red Lion, and married him a month after Matthew's return home.

It was a few days after that when Bernadette received a letter from Cumbria that was not from her sister Marie. Recognising the spidery handwriting, she decided to take the letter to Glynn's cottage so they could read it together, and made her way there after breakfasting with Louise and Shaun.

"Good morning, my love." Glynn opened the door to her with a cheerful smile before she could even knock. "No herb basket today?"

"Only this." She brandished the envelope. "It's from Ruth."

She and Glynn had sat down with Shaun Jackson after their return from London and confessed that they had discovered Reverend Millings' killer… and then they'd let her go free. Shaun had listened carefully, his big fists clenching with fury when Glynn explained what the vicar had been doing to his daughter, and finally nodded.

"Justice was served," Shaun said with quiet approval, and Bernadette breathed a sigh of relief. The investigation was closed, and she was pretty sure nobody in Hatfield regretted Reverend Millings being replaced with Mr Charles, anyway. Church on Sundays was much more enjoyable listening to sermons about loving thy neighbour and welcoming strangers as brothers.

"Did you read it yet?" Glynn asked, and Bernadette shook her head. They headed into the kitchen together, with a brief pause as Bernadette almost stepped in some mouse entrails and Glynn reproached Byron for leaving a mess and found some rags to clean up.

They sat down at the table and Bernadette broke the seal on the letter, laying it flat on the table so they could both read together.

"Dear Bernadette," Ruth had written. *"I am writing to let you know that everything is quite all right for Mother and I. The Charles family are very kind, even though I cannot understand much of what Mrs Morag Charles says, but she hugs me a great deal. I have decided I don't want to keep the baby when it comes and Morag is going to raise it as her own. It is cold here now and nobody travels much, so hardly anyone even knows we are here. It is for the best really. Marie - or Lady Renwick as I must call her now - came to see me, and after the baby comes and we are ready to leave, Mother and I are going to move to Alston Castle. Mother is going to be the assistant housekeeper and I will be Lady Renwick's companion, which will be lovely. Lady Renwick says they have ever so many books in their library and I can read whatever I like!"*

"That poor child," Glynn murmured, echoing Bernadette's sentiments. Ruth really was still only a child, but Marie would take good care of her, even finishing her education in the guise of providing reading matter from

Renwick's library. And Mrs Millings could find purpose without fear as assistant housekeeper at Alston, reserving her small jointure for a more comfortable retirement in the future.

"The best thing for her, to give up the child," Bernadette murmured, skimming the rest of the letter. "She has a better chance at marriage in the future, without a child with such a dark history clinging to her skirts."

"Do you think she'll ever marry, after what her father did to her?" Glynn asked curiously.

"Perhaps. She's very young… and people are resilient. I wish she had told me the truth before she got pregnant, but at least she has a chance at some sort of future, and so does Mrs Millings."

"We did good." He nudged her shoulder lightly with his, and she smiled.

"We make a good team, you and I."

"Indeed we do!" He leaned in for a kiss, but they were interrupted by a knock on the door, and Glynn sighed. "The first patient of the day, I'm afraid. Will you stay and consult with me? I would value your opinion in this case; a child with a mysterious illness."

"I should be delighted!" She stole a quick kiss anyway, and scooped up Byron the too-big-to-be-a-kitten-anymore as he darted past her feet. "And what are you up to, you little monster?" She bestowed kisses on the cat's head. All Byron's littermates had found good homes too; Louise and Shaun had taken his sister Evelina, Cecilia had gone to Ferndale Hall with Estelle and Felix, Waverly to the vicarage with Mr Charles, and Smollett with Mrs Poole when she married Mr Thomas. The mice of Hatfield would be terrorised by Crafty's offspring for many years to come.

Byron was of use in Glynn's practice as well, providing an excellent distraction to the little boy who had been brought by his mother for a consultation. After a great many questions, Glynn and Bernadette eventually diagnosed a diet lacking in fresh fruits and vegetables, and Bernadette promised to drop off a tonic of rosehip syrup to boost the child's health, as well as recruit some of the ladies of Hatfield to supply fresh produce from their gardens and help the fretful young mother learn the best ways to prepare them.

"It does feel good to help," Bernadette said after seeing their fourth patient for the morning.

"It truly does," Glynn said, as he delivered a smile her way. Not content with merely smiling, he stepped closer to deliver an embrace.

Byron pounced on his boot and attacked his laces. He kept walking to Bernadette, cat riding on one foot as he adjusted his gait to close the distance.

They giggled and laughed together, then stole another delightful kiss before Glynn carefully stepped back. Slowly, he lifted his foot, bringing the cat higher. "Now look here, your job is to keep the rodents away, not trip me up. Oh, I nearly forgot, how many printed record sheets do I have remaining?"

Not hindered by a maniacal feline, Bernadette opened the drawer and quickly counted. "There might only be about twenty pages here?"

"In which case, I should put another order in with Mr Black."

"I can do that if you like? There's a magnificent rose bush along the way, I'll see if it has any ripe rosehips."

She turned around to see Glynn had already anticipated

her need to gather ingredients, for he had a harvesting basket already in his hand.

She loved this about Glynn. He anticipated what she needed almost before she did sometimes. He made her so happy, her face ached from smiling. He'd proven his willingness to woo, she'd be more than happy for him to ask her to marry him, whenever he felt like it.

The sooner the better, really.

"I'll be back in a little while," she said, taking the basket from him and a blank patient record.

When she opened the door, she gasped.

There was her brother-in-law, Felix Yates, galloping down the street towards them as if the devil was on his heels.

His hair was wind-tossed and damp from sweat, and he wasn't even wearing a hat!

"Felix?" Bernadette called out.

He spotted her and pulled his horse up. "Hurry!" he cried out, "is Mrs Bell with you?"

Bernadette shook her head. "I'm sure she's at home."

Glynn stepped out through the door, Byron clinging to the bottom of his trousers. "Hullo there!"

Felix didn't respond to the cheerful greeting, he just said, "I'll get Mrs Bell, you two make haste to Ferndale Hall. The baby's coming!"

Bernadette immediately agreed. She put the basket and the patient record back inside and said, "The rosehips can wait, my sister cannot!"

Christmas at Ferndale Hall

"No, thank you, I could not eat another bite!" Bernadette said as Glynn offered her the plate of decadently sweet dessert pastries. He smiled and took another for himself before passing it across the table to Shaun Jackson.

"I have never known a Christmas like this," Glynn said to her in a soft, wondering tone, and Bernadette smiled, taking his hand in hers under the cover of the tablecloth.

"Nor I, to be entirely honest!" She had celebrated Christmas at Ferndale Hall last year, of course, but it had been a far smaller gathering. Today, every leaf had been added to the grand dining table, and a second table set at the side of the room for the youngsters. They were still a little crammed in, jostling elbows as they ate.

Lord Ferndale presided at the head of the table, beaming constantly at his house full of guests. All four Baxter sisters, three with their husbands and one with a fiancé, Matthew Baxter and his new wife Céline, and several dear friends like Riot and Rosie Jones, the former Mrs Poole with her new husband Mr Thomas, Mr Charles the vicar and Mr Lennox the apothecary, and of course Miss Yates in the hostess's chair. The five boys at the other table, Brutus, Philippe, Pierre, Richard and George, had eaten together very nearly as much as the adults, and made just as much noise, though they were settling down now into quiet contentment with full stomachs.

Between courses, Glynn leaned over and whispered into Bernadette's ear, "Come with me to the foyer. I spotted something there I think you'd like."

Intrigued, Bernadette accepted. There were so many people, surely nobody would notice their absence for a little while.

Glynn took her hand in his and they slipped out of the room. He was being mysterious and romantic, and she loved that about him.

But when they reached the foyer, they stopped in their tracks. They hadn't noticed that Shaun and Louise were also not in the room. They were right here, in the foyer, kissing under the mistletoe.

"Oh for heaven's sake," Bernadette giggled. "They stole your idea."

Louise and Shaun broke apart with a laugh.

Shaun pointed to the weedy greenery above him with its white berries. "Can you blame us? There wasn't any here last year."

"We can come back later," Glynn suggested to Bernadette with a shrug.

"Much later, please," Louise said with a naughty giggle.

Bernadette rolled her eyes and made a little snort of laughter. "I shall find us some mistletoe, there's a row of apple trees where…"

Glynn didn't wait for her to finish the sentence, as his lips descended on hers. For as long as she lived, Bernadette didn't think she'd ever grow tired of kissing Glynn Williams. When they did pull apart, they slipped back into the dining room, grabbing their chairs so they could sit near the boys and join in their conversations. It was fun to hear their tales of adventure and heartening to see how well they were bonding. They were looking forward to the new school term at Eton and Bernadette feared the headmasters would have their hands full with these headstrong lads.

Movement at the door caught Bernadette's eye, and she saw a maid slip in, a blanket-wrapped bundle in her arms.

"I'll take him," she said quickly, rousing groans of envy from several around the table as the bundle was laid in her arms. Everyone wanted a turn to hold Estelle's beautiful son! She walked back to the long table and Glynn brought her chair back for her to resume her seat.

Little Harry Yates blinked long lashes at her as the maid handed him over, and then yawned.

"Did you wake up from your nap a little early?" Bernadette rocked him gently. "We are almost done with lunch; your mama will be coming soon!"

Harry did not cry, just looked around as she propped him up against her and let him look about the table at his family. He was exactly two months old, born after a surprisingly easy labour for a first-time mother. Bernadette and Mrs Bell had only just made it to Ferndale Hall in time to help, and Mrs Bell had firmly warned Estelle that if she had any more children, she would need a midwife living with her for the last few weeks or risk giving birth without one!

"Ahem," Lord Ferndale said at the head of the table, standing up. "If you all do not mind, I should like to say a few words." He looked around at them, and Bernadette swore his eyes were glistening with tears behind his glasses.

"I do not think Florence and I could ever have imagined that our family would expand in such a magnificent way," the old baron said at last. "Matthew has been my good friend these many years, and to see you safe home again and have our families combined is a blessing and a great joy."

"Hear, hear!" several voices exclaimed.

Bernadette saw Louise and Shaun quietly walk back into the room, her sister looking thoroughly kissed. Louise caught her eye, and grinned unrepentantly.

"I hope this will be only the first - and smallest! - of many such gatherings at Ferndale Hall for Christmas. Felix, you are charged with the duty of gathering them all here every year once I am gone."

"I shall solemnly accept, but Grandfather - you are hale and hearty yet. It will be many years before I am in your seat, I hope!" Felix exclaimed.

Lord Ferndale did actually look better than he had in quite some time, Bernadette thought, and so did Miss Yates. Having Felix home and taking on more responsibility, and Estelle taking up the reins of managing Ferndale Hall, had lifted a good deal of weight from the elderly pair's shoulders. She had not heard Lord Ferndale cough once this winter, and she had spent a good deal of time at the Hall with Estelle since Harry's birth.

Lord Ferndale concluded his little speech with a toast to his great-grandson, and they all drank to Harry's health. Bernadette cuddled her nephew closer, kissing the soft blond curls escaping his knitted cap and breathing in the sweet new-baby scent of him.

Beside her, she heard Glynn let out an odd little sound,

and looked up to find his eyes fixed on her, the softest expression on his face. A little blush warmed her cheeks as she wondered if he was imagining her with *their* child. Though they had an understanding, no date for the wedding had yet been set; Matthew was insistent that they should not be in any hurry.

Still looking at her, Glynn rose to his feet as Lord Ferndale sat down. "If I may beg your indulgences, I have some news I'd like to share," he said, and everyone quieted and looked at him with interest.

"I think you all know my story; that I apprenticed to my father as a surgeon and joined the army," Glynn began, "and that quite by coincidence, I happened to save the life of a very eminent gentleman when I treated wounds he received in battle. I have always honoured his request to remain anonymous, but it was he who paid for me to return to England and attend medical school, and I should certainly not be in my current position without his generous treatment."

"Well, nor should he be alive without your skills, so a fair trade," Louise said, and there were murmurs of agreement and nodded heads around the table.

"Sadly, I received a letter a few days ago with the news that he has passed away," Glynn continued. "Not due to any lingering effects from his injuries, but from pneumonia which set in after an influenza."

"Oh, I'm so sorry!" Bernadette said, feeling for Glynn. He had always spoken with utmost respect for his benefactor, while protecting the man's identity.

"I wish he had sent for me," Glynn said with a wry twist to his mouth, "but I cannot change the past, and it transpires that my benefactor had one more gift for me." He looked down at Bernadette, and smiled. "In his will, he specified that I should receive the sum of five thousand pounds."

Gasps went around the table in the wake of this startling announcement, and Glynn looked at Matthew. "And while you have been more than generous in your offer of a dowry for Bernadette, sir, I am glad to say that I will not need to use it to provide for us. I have already completed negotiations with Lord Ferndale to purchase my cottage, and as a gift for Bernadette, I plan to begin construction of a glass house in the garden, so that she may grow her own ginger!"

Bernadette gave a little squeal of joy. Marie, sitting on her other side, deftly scooped baby Harry out of her arms so that Bernadette could jump to her feet and throw her arms around Glynn. He embraced her most satisfactorily, and then, grinning down at her, said;

"Will you marry me?"

"It's about time!" She laughed up at him. "Of course I'll marry you, you foolish man!"

He kissed her, and then everyone was swarming around to congratulate them, to embrace her and shake Glynn's hand and welcome him properly to the family.

"At least I will get to walk *one* of my daughters down the aisle," Matthew said, kissing her cheek tenderly.

"We shall all be there, I would not dream of marrying without my sisters beside me!" Looking around at them, Bernadette had a sudden, wonderful idea. "You could walk each of us down the aisle, Papa! It might be only me getting married, but I am sure Mr Charles would not mind including a blessing for each couple in the service - and for you and Céline too, since we missed your wedding!"

"What a capital idea," Mr Charles said immediately.

"You would not mind sharing your wedding day, Bernadette?" Marie asked.

"We didn't get to see your wedding either, since you and Renwick ran off to Gretna Green because of Cousin Joshua being awful, and you and Estelle missed Louise's too! I think it would be the most wonderful thing imaginable for us all to celebrate together."

"And Ferndale Hall will host you all again!" Miss Yates cried with delight.

"Oh, please say it will be when we are on school holidays so we can come?" Brutus begged earnestly.

Bernadette smiled, but did not laugh, at the lad's apparent sentimentality. It was quite the turnaround from someone who had recoiled at demonstrations of affection.

She had hoped to marry sooner, but looking at Brutus and the rest of the boys looking so hopeful, she could not deny the boys the opportunity to attend.

"Perhaps just after Easter?" she suggested. "We can't marry during Lent, but the banns could be called?" She looked hopefully at Glynn.

"That sounds perfectly wonderful to me," he said obligingly, "and will give me time to have your glasshouse completed as a wedding gift!"

"And time for us to properly prepare your trousseau!" Céline declared, and Bernadette laughed as her stepmother and sisters converged to begin talking of silk and lace.

She didn't care about silk and lace. She'd marry Glynn in her oldest gown, stained from making teas and tonics, and she was very confident he would not love her any less. Having all her family and loved ones around her while she married her beloved, her true partner in her life's work?

That was a gift beyond price, and she would treasure it forever.

After the year they'd had, never did Bernadette imagine how happy she might be. Looking about her, her body replete with delicious food, surrounded by family and love and a crackling fire, she started to think she could become used to this level of contentment for many, many years to come.

Good Golly Miss Molly

CATHERINE BILSON

CHAPTER 1

April, 1811. Belle Haven Estate, Hampshire, England

The first rays of dawn stretched lazily across the expanse of Belle Haven's rolling acres, casting a delicate golden light through the stable doors as Molly Bell strode in briskly, her sharp eyes scanning the rows of stalls bathed in the serene morning light. She took a deep breath, savouring the familiar, earthy scent of hay mingled with leather and the musky aroma of the horses.

"Good morning, my beauties," she murmured, reaching to stroke the nose of a pretty bay as the mare whickered a greeting. "Ready to start the day?"

With practiced efficiency, Molly moved to the feed room, her footsteps barely audible on the straw-laden floor. Her hands worked swiftly through her regular morning routine, measuring out and mixing the correct feed for each individual animal, delivering the buckets and then checking the horses over while they ate. Each task performed with a precision that spoke of years of practice and an innate understanding of her charges. The horses responded to her presence, their ears flicking forward, nostrils flaring as they acknowledged her care.

"Easy there, Apollo," she crooned to a particularly spirited chestnut, who sidled away as she stroked down to his fetlock and encouraged him to pick up a hoof. "I'm not keeping you from your breakfast."

Apollo snorted, his dark eyes following her every move as she continued her morning routine. Molly's strong, capable hands moved over the horse's coat, checking for any signs of distress or injury. Satisfied, she gave him a pat, earning only a grumpy snap of teeth in her direction for her troubles.

"You're a rascal, you know that?" she said with a chuckle. "There'll be none of that when you get to Sandhurst, my lad. Save it for the French."

Molly moved with fluid efficiency from stall to stall, confident around the large animals in a way that spoke of her familiarity with them. The scent of fresh hay mingled with the earthy aroma of the stables, a comforting blend that spoke of home and purpose. Each horse received a gentle touch, a murmured word, and a careful inspection.

"Easy there, Bramble," she cooed to a spirited bay mare, who tossed her head but settled under Molly's calming presence. "You're as feisty as ever, aren't you?"

Bramble nickered softly in response, nudging Molly's shoulder as if to agree. With a final pat, Molly moved on, her mind already shifting to the tasks ahead.

The preparation for delivering these horses Sandhurst was no small feat, and Molly knew every detail had to be perfect. She made her way to the tack room, where rows of bridles, saddles, and grooming kits were meticulously organised. She pulled out a well-worn ledger, flipping through pages filled with neat, precise handwriting.

"Three-year-olds for Sandhurst," she muttered to herself, running her finger down the list. "Apollo, Bramble, Thunder... all fine stock."

She checked off each name, mentally reviewing their training progress and temperaments. These horses were more than just animals to her; they were partners, each with their own quirks and strengths. Apollo's unbreakable courage, Bramble's fiery spirit, Thunder's raw power—each would play a crucial role in their destiny as war chargers for the officers of the British Army.

Molly tried not to think too hard about the brutal truth that few of the horses Belle Haven delivered annually to the Army would ever come home again once they were shipped to the Continent. After ten years, she had learned to harden her heart.

"Now, let's see about your gear," she said, moving to inspect the equipment laid out for the journey. Saddles were checked for wear, bridles polished until they gleamed, and grooming supplies packed with care. She paused to ensure every item met her exacting standards, her mind a whirl of logistics and schedules.

"Mustn't forget the medical kit," she reminded herself, tucking a small wooden box filled with salves, bandages, and other essentials into the saddlebags her own horse would carry. Her thoroughness was born of experience; she knew how quickly a minor issue could become a major problem without proper preparation.

Stepping back, she surveyed the organised chaos with a critical eye. Everything seemed in order, but there was always one more thing to consider, one more detail to perfect.

"Good morning, Molly." Clara's soft voice broke through the rhythmic sounds of horses munching on hay and the clinking of metal harnesses.

"Morning, Clara," Molly replied, looking up to see two

of her sisters approaching, Clara wearing a wistful expression. Anna trailed behind, her hands clutching a small notebook.

"Reviewing the list for Sandhurst?" Clara asked, resting one hand on the stable door as she peered inside.

"Yes," Molly said, holding up a list that detailed each horse's name, age, and condition, as well as the rider they were destined to be paired with at Sandhurst. "Just making sure everything is in order. We can't afford any mistakes - every one of the horses has been paid for already and we don't want to have to pay anyone back!"

"Of course," Clara sighed, her eyes lingering on the list before shifting to the horses. "I wish I could come along. It seems like such an adventure, helping to get the horses settled in with their new partners!"

"Maybe next time," Molly said gently. Clara was only seventeen, to Molly's twenty-three; Molly did not see their father allowing Clara to make the trip in the next year or two at least. "Your presence here is invaluable, you know."

"That's what everyone says," Clara laughed lightly, "but it doesn't make staying behind any easier."

"Well, I've completed the feed calculations," Anna interjected, waving her notebook slightly to catch their attention. "Each horse will have precisely the right amount for the journey and the first week at Sandhurst. No need to worry about them running out or overeating, and then you'll have the information for Sandhurst to order the correct quantities going forward."

"Thank you, Anna," Molly said, genuinely impressed by her sister's meticulous work. She took the offered notebook and scanned the figures, nodding approvingly. "These are perfect."

"Anything to contribute," Anna said with a modest smile, but the pride in her eyes was unmistakable.

"Clara, do you mind helping me pack the rest of the equipment?" Molly asked, turning her attention back to her eldest sister. "There's still quite a bit to organise."

"Of course," Clara agreed eagerly, stepping closer to the pile of gear. "Show me what needs to be done."

"Start with these saddles," Molly instructed. "Make sure the straps are secure and the padding is intact. And if you find any worn spots, let me know immediately."

"Got it," Clara said, rolling up her sleeves and getting to work. She handled each piece with care, her fingers tracing the leather as if committing it to memory. Anna joined her, turning a heavy saddle upside down and holding it so Clara could inspect the underside.

"Wonderful," Molly commented, feeling a surge of gratitude for her sisters' support. "I don't know what I'd do without you two."

"Well, we're a team, aren't we?" Clara said. "And even if I can't be there in person, I'll be with you in spirit."

"Same here," Anna added, her voice soft. "Just remember all our hard work when you're impressing those officers at Sandhurst."

"Believe me, I will," Molly said, her heart swelling with affection for her family. "Every step of the way."

"Good morning, girls," came a familiar voice from the stable doors.

Molly straightened up, wiping a bead of sweat from her brow as she turned to see her adoptive father, Lord Richard Bell, striding towards her. His dark hair was tousled from the breeze, and his clear blue eyes held a warmth that never failed to put her at ease.

"Good morning, Pa," she replied, a smile tugging at her lips. "I trust you slept well?"

"Indeed, I did," he said with a chuckle. "Though I must admit, thoughts of this Sandhurst delivery kept me awake longer than usual."

"Understandable," Molly said, nodding. "It's a significant undertaking."

"That it is," he agreed, stopping beside her and reaching out to give her shoulder a quick squeeze. "And I wanted to go over the logistics with you one last time before you set off. Your meticulous planning has been invaluable, as always."

"Thank you, Pa," Molly said, feeling a flush of pride. "I've made sure everything is in order. The horses are in top condition, and we've packed all necessary equipment and provisions for the journey."

"Excellent," Richard said, giving her a reassuring smile. "I have no doubt that you'll manage everything beautifully. You've always had an extraordinary way with these horses."

"Years of practice," she replied modestly. "And a deep love for them, of course."

"Which is precisely why I trust you implicitly with this task," he said, his tone serious. "Your expertise is unparalleled, Molly. Now, let's review the training schedule and the specific needs of Sandhurst."

"Of course," Molly said, reaching for a leather-bound notebook on a nearby workbench. She flipped it open to a page filled with neatly written notes and charts. "Here we are. I've outlined the training regimen for each horse based on their current progress and the requirements of Sandhurst. Of course, it will be dependent on the abilities of the recruits they are paired with, but I can't imagine any of them will be unable to ride."

"Indeed, they will all be the sons of gentlemen; most of them will be excellent riders, though you might have a few London lads who think a gallop in Hyde Park is a hard work out. This is impressive," Richard murmured, scanning the pages. "You've considered every detail."

"Naturally," Molly replied, her eyes twinkling. "We can't afford any missteps, especially not with the reputation of Belle Haven at stake."

"Quite right," he said, nodding appreciatively. "Let's start with Thunder. He's shown remarkable improvement since his last assessment. You know I've no liking for breaking them in as two-year-olds; they're not truly grown into their bodies yet, but the Army's needs..." he trailed off with a regretful shrug.

"Thunder's muscling up well," Molly said, her voice equally regretful for the necessities they were forced into by the exigencies of the war. "I've adjusted his regimen to include more endurance exercises, which should prepare him perfectly for the rigours of Sandhurst."

"Smart thinking," Richard said. "And what about Apollo? He had some issues with his left lead canter transition, if I recall correctly."

"Ah, Apollo," Molly said with a fond smile for the temperamental chestnut. "I've introduced a series of targeted drills to correct that transition. It's a slow process, but he's making steady progress."

"Wonderful," Richard said, his expression softening. "Your dedication is truly remarkable, Molly. I don't know how you do it."

"Passion and perseverance, Pa," she said simply. "Our precious horses deserve nothing less."

"Indeed they do," he agreed, closing the notebook and meeting her gaze. "And so do you, Molly. Your work here is invaluable. Now, let's ensure everything is ready for this journey. Sandhurst awaits, and I have no doubt you'll make us proud."

Molly knew Richard would have preferred to take the horses to Sandhurst himself, as he had every previous year for the past decade, but unfortunately, the Prince Regent had sent a letter just two days ago requesting his presence in London. Belle Haven's very existence depended on the Prince's continued patronage - more than once the Army had attempted to requisition the mares and stallions who were Belle Haven's essential breeding stock - and only the Prince's direct order had prevented it. When the Prince called, Richard had to go.

Molly, however, had assisted Richard in delivering the horses to Sandhurst and settling them in with their new partners for the last four years. She knew she could handle the job alone, and she was extremely proud Richard had agreed to let her try.

Richard nodded to Molly before heading to the stallion barn, where he would spend most of his day exercising Belle Haven's four resident stallions, ensuring they did not get bored or frustrated in their stalls waiting for breeding season to begin. Molly was about to return to her work when she spotted Lady Theresa Bell, her best friend and adoptive mother, approaching from the manor house. She balanced a tray laden with fresh bread and steaming tea, her face lighting up as she saw Molly.

"Theresa! You've read my mind," Molly exclaimed,

wiping her hands on her apron and reaching out to take the tray.

"Well, I thought you might need a little sustenance," Theresa replied, her voice warm. "And perhaps a bit of company?"

"Always," Molly said, leading her friend to a nearby bench. The aroma of freshly baked bread mingled with the earthy scent of hay and horses, familiar and comforting.

"How are things shaping up for the trip?" Theresa asked, pouring tea into two cups.

"Busy but smooth," Molly replied, taking a sip of the warm tea. "We're nearly ready. We;ll be ready to leave before dawn tomorrow, with seventeen horses to deliver. With thirty-eight miles to Sandhurst, we should be there by mid-afternoon."

"That's wonderful to hear," Theresa said, her eyes twinkling. "You know, sometimes I wish I could be as brave and capable as you. I like to ride, of course, but taking a string of half-trained war horses to a military college…" She shook her head.

"Don't sell yourself short, Theresa," Molly chided gently. "Belle Haven could not function without you at the heart of it."

"Thank you, Molly," Theresa said softly, looking down at her cup, a blush creeping up her cheeks. "Here's to safe travels and a successful season at Sandhurst."

"Indeed," Molly agreed, raising her cup in a toast. They shared a moment of comfortable silence, savouring the simple yet profound bond that had been forged between them in a London orphanage, and endured through the years since.

The serenity was suddenly interrupted by a sharp

whinny from one of the stalls. Molly's keen ears instantly picked up on the distress in the sound. Setting her cup down, she hurried to the source of the noise.

"What's wrong, girl?" Molly murmured soothingly as she approached a young mare, Dulcinea, who was shifting uneasily in her stall. A quick examination revealed a small cut on the horse's rear leg, just on the hock.

"Now how did you do that?" Molly said with a half-laugh. "I swear, horses can injure themselves on thin air!" She looked about before finding a small splinter jutting out of the wooden partition between the stalls. "Was that it? You silly filly!" Carefully, Molly removed the bloody splinter, putting it in her pocket to dispose of safely later.

Theresa laughed, going to the tack room to fetch the medical bag before returning to hold Dulcinea's head and keep her still for Molly to work.

"Hold still, sweetheart," Molly cooed, her touch gentle as she expertly cleaned the wound with a damp rag before rubbing in a salve, all the while murmuring reassurances. Dulcinea gradually calmed under Molly's deft care, her eyes softening with trust.

"Is she going to be alright?" Theresa asked from Dulcinea's head, her brows furrowed with concern.

"Yes, it's just a minor scrape," Molly replied. "She'll be good as new in no time. I'm not even going to bandage it, just keep putting salve on it for a few days."

"You're amazing, Molly," Theresa said, awe evident in her voice. "You're as good with the horses as Richard... it's like the two of you can speak their language."

"Maybe I do," Molly said with a wink, giving Dulcinea one last pat before returning to Theresa. "Or maybe they speak mine."

"Either way, it's a gift," Theresa said. "And one that will serve you well at Sandhurst."

"Let's hope so," Molly said, her eyes drifting to the horizon where Belle Haven's green fields met the morning sky. "Because I'm ready for whatever comes next."

"Safe travels, Molly," Theresa whispered, her hand squeezing Molly's in a silent vow of friendship and support.

"Thank you, Theresa," Molly replied, her heart swelling with gratitude. "For everything."

"You are most welcome, dear one." Theresa put her arm around Molly's shoulders. "Now. I know you've packed everything for the horses; you will not have left a single thing to chance. But have you put even one single item of clothing in your own trunk?"

Molly's guilty expression told the truth of it, and Theresa's laughter rang out. "Miss Molly! Get yourself up to your room right now and get packing! The baggage cart's leaving this afternoon to be there ahead of you, and I'll not have you at Sandhurst with only whatever gowns you can squeeze into your saddlebags!"

"I've work to do yet," Molly demurred. "I'll pack before the cart leaves. I promise."

"See that you do." Theresa's glance was gently admonishing, but she did not press further, instead picking up the used teacups and tray and returning to the house, leaving Molly to continue with her morning routine.

<hr/>

Molly's room was a modest one at the back of the manor house, but it had the charm of her personal touch. The afternoon sun filtered through the lace curtains, casting delicate patterns on the floor. Molly knelt by her wooden trunk, neatly folding her clothes and placing them inside with care. Each item seemed to carry a memory, a piece of her journey from London to Belle Haven.

She picked up a well-worn book on horse anatomy which Richard had given her, its pages dog-eared and filled with her scribbled notes. A smile tugged at her lips as she added it to the trunk. How many nights had she spent poring over its contents, eager to understand every nuance of her beloved horses?

"Need any help?" Clara's voice broke the quiet, and Molly turned to see her sister standing in the doorway, her fair hair glowing like a halo in the sunlight.

"Always," Molly replied, her eyes twinkling with affection. "You know I'm hopeless at packing efficiently."

Clara laughed. She crossed the room and began folding a dress that Molly had haphazardly tossed onto the bed.

"Do you have your bonnet?" Clara asked, glancing at Molly's thick black hair, which was currently loose and tumbling around her shoulders.

"Of course," Molly said, fetching it from the dresser. "I wouldn't dare face the Sandhurst officers without it."

"Not with that wild mane of yours," Clara teased gently. "They'll think it's a horse's tail!"

Just then, Anna appeared, her delicate features set in a serious expression. "Don't forget this," Anna said, handing Molly a small, intricately carved wooden box. "It's your lucky charm."

"Ah, yes," Molly said, taking the box and opening it to reveal a tiny silver horse figurine. "Wouldn't want to leave without it."

"Remember to keep it close," Anna advised. "It'll bring you good luck on your journey."

"Thank you," Molly said, touched by her sisters' thoughtfulness. She would miss them for the month she was expecting to stay at Sandhurst.

As they worked together, the room buzzed with activity and laughter, each sister contributing in her own way. Finally, the trunk was full, and all that remained were the items which had been rejected for the trip, scattered around the room waiting to be put away tidily.

"Let's get these loaded," Clara said, and she and Anna hefted the trunk between them. Molly smiled fondly as she watched them haul it out of the room. Anna was a tiny thing, half-Chinese in ancestry, and Clara not much bigger, but growing up on Belle Haven they handled horses who outweighed them ten times over without a blink and were far stronger than they looked.

They made their way down to the courtyard between the house and stable, where the wagon stood ready. Two draft horses were already hitched, their glossy coats gleaming in the sunlight. Molly felt a surge of excitement mingled with responsibility as she helped secure her belongings among the piles of tack and bags of feed.

"And now, time to change for dinner." Anna tugged at Molly's hand. "Come on. Mama's ordered a special farewell dinner for you and Pa, before you leave in the morning. There's roast lamb, and treacle tart!"

"Two of my favourites," Molly laughed, her heart swelling again with love for her family. "I should check on the horses again, though…"

"You should not." Clara laughed at her, seizing her other

hand. "Come on! We'll help you wash your hair. You should do it before you go!"

It was pleasant to spend an afternoon with her sisters, Molly conceded, as they helped her bathe and dry her long, thick black hair before the fire before dressing for dinner. And it was even better to spend the evening with her family, enjoying a wonderful dinner in the dining room before sitting in the parlour talking and laughing together for hours, Richard and Theresa on the sofa side by side as always, their daughters clustered around them. Watching Richard take Theresa's hand when Theresa set down her teacup, Molly wondered privately whether the two had ever regretted not having any children of their own. Six daughters, and every one adopted.

But as she observed the easy affection and understanding between them, she knew that biology did not define true family. The bonds they shared, forged through love and care, were stronger than blood.

As the hour grew late and the younger girls were sent off to bed, a gentle quiet settled over Belle Haven. The warmth of the fire cast a soft glow across the room, and Molly sat gazing into the flickering flames, savouring these precious moments before her journey to Sandhurst.

"Molly," Richard's deep voice broke the silence, and she looked up to meet his eyes. "You know how much we trust your judgment and skill with the horses."

Molly nodded, her heart swelling with pride at his words. Richard was not one to offer praise lightly, but when he did, it held immense weight.

"We have every confidence in you," Theresa added softly. "But remember, you are not alone. We are always here for you, no matter what."

Molly's eyes glistened with gratitude as she absorbed their words, feeling the weight of their support and love. "Thank you, Richard, Theresa. I couldn't have asked for better family, for more than what you've already given me."

Theresa reached out, her hand finding Molly's and giving it a reassuring squeeze. "You've worked so hard for this, Molly. Your dedication and passion shine through in everything you do. Sandhurst will see that, too."

Richard's gaze was steady, filled with a mixture of pride and concern. "Just promise me one thing, Molly," he said, his voice gentle. "Take care of yourself out there. The horses will heed your command, but don't forget to look after your own well-being. Don't let those recruits try and boss you about just because you're a woman. I know full well there's no better rider in England than you, and they'll soon know it too."

Molly nodded solemnly, feeling their care envelop her like a warm embrace. "I promise," she said, before giving a cheeky grin. "I'll try not to show them up too much!"

Richard and Theresa's warm laughter followed her as she bade them goodnight and made her way upstairs to her room, the same she had occupied ever since she came to Belle Haven as an orphan runaway. Theresa had many times offered her a better room, but Molly preferred this one… none of the family bedrooms offered such a good view of the stables.

She sat at her window, the cool night air carrying the soft sounds of the horses rustling in their stalls below. Moonlight bathed the courtyard, casting long shadows that danced like spectres across the ground. Too full of anticipation to sleep yet, she sat drinking in the familiar, beloved atmosphere until her eyelids began to droop, and at last, she took herself off to bed.

About The Authors

Catherine Bilson and Ebony Oaten are long-time collaborators, creating bestselling multi-author Regency romance anthologies over many years.

At the 2024 Romance Writers of Australia conference in Adelaide, they were busy running the Indie Book Store when they came up with the idea for this series. A bookshop would feature strongly - they were living their fantasy of selling books to readers anyway.

Why not set an historical series in a bookshop itself? With sisters who each find love in a bustling town. Instantly they brainstormed complications and issues - what if their father raced off to France after Napoleon was exiled away on Elba, to gather rare books? The characters weren't to know Napoleon would escape only a few months later and wreak havoc on France!

Also, at this conference, Catherine won the RUBY - the Romantic Book of the Year award - for her novella *The Bride Said No*. This novella had started life in one of their collaborative anthologies, of course.

Ebony had also won the Ruby several years earlier, for one of her sweet romance novels, *The Girl and The Ghost*.

With their powers of romance combined, surely they could come up with something wonderful.

You can follow the authors by heading to their respective websites and joining their newsletters.

Catherine is here:
www.catherinebilson.com
Ebony is here:
www.ebonyoaten.com

ABOUT CATHERINE:

"I grew up in a 14th century manor house in North Wales and spent most of my youth making up stories about the people who might once have lived in it. I ran off and married a handsome Australian a few years later and now live with him and our two sons in the permanent sunshine of Queensland.

I write original Regency romance, Austen-inspired variations, and Pioneer American romance. I also write contemporary romance and romantic suspense under the pen name Caitlyn Lynch."

ABOUT EBONY:

Ebony is from Melbourne, Australia and used to be a journalist at several suburban newspapers across the city. Then she turned her hand to writing romance and hasn't looked back. She married a Welsh 'boyo' and they are raising their son in Melbourne, where it can be stinking hot one day, pouring with rain the next.

The Bookshop Belles

NOVELS:

Estelle's Ardent Admirer

Marie's Merry Gentleman

Louise's Christmas Champion

Bernadette's Dashing Doctor

EXCLUSIVE BONUS NOVELLA FOR SUBSCRIBERS:

Matthew's Willing Widow